THE LONG JOURNEY BACK

Other books by Robert Mendelsohn
published by Prion

Footsteps on a Drum
Clash of Honour
The Red Pagoda
The Hibiscus Trail

THE
LONG JOURNEY
BACK

Robert Mendelsohn

PRION

First published in the United Kingdom 1995 by PRION,
an imprint of Multimedia Books Limited,
32–34 Gordon House Road, London NW5 1LP

A catalogue record of this book can be obtained from the British Library

ISBN 1-85375-193-6

Typeset by Books Unlimited (Nottm), Pleasley, Notts NG19 7QZ
Printed and bound in Great Britain at the University Press, Cambridge

'Dedicate the next one to me,' my father said. I looked at him and saw that he knew what I thought. Then he smiled and he said, 'in that case just leave it on the terrace.'
I am leaving this novel on the terrace for you, father.

CHAPTER ONE

———— ■ ————

They were only voices and echoes and they always hit him in the dark. Sometimes they made him laugh and sometimes they made him cry. They were deep, confusing sounds and sights without shapes or faces. They came at him from the edge of his dream, and he saw muted figures in an arid landscape and heard the crackle of burning fields. Passionate groans of distant ecstasy and stark grimaces of pain fleetingly converged on him then disappeared.

He floated between sleep and awareness and flew over contrasting scenes of delight and desolation. He struggled to retain some of what he had seen and heard but he could not connect any of it. It was there and gone in seconds.

He thought he was awake but his eyes were closed still. It was all over now and packed away in a bundle of unwanted memories, yet the lingering of it persisted and he knew it came from somewhere inside him.

The full moon had come and gone. He slept through all the cold drops of sweat that rolled down his neck, and then came the shriek of the morning wind outside and he awoke with a jerk. His mind was a blank.

Had she been there, Annie would have put on the light to ask him what the matter was, but he was alone. He opened his eyes and stretched and he looked about.

In front of him, behind the mist that covered the grey Caribbean, the sun was trying to penetrate a reluctant horizon. He was exhausted because the mystery of these images had woken him before it was time. There would be no more sleep for him now.

He had nothing to hide, he thought, as he slid out of the large bed. Just scared of the dark, like any child. But the tall, overweight figure that was reflected in the large window he was approaching was that of a grown man. He came closer still to examine his face. He yawned, his nose touching the cold glass. A liquid world extended down beyond the garden. He looked at it through tired, dim eyes, and then the energy came, the power that forced him to scream every time the vision was over.

No one would hear him at this hour, something within him whispered, and he yelled at the view. He did not know why he chose that same sentence every time, yet the words came out in a shriek that said 'That was not ME!!!'

The vigour in his own voice shook him. He was fully awake now.

There is no echo by the seaside, yet he expected one, and he growled those same words again and again until his depleted throat felt sore. The kind of feeling you get when you've been smoking too much or singing all night or something.

Through a narrow slit in the window he could smell the early morning perfume. It drifted from the sleeping flowers behind which spread the lawn that led to the precipice. A sheer drop at the end of the garden. Hundreds of feet falling straight down on San San Bay. He knew the brink was there because he had seen it the day they had shown him around the house. He was not really afraid of it. All he needed was a good night's sleep with no interruptions from within. There would, he knew, be no more voices until the same time tomorrow. Along with the dream, that terrifying experience that had come back every night ever since he was young. He had, as always, forgotten what it was, but he could count on it turning up again as soon as it was bedtime. He could set his watch by it.

Clockwork nightmare.

In the bathroom his face looked back at him with defiance. A strong chin, bloodshot eyes. He had at least another hour before they came in with his breakfast. Bacon and eggs and freshly ground Blue Mountain coffee and toast. He could walk about and listen to the radio or watch the television or look out of the thick glass and read books. He could pick up the telephone and ask for things. They were always there and he could have anything. Anything at all.

He could do anything he wished, except leave.

The house was large enough to get lost in. Oak panelling in the library and paintings of old ships and horses. Deep leather chesterfields and brass bits and pieces by the fireplace. Lush carpets beneath the air-conditioned living-space. Dark green, living tropical plants stuck indoors just like himself. Maps and prints of old Jamaica hung over ornamented oriental pottery. They knew what turned him on. He had said he liked the house as soon as he saw it and he had agreed to buy it. Clever bastards. At the time he did not notice why he liked it. Clever bastards, he told himself as he switched on the electric shaver.

They knew all there was to know about him. The foods he craved and the magazines he read and the art he felt good with. They knew the furniture he liked and the books and the colours and they were all there.

The Remington zoomed along his skin and he thought of open spaces. Careless days on wooden decks with tight sails above and the laughter of pretty girls. Humphrey Bogart lay packed in plastic cassettes under the television set as did Clint Eastwood and all his other heroes. There were, outside, mountains he could not scale and royal palms he could not touch and, closer, there was the fragrance of his favourite flowers.

He showered and dried himself with brisk, intensive strokes of the towel. He sprayed the green Guerlain on his face and the smell of vetiver came to him. Even that was there in the bathroom that first day, and his brand of soap. Clever bastards.

For a long time he had been able to go anywhere he pleased. Ever since he got out of silver at the top, just before it crashed. God, how he was hated then. How many anonymous letters were written to him. How many threats. How many bankruptcies he was blamed for. It wasn't fair. He had warned people to sell while silver was up but they were greedy. They thought it was going to go up forever. And those who had listened to him and had sold when he had told them to sell did well. It was their testimonies that had enabled him to stay in business, but he knew he had made enemies.

Could one of those have arranged for this? His clients were astute people and all this took some doing. Was this internment their way of settling an outstanding account? A belated revenge from those who had lost their shirts? Impossible. All that was far behind him now and the City had forgiven him.

No matter. He had warned people and as long as he was known and welcomed in all the fashionable places those others did not count. He had credit all over the place. Maîtres everywhere had a table for him without prior reservation. He never did like staying in one house too long and yet, to his own surprise, he had decided to buy this one.

'My wife has been nagging me for years to get a place in the sun,' he had lied. 'I suppose I should bring her here first.'

'What the hell,' he had said, 'she is going to love it sight unseen.'

She would have hated it.

In any case, Annie was dead and what she would have thought of the house didn't matter any more.

He went back to the bedroom to dress and he remembered how they had set the trap. They had laughed and nodded and agreed with everything he had said. Perhaps too quickly. They never intended to let him go. Not once he was inside. God, how could he have been so dumb? Easy, that's how. You try walking into a place and suddenly everything about it seems familiar and safe. Everything pleases you. It's far from home so you do not notice someone has made all your dreams come true. Everything that ever delighted your eyes and your nose and your ears is laid out right in front of you. Anyone would have fallen for this. He must not lose his self-esteem. Keep cool. Think. This could happen to anybody. They had it all there waiting for him, making him feel he belonged there. No one could resist such a lure. He had said the place was so perfect it could have been custom-made for him. It was. Of course it was, but how was he to know it was to be his prison?

Hindsight is a Mr Smartass.

Grey flannels and a striped shirt. Made him look slimmer, Annie used to say, blowing kisses at his bulk. Blue Valentino blazer. The red tie. No. Polka dots. He did not remember how much he had packed in his suitcase, but the cupboard was full of his clothes or identical ones. His shoes, his socks, his underwear. Who was he dressing up for? He might as well stay in his pyjamas.

But he dressed all the same and he stood in front of the long lit mirror and looked at himself. The pants were no longer tight and there was space inside the buttoned-up jacket.

Below, in San San Bay, the sea turned emerald green to greet the sun. In the garden, the bright red hibiscus replaced the shadows. The dew had spread wet diamonds on the grass and he watched the glitter of them and waited for the boats. They passed his window every morning. A myriad of coloured spinnakers flapping with the wind not a mile away, and free to go where they pleased.

They couldn't keep him there forever. A man in his position would be missed. People must be looking for him. Asking questions. The press would be on his trail. It was all a big, fat mistake. Maybe they had taken him for someone else.

And then he looked around him again and he saw the familiar signs and sights of his vanity and remembered. The house and whatever was in it was created for him alone. It was him they were after all the time. Except he did not know who they were or why they wanted him. There was no cause for anyone to keep him there. Not unless they knew everything he had done and were looking for revenge. But no one knew.

He heard the car and then the slamming of the door. The dogs were barking. Big, menacing Rottweilers that roamed the grounds day and night. He had seen them tear a rabbit to shreds the other evening. Man's best friend, my eye. It was him they were after. Whoever kept him there knew about the dogs. Knew he had always been terrified of dogs.

Ever since the family Alsatian bit him in the thigh. He was ten years old at the time, eleven perhaps. His father had bundled him off in the Bugatti to the doctor's. In spite of his family's name and influence they had to wait forever and he was in pain. Perhaps the doctor was too old or too busy or both. They had to show him the dog's body before he calmed down. The injections nearly killed him. The scar was still there.

He had a different name then. Spoke a different language.

Another country, another time. A world away.

He heard the front door open, then their mocking sing-song voices. They always talked to each other before they came in. He saw them enter.

'Breakfast, Mr Gordon, sir.'

Always two of them. Different ones each day. Always large and agile and oozing power. He must have seen tens of faces by now. A fucking private army.

He walked into the dining-room and sat down as they lifted the silver cover for his inspection. It was all there, including the rose that stared at him by the orange juice. Stiff napkins and the crisp, unopened *Daily Gleaner*.

'Breakfast, Mistuh Gordon, suh.'

That was all they were going to say. Four words. One to do with a necessity, two for his name, and one of make-believe respect. Four miserable words. That was all he had heard ever since they locked him up. And that but once a day, at breakfast.

They had been very talkative on the first day. They had to be. They were selling. They had talked of this island paradise. The history, the pirates, the great sugar estates. The endless white sandy beaches and the palm forests and the mountains. They had talked about land and value and low taxes. They had shown him the house and he had asked to use the bathroom. 'Yes, of course,' they had said, and that was how it began. He remembered how they took him to lunch and then back to the house. He had drunk a lot of rum punches and had asked to go to the bathroom again. Weak bladder, he had said, and they smiled and, as he flushed the toilet, he heard the door and then the car and then the place fell silent.

That was six weeks ago.

'Breakfast, Mr Gordon, sir' was the only human sound he was to hear after that. Of course, there was the telephone, but that was his own voice asking for something. They had granted his wishes without a word. Their faces had constantly changed as they came in and out of the house, but while serving his lunch or his dinner they did not talk at all. There was Bogart's lisp in *Casablanca* and *The Maltese Falcon* and those other loathsome voices in the night, but they did not count.

Now they stood over him as he ate, muscles bulging through unmarked tee-shirts. The taller of the two handed him a slice of toast. A drop of molten butter appeared on his napkin and the shorter one replaced the white cloth instantly. Of course, he had tried to humour them at the beginning, before he knew better.

'Take me to your leader,' he had said a million times, but no one laughed.

'When am I leaving here?' he had asked a million times.

'Anyone for tennis?'

He asked many questions but he never asked who had hired them and why they were holding him. He did not ask these most important questions because he had made up his mind to find the answers by himself. By going through his past life and working out which of his enemies had finally caught up with him. Which of the dark secrets he had carried was exposed. He had not been able to do that during these past six weeks because at first he was convinced someone was playing a joke on him, and when he realised he was in real trouble he entered into a state of shock. He recovered, and then something else happened that jolted his common sense: for the first time in his life he missed the company of people. He craved someone to talk to him. Make any stupid small chatter just to confirm his existence as a human being. But no one had spoken to him and in time the silence began to harass him. He had never known how much he needed other people.

'You don't need anyone,' Annie had said. 'You collect people with that Central European charm of yours. You use and abuse and drain them and then you drop them. You're a loner. You will end up all on your own. That is how you want it.'

She would never know how wrong she had been.

* ★ *

The aroma of the coffee was fresh and pungent and the expectation of its taste revived him. He thought his old self-reliance was back. In his bones he felt this was going to be a different day. He asked:

'Is there a plane for London?'

They rewarded him with their usual blank silence and he said, 'Not today, Josephine', and knew he was corny, and that embarrassed him and he laughed. They would soon leave and he waited for the depression of loneliness to fall on him. And then the woman came in from the kitchen.

She was tall and she wore a clinging grey flannel suit, a beige silk blouse and red shoes that matched the scarf around her long, suntanned neck. He got up and the plate fell to the floor, spilling yolk over the carpet. He was too surprised to notice but her presence injected a measure of boldness into him.

'What have we here?' he asked, his hand covering the bald patch above his forehead. She came over and sat by his side, displaying a pair of exquisitely shaped legs. She extracted a cigarette from somewhere and someone lit it for her. They cleaned the carpet and took the tray out of the room and he heard the front door shut. Soon the engine invaded the silence and he knew they were gone. This was the moment he dreaded every morning, the moment his solitude would usually resume, but perhaps the war had come to an end.

'And who are you?' he asked as he pushed the ashtray towards her. She did not answer. She had thick pepper-and-salt hair that fell neatly onto one shoulder and a generous, curly mouth that sucked the tobacco and exhaled a funnel of smoke into the air.

'I gave that up years ago . . .' he started to say, and he noticed there was something familiar about her. Maybe not. Maybe just her well-dressed shape and proud posture. Or the cool, elegant, bemused face. She wore a pinkish pearl necklace and matching earrings, long, manicured fingernails and a ruby ring and lipstick that left a mauve label around the filter of her half-smoked cigarette.

'You must be the entertainment,' he said. 'Good thing I got dressed.'

Her skin was smooth and silky and it loved the sun. She had a snub nose and a pair of cobalt-blue eyes that hovered about him. Not too young. A sophisticated late thirties.

The type of woman he had chased and liked to be seen with before Annie had left the first time. They knew. Clever bastards.

7

'I am travelling alone,' he said. 'But I expect you were told about that.'

She didn't even nod.

He wasn't going to fall for this one. Not him. Not today. He could be quiet too. But what the hell for?

'Would you like to see the house? I would take you out for the view, but . . .'

What *did* they expect him to talk about? Nothing probably. Maybe they were just being nice to him. Maybe this was a hooker dressed up for the occasion. Or was she a dream come true? Some wish he had expressed and had forgotten? Was she going to stay the night?

The sun had just come up and this was his kind of woman and he was not going to make conversation. If she had a job to do she would have to begin. He got up and walked into the library. He took the newspaper with him. The deep carpet absorbed her footsteps as she followed. He sat down and slipped his reading-glasses down his nose. He stretched the paper and he saw the headlines. Something about the price of sugar. He tore the date off and put it in his pocket. He did that every day. He smiled sheepishly at her.

'My way of keeping a check on time,' he mumbled.

By now he would have settled to read the paper front to back had she not been there. She was just another trap they had set for him. Perhaps he should go on regardless. Pretend he was alone. Make them see the stuff he was made of.

He was looking at the paper and he watched the fresh black print forming into letters. He recognised some of them and some of the words they had grouped into but nothing made sense to him. Something about the price of sugar was all he could retain. The rest was all her.

She was there close to him, exquisitely chic and aloof, but her vibes gushed at him, caressing him as they washed over his body. They spread under his skin as if she was a part of him. Teasing scents of familiar, expensive perfume and the bitter-sweet smell of woman. He tried to concentrate on one paragraph and he read it many times and all the while under the onslaught of her presence he was thinking 'For Christ's sake say something to me' and he took nothing in. Maybe there was a war in the world or a revolution. Other people's blood spilling in some faraway field.

Who cares? With the rapture of his mind's eye he saw her lingerie and imagined it to be of flesh colour. Soft beige see-through material that hugged her hips and touched that deliciously exciting mound of her crotch. He read the paragraph again. A bundle of optimistic nerves palpitated under his groin as he thought of her breasts and imagined her nipples hardening to his touch. He was almost in pain as pictures of what might come burst in upon him. No foreplay. Just him slipping into that temple of moist passion. Just him plunging to and fro inside the maddening heat of her.

He watched a tiny drop of sweat roll down from under her arm and touch her bra. Soon she was bound to want to talk. Something must be bothering her, making her unhappy. Otherwise she would never have taken this job.

Like all the women he was attracted to, she must have been unfulfilled. Misunderstood.

Bored. That was it. She must have a grudge against something. A husband, a lover. Someone. She was not from these parts. Could be an American. Came here to find herself and landed on his doorstep. Once she thought she had his ear, his sympathy and understanding, she would tell all. They always did, and remembering that encouraged him. Talking to her would make him whole again and enable him to find out the most important thing in the world. What they wanted with him, who they were, and why he was here.

Now that he felt so good he would soon be able to look for answers. The original shock of his captivity had not lasted that long, he thought. Nor was he that helpless any more. Or maybe he felt that because the woman was there with him.

At the beginning he had not cared about the silence because he had never known total isolation before. There was something relaxing about it. They did not talk but he did. He talked and teased and bullied them. For a while he had practised his German and French and Italian on them, and then he began to learn how to talk to himself. More than that. He began to listen to Annie talking at him. And with her sound she came alive.

'You blame me for everything,' Annie had said long ago. 'You hate moods and you say I inhibit you. You think I envy your success.'

He had tried to calm her down. Reason with her. It was true he had said those things.

'I didn't mean it,' he would usually say, and her reply would always be the same.

'Look into yourself for a change.'

9

He had done none of that. Maybe his past frightened him.
Not now, Annie, he thought. Don't barge in now.

The woman kicked her shoes off and came to him. She sat on the floor
and she rested her head on his knees. Her hand climbed up his leg and
he flexed his muscles to hide his varicose veins. Her other hand crawled
above his knee and along his inner thigh and then she touched it. He
had expected it and the anticipation of it should have excited him, but
nothing happened. He was actually going softer there.

'You only married me because you thought I was pregnant,' Annie
had said.

What a time to think of that.

That wasn't true at all, he used to answer, knowing she was right;
and when he felt hard done by he would snap at her and utter ugly
words. She was hard-headed and unfair. After all he had done for her.
After the way he had elevated her. He was the big boss and she was a
typist in the general office when they had met. Not even a secretary.
Within months he had given her his name and the world in exchange
for her hand.

This woman here knew how to touch and where to probe and where to
stroke. She was a pro. They were paying her, and yet she did have class.
She had to be a whore. Who else would have agreed to come and spend
time with the bore he had become? Any minute now she would realise
she wasn't doing very well. They would expect her to deliver. It isn't you
at all, he wanted to say as he felt his manhood shrink further.

'Why don't we talk a little first,' he heard himself think. Maybe he had
said it. It had been years since he had heard these words. Annie had said
just that on their first date. When he tried to kiss her.

'What do you want to talk about?' he had responded.

'Anything,' Annie had said. 'I love listening to you. You have such
depth. You're so different. The sort of life you've had makes me see how
lucky I've been. You give me such peace. Please talk to me some more.'

He talked all night and got nowhere.

Could that be why he kept on talking all the way to the altar?

'I can't stand the sound of your voice.' She had said that too, but
years later. Towards the end.

Another fairy tale that ended in the shit.

CHAPTER TWO

—■—

This one wasn't shy at all. She had a job to do and she put her all into it. Her face was flushed and smudged and there was nothing to show for her efforts. He had been celibate for so long they must have reckoned he would climax as soon as he saw her flannel-covered shape. She looked at him and she smiled. Any minute now she'd say something to show her understanding. She'd suggest they went to the bedroom. She would tell him to relax. Take your time, this can happen to anyone, she would say. She would suggest she slipped into something more comfortable.

But this wasn't a movie. She didn't suggest anything.

Oh well, she wouldn't. No talking. This must have been part of her brief. They would have told her that he needed to be the bandleader. She expected him to give the orders. Everybody knew what a powerful man he was, and now she did and she was acting accordingly. They only wanted to humiliate him but they could all go jump in the lake. First he'd wait for her to talk. To tell all. They had had it their own way long enough. Just like he had, according to the note Annie had left behind when she had walked out on him the first time.

His face must have betrayed his thoughts. The woman looked up at him and for a split second he thought she was going to speak. He held his breath in anticipation and then he saw a flash of compassion behind her eyes. She was feeling sorry for him.

Oh no you don't, he said without a voice. His lips extended into a smile that was false. He stroked her hair, gently guiding her head back where it had been. He leaned back and stared into nothing and felt the moist heat of her lips engulfing him. Nothing.

His head ached. He remembered how Annie used to massage the back of his neck in the early days.

She knew where and how and when to do that.

'It's nerves,' she used to say. 'You work too hard. You take it all too personally.'

She would then undress him and bath him and wrap his body in a giant towel.

'Go sit on the bed while I fix you a drink,' she used to say. She'd call him darling, looking as alluring as if she'd just stepped out of a fashion show.

She spoiled him. He had loved every minute of it but had never said so.

Funny how he couldn't remember Annie's face. He was sure he had the day before. Round about this time, while reading the paper. He remembered what it was he had read. A discourse about the visit of an American secretary of state. Maybe he remembered it because they showed it on the television later. It had been a long time since he had thought about her. He had more pressing problems on his mind.

He had spent almost six weeks trying to work those out.

The pepper-and-salt hair was in his lap still and he could touch it, but the silence had scrubbed his desire clean away. He looked at his watch. Less than an hour had passed since the last 'Breakfast, Mistuh Gordon, suh'. Outside, the sun came down hard. He could almost feel the tips of the grass turning yellow then brown before they split.

He was going to put an end to this. He'd call them.

Steam collected over his glasses and he stretched his hand to lift the receiver.

'Tell the boss I am ready to talk,' he said, and he knew someone was listening because the thing clicked. He had never tried that one before. He had no idea what he was going to tell them. He did not remember what Annie had looked like but he could always start with her. Tell them she'd bail him out of whatever they thought he was guilty of.

Safe enough, that. They would not know she could never be called upon to back him up or contradict him. Or would they? They knew everything else. Would they have known about Annie and what had happened? The phone clicked and no one answered.

He pushed the woman's head away. Brutal, he thought. Maybe not. She was soon going to give up. He crushed the newspaper into a ball and threw it into the fireplace. The woman's eyes expressed no emotion at all. She calmly zipped him up, took a match out of her bag and turned her attentions to lighting the fire.

She did not look rejected at all.

'That's not what I had in mind,' he said, and got up. He looked at her elongated shape on the floor. 'Some other time maybe. You don't need the fire here. It is indeed winter but this isn't Europe.'

He wasn't sure whether or not she was paying any attention to him and he didn't much care. Must concentrate on Annie. He could hear her hesitant soft voice of old, and his hands remembered the silky feel of her skin.

Annie is at the back of all this, he thought. Must be. Can't be. All he needed to do was see her face and look into her eyes and he'd know. He could make it easy on himself. Look at her photograph. A small glossy square stuck above her signature on page three of her passport. He had the dark blue document in his attaché case by his bed. No way. He couldn't do that. He wasn't senile yet. Why should he need that? Annie was the passion of his life. She meant more to him than anybody. He needed her. He needed her now and always. He must try and remember her without looking. Must remember Annie of all people.

The only woman he ever loved. Everybody knew that. She was the only woman who understood him. The only woman he ever married.

The only woman he ever killed.

Caused her death, not killed, he thought, trying to console himself.

Same thing, he heard himself answer. No comfort there.

The yellow flame spread into the newsprint and a small segment of it hit the dry log. Soon it would turn orange and nibble at the wood with a crackle. Nothing smells quite like a log fire, he thought. The burning pulp hit his nostrils and with it came the memory. Pictures of a long-gone morning floated before his vision and hovered about the room. There might be a clue in that. He might be ready to think of his youth now. That long-gone time when he started to break the law. Maybe it wasn't as bad as all that. He sat down again and leaned back to watch and savour his past, where that other fire was.

Savour? There was nothing pleasant about that time or place, and it had nothing to do with Annie or her forgotten face, but he smiled nonetheless. They didn't know everything. He had at least one up on them. Had it not been for that particular morning long ago nothing would have happened. He would never have been forced to flee the country of his birth or change his name or meet Annie or be in this luxury hell-hole.

Not yet. Not yet. He managed to stop the pictures from flying into his head, and he looked at the woman. He looked at her carefully and for a moment he did not know her. The fire must have gone out since she was trying to rekindle it. She was striking matches and throwing pieces of paper and she was blowing. The sweet smell of burning wood gave way to the suffocating stale scent of burning paper.

He must have been gone for a few minutes, but he did not know where his memory had tried to take him. He wanted to rub his eyes but his glasses were in the way. Thirty years gone with a wink.

He had been kidding himself. Of course he had been alone before. Maybe he was always alone while the rest of the world marched on all the way in pairs. Someone, he had forgotten who, had told him that nothing was for ever. He used to think he had conversations and relationships with people, but perhaps it was all an illusion. Relationships and people were a brief experience for him. No more than a few black and white spots that grouped together for a little while. They were just images on a small screen one could switch off. This is all there is, he thought, the present. The house, the woman, his craving for conversation and the dogs prowling outside in the garden.

The now.

During his short absence the sky had collected a black curtain of rain clouds and inside, across the carpet, the fire was going again. He saw the woman's face quivering in the shadows while his eyes were aflame. Had he been there all this time? All what time?

There was nothing in her face to suggest he had been anywhere but here. Not even in his head, visiting his youth. That scene of his first mistake.

He sat down. Outside, the rain refused to come down. The sun came through the large bedroom window and set her hair alight. He looked at her long bronzed neck and he saw the pearls and further down he saw the flesh colour of her lace-framed bra. He took his glasses off and stretched his hand to her and smiled. With the soft touch of her skin he felt the hardening under the cotton of his slacks and then she was there with him and she touched.

The vigour he had lost was now thumping hard as their probing lips gave chase to each other. A wet volcano formed about their faces and his breath came in short bursts as her hands undressed him.

'Annie,' he groaned. 'Come to me. I want you. I must have you now, Annie.'

Her face recoiled from his as the silence exploded.

'I am not Annie,' he heard the woman snap. 'I am . . .'

The shock of another voice was too sudden.

There was more than a hint of anger in her voice.

Maybe she had told him what her name was, but he had not heard. He heard nothing but the sweet, unexpected sounds of words. Not imagined, not seen in a book or a screen, but spoken.

He was stark naked now. He looked at her. He wanted to believe there was urgency in her eyes. He was hardening at last. She lay back and wrapped her legs around his body and he entered her. He felt the burning, moist softness of her as the universe went mad. He heaved and she gyrated and they both screamed. Her nails dug into his back and his body was taken over by a long shudder and then there was calm.

'I am sorry,' he said. 'It's been weeks ...'

'Me too,' she whispered, and she kissed him. She cupped her hands around his head and she lifted it. 'Let me look at you. Your name is Peter, isn't it?'

'Yes. Peter.'

'It's a nice name. A strong name.'

He was taken with the disappearance of the old intensity from her lips and did not notice she was talking to him.

Then they lay on the couch for a long while and they talked. Listening came surprisingly easy to him. They talked trivialities. The rain that was about to come and the sea and the fire and the island of Jamaica and diets. Famous restaurants and landmarks and airlines. They talked like any other couple would while he waited for his energy to return and conquer and last.

Then he heard the car and she jumped up and collected her clothes. Two men burst into the room. He was on the point of asking her about herself.

He did not expect anyone at this time of day but he felt easy. He chuckled at their indiscretion. They looked at him and the woman as if they were part of the decor.

'Manners,' he said with a grin. 'Manners.' The shorter man pulled a gun.

'You've been watching too many movies,' he said. He could hear the woman's pulse quicken as he held her hand. She looked terrified. She slipped away from his grasp and straightened her hair and her skirt.

'That's enough,' he said. 'You're frightening my friend here ...'

'I haven't told him a thing,' he heard her say, and then the man took aim and shot her between the eyes. She fell to the floor.

The taller man bent over her and lifted her up. Before he could react they were gone.

This couldn't be happening here. Must be some old black and white melodrama he'd been watching on the box. The week before, he thought he saw James Stewart walk out of the glass and sit with him. He heard his soft, captivating drawl say things to him. Maybe it had all happened on television. Maybe the woman was never there. His mind was hazy. The whole thing had never happened. He had confused the screen with reality before. It could happen to a man after six weeks in solitary. He yawned and got up to turn the set off. He wasn't sure whether it had been switched on. He went back to the chesterfield and felt the cold leather touch his back. Then the shorter man came through the door and handed him his kimono.

He smiled in his direction and was gone again.

He was tired. It was a dream. He must sleep the whole thing off. Sleep it out of his mind. Maybe he hadn't got up at all this morning. He tried to think but tiredness raced through him. What if it was night still? Would the voices be coming later to drag him from his bed?

He was exhausted. He lay down but his eyes refused to stay shut. On the carpet there was a spot. He touched it. It was blood. It was only a tiny spot but for a long moment it became the very centre of the minuscule world he was living in.

He lay face down on the leather, his body soaking in an irritating film of sweat. He touched the spot again and tasted it and a sharp shiver sliced through his body. It was there and real. It did happen. They had made their move. They were committed to it up to their eyeballs. Things must come to a head now. He would not be allowed to sleep. But his eyelids were heavy and he remembered the bitter water they had given him. They had drugged him. He couldn't help but sleep now. He'd work it all out later.

It could be a political thing. Maybe they did know where he had come from. Maybe there was something he had forgotten. Someone. There had been this scandal just before he had left on this trip. Some woman was found dead in some hotel in Warsaw, together with a British businessman who was thrown out of the window twenty floors up. The man had worked for his company once but was on his own now. Still, the government reacted. A whole litter of diplomats was kicked out of the country. In the wake of their departure the Poles had one general executed and two junior ministers put in jail.

Nothing to do with him. There was nothing political about him or his business. He had managed to stay in England as a political refugee, but that was because of his family. What else could he have told them at immigration? The truth?

* * *

'You mean you really are a baron?' Annie had asked on their first night out. God, how easily impressed she was.

'Only half a baron. My mother was a commoner,' he had answered to shut her up, but she persisted.

'In this country you could have made *The Tatler*.'

'There were plenty of barons where I came from. The King of Rumania gave titles away any time he felt like it. Like lollipops.'

'You are funny,' she had said. 'Do you have a coronet somewhere?'

'If it turns you on I can have one embroidered on my underwear.'

'What about your uncle ... Is he?'

'No. He is my mother's brother. Common as dirt.'

'Is this why you get to run the company?'

'No. I get to run it because I am good.'

'Still. Lucky for you to find him.'

Not luck at all, he remembered. A good bit of detective work, though. All he had when he got to Venice was his uncle's name and a hundred dollars. A single, sweaty bill that smelt foul. The commercial man at the British consulate had never heard his uncle's name before, but he said he'd check.

'I have no address but my uncle came to England many years ago. He's a big businessman there now.'

'Everyone wants to come to England,' the diplomat moaned. 'God only knows why, given the weather.'

But two weeks later the diplomat was all smiles. They sent him a postcard and asked him to come to the consulate at his earliest convenience.

'Your uncle is coming out here to meet you,' the commercial attaché said.

'When?'

'Tomorrow.'

'I must be the only relative he's got.'

'Your uncle has connections, my boy. Big connections. We are authorised to put you in funds. This is exciting. A human interest story. A real reunion. Where are you staying?'

He couldn't tell the man that. It was time he got out of Italy anyway.

'I don't need any money, sir.'

'Suit yourself.'

The English never get involved. He liked that best about them.

Annie was different. She had read all about Rumania and the landed gentry there before the war. How the Duke of York went there for a wedding. How their royal family was related to the Windsors. She knew and she tried to learn more. One evening she opened her door for him dressed up as a Carpathian peasant woman. She learned to make mititei meat balls and she fed him on them one weekend with a bottle of Molfatlar wine to wash the spicy meat down. She had tried to invade his insides. Knit herself into him. In trying so hard to please him she did not realise he wanted no part of the old country. He was going to be British. Just like everybody else. He took elocution lessons three times a week and by the time they met he had almost lost his accent.

'I would never have known you were foreign,' she had said when she found out where he was from. Way back at the beginning of their affair. A relationship that started a few weeks after he had first seen her. When they sent her in to him because his secretary was off sick. He spoke English well by then, a far cry from that first meeting with the English in Venice.

He could hardly pronounce 'good morning' properly then. Funny how his uncle had refused to speak Rumanian to him when they met at the Lido. Or even French, the language everyone in Rumania had learned at school.

His uncle had created this investment consultancy business and had other people's money floating about everywhere. He was an expert in maintaining the value of inherited wealth. He was a sharp dresser and could play the piano and owned a priceless collection of antique clocks and paintings. He was a little pompous with it all but he had been kind to his nephew and had installed him in an apartment of his own right from the beginning.

'You must be independent, my boy,' he had said. And for a long time Peter had thought his uncle was motivated by generosity alone. Until he found the old man in bed with his twenty-five-year-old tennis coach. They were both asleep and the young man's golden head rested on his uncle's bare shoulder. He was relieved they didn't see him and thought he would scream but he kept still and tiptoed out of the room. His heart was palpitating. He had not expected that. Of course, he knew what a liar his uncle had been. He used to talk about his mother with tears in his eyes. He said these awful things about the way she had been treated by his father's family.

'My poor sister was deserted,' he often lamented when he'd had a few drinks. 'Just when she needed your father most.'

His father, the Baron, would have shot him for that, had he been around.

But Peter took his time and everything else he was offered.

He often wondered where the bastard was hiding his mother and why. But he was patient by nature and he didn't want to see her anyway.

After all, he was only twenty-five years old and already a director of the firm.

And by the time Annie came into his life from the general office he had made up his mind about the old man.

The sky had opened up above the house that was his prison and lightning shot across the room. Then came thunder. The electricity went off. He braced himself for a downpour. He was cold. But he was awake and he knew he had just witnessed a killing. Perhaps it would be his turn next. Perhaps she had been a prisoner too. Could this be a place where they killed people? A sort of designer execution ground? Contract killing. Keep someone and treat him according to his sins. Get them to talk then bump them off. Could be. Lots of people paid to get rid of someone. A disgruntled customer. The competition. Someone's husband.

These thoughts troubled him because he knew he had enemies. Was that why he was here? No, no, no. They might have known a lot, but they did not know it all.

'Who can sleep at this time in the morning?' he growled into space. The room basked in the mystery of daytime darkness. Strange for this part of the world, he thought. The fire was going strong. He had not seen who lit it or when. The wood crackled and the heat floated across to him.

Then the first drop of rain fell on the slated roof. It was soon followed by more. It came down like a barrage. More and more of it fell and it sounded like machine-gun fire. Or something else, buried deep in the dark catacomb of his memory. The past he had so desperately tried to erase was knocking on his door.

No you don't, he decided, and tried to think of something else. But there was no stopping it. He was transported far away, onto a pine-covered slope on another continent. Another time. He had another name. He was young. He was in uniform.

His yesterday came to him with a bang, sharp and raw and clear.

CHAPTER THREE

———■———

'You're a liar,' the corporal said. 'A goddamned mother-fuckin' liar.'

A grey cold dawn descended from the treetops and the fire they had lit the night before was dying at his feet. Its scent mingled with the strong odour of pine. There was no one else about. Staccato shouts of command invaded the forest and in his mind he saw the others sweating at their push-ups or jogging over the fern.

'I'd better join the platoon,' he said in hope, but the corporal shook his head.

'PE is too good for you, Gordonitzu. You're going to rot in jail forever. The army knows how to deal with your kind. A military jail is worse than death. People go there for less than what you've been doing.'

The man is faking, he thought. He wasn't angry enough to be honest. He knew nothing.

Below, fifteen small tents stood neatly around the clearing. Dead centre, amidst a square of whitewashed stones, stood a makeshift wooden pole. Two flags, the red one for the party and the other with the battalion's insignia, fluttered gently in the rising mist. In the corner, by the field kitchen, two soldiers polished a huge aluminium pot. They were out of earshot.

'You're scum, Gordonitzu. A traitor. Rumania is a socialist country. No private income, no private enterprise allowed, remember? How much money did you make?'

The words hit home and made his heart palpitate. The corporal did know something but he must not panic. He could be playing a guessing game. Maybe he knew a little and was trying to find out more. His language was foul but that was not unusual.

'What money?'

'Foreign money, you Jewish shit. D. marks, sterling pounds ...'

'I am not a Jew.'

'Oh, pardon me ... Of course you're not. You're from history. You think you're allowed to be different. Ignore what goes on around you ... Ignore the rules and regulations. You're some sort of an aristocratic blue-blooded parasite, aren't you?'

'My father is ... was a baron.'

'Barons, Jews, all the same. Enemies of the state.'

'Not the same, Comrade Corporal.'

'Who cares? Were you thinking of starting a bank maybe? Right under the nose of the Rumanian army? You can't have two jobs, you know. Banks are no longer private.'

The voice was too gentle. Humorous, if anything. The man *must* be bluffing. He would never miss the opportunity of doing this in public otherwise.

'I don't know what you mean, Comrade Corporal. I hope you do.'

By rights the corporal should have hit him across the face for insolence. But he was smiling. He either had no proof or else he wanted something. Must try. Go on the offensive. This was an army of equals.

'If you feel I've done something wrong you should report me to the comrade lieutenant.'

'No profit in that, Gordonitzu, is there?'

'Comrade?'

'It's the share of the cash I am after, little Baron, not glory. A bit of that thriving business of yours, you understand? Of course I can go and talk to the comrade lieutenant, but only if you force me to go on living on this crappy pay. I'd rather you paid up ...'

'I could deny everything.'

'Not when they see what I've got.'

The corporal took a bunch of photographs out of his pocket and showed him the one on top. He knew, all right. He knew it all. There was no sense in further pretence.

'Where did you get these pictures, Comrade Corporal?'

'Photography is my hobby, Gordonitzu. Good, aren't I?'

'What now, Comrade Corporal?'

'I'll soon let you know, Gordonitzu. Very soon. Now go join the others and get some exercise. Makes you think better, a little sweat does ...'

'But Comrade Corporal ...'

'When we're alone you can call me partner.'

Peter saluted and, following his comrades, he sprinted into the woods. He was eighteen years old and broad-shouldered and always taller than others his age. His father was proud of his looks, his muscle and his talents. He needed to see the old man now. Ask for advice. He could get leave now that he had a friend in authority. The old man would know what to do.

'You get your looks from me but your brains are definitely from your mother's family,' his father used to say, but then he was being modest.

He was always modest when he wasn't gambling. He was educated and he loved to talk. Politics, stamps, hunting, fishing, sailing boats and cars and French cuisine. He never talked about Peter's mother unless he was totally drunk, which was rare nowadays.

And then he would remember her, the woman he divorced when his son Peter was four years old. Remember her, and talk of how she had left him, and cry.

His father, too, had spent time in uniform when he was young. That was a different army altogether, if it was an army at all. People did not talk of his father's army any more. Nor of the last king or of titles. Such talk was against the law now. The changing fortunes of Rumania did not affect his father too much. Incredibly, he was still living where he was born, on the family estate. Perhaps the corporal knew about that too. He certainly knew about his mother. Why else would he have called him a Jew?

He ran down the hill to catch up with his comrades and the old notion of his mother's secret origins began to prick his conscience.

Not so secret origins. His mother was born Jewish and had converted before marrying his father. He never knew why things did not work out between them. After the divorce he was sent to a boarding-school.

Sometimes he was brought to see her in a small apartment in Bucharest, or so he had been told. He stayed with her there too. Something about soldiers taking her away had often entered his mind but never lingered. He had been told she took off one day and left him and was never seen again. They said she left in 1942 to go to a brother she had in England. A big businessman there. 'Brains of a professor, your uncle has,' his father always said. He used to wonder why she never tried to make contact after the war. Even dogs look after their young. Maybe his mother was just bad. He had come to that conclusion himself. His father did not contradict him and others did not talk of her because they were afraid or did not remember.

Well, he was eighteen years old now and a soldier in the Rumanian People's Army. He had been operating an illegal foreign exchange business for four years. Now that he had been found out, he had problems.

Later that day the corporal cornered him again. It was five o'clock in the afternoon, the sun was down, and the air had become progressively cooler.

'Let's walk around the perimeter,' the corporal said. 'We must talk about our future.'

When they got to the lake the corporal said:

'It will freeze over tonight for sure. Say, Gordonitzu, how much money do we have?'

'I cannot say for sure. I don't keep the books here.'

'That much, huh? So there're other people involved?'

'Only my father ... and his manservant ...'

'Manservant? Nowadays? Your father has a manservant?'

'Not exactly ... sort of manservant. He lives with my father.'

'Your father keeps the money?'

'No. The money is on the streets.'

'Our money on the streets? Are you crazy?'

'On the streets, Corporal. Circulating ... Working for us. Changing hands.'

'Is that good?'

'It's the way my business operates, Corporal.'

'Our business, Gordonitzu. Ours. You'll have to explain it to me one of these days.'

'I can do that now.'

'No need. I trust you. There is honour amongst thieves, right?'

They walked and they talked about this and that. Gordonitzu figured the corporal was greedy, but not as clever as he had thought. He came from Ploesti and his father had worked in the oil fields there. He was going to make the army his career, he said, but he would give it a miss if he could make his fortune elsewhere. He was born lucky, he told Peter, and the further he was from Ploesti the luckier he felt. There was a branch of the People's Bank across the street from their flat in Ploesti. The people who worked there were always smartly dressed in suits and ate in the finest restaurants. He would have liked to have been a banker and now he was, wasn't he? His life would change. He would be able to buy some decent clothes and travel and visit the Black Sea coast and see the foreign tourists who went there. Buy a Leica camera. Go to the West ... Meet a foreign woman and maybe marry or go to America.

Until now he hadn't been able to do that. He had thought of ways of improving his life, but in the meantime there was always the army to fall back on. You could make yourself invisible and stay on for years, living off the fat of the land. The People's Army was a holy institution. No one would suspect you of anything as long as you were in uniform. The important thing, he said, was to learn to keep your mouth shut in the army. Keep to as low a rank as possible. Do what you were told and stay there forever. That way nobody noticed you and nobody knew you were even there. The corporal talked a lot that day.

The old man would know how to deal with the situation, Peter kept telling himself as the evening wore on. He would get his pass all right. The corporal's greed would mar his judgement. It would be easier to sort things out in the country, with his father.

'The first thing I'll do with my money is buy myself a motorbike,' the corporal said.

'You want to spend money?'

'Sure. What else is money good for?'

'You'll make more if you keep your share in.'

'Where are the books?'

'My father keeps them up-country.'

'You're a clever fellow, aren't you, Gordonitzu?'

'Would you like to come with me to see my old man? You would enjoy where he lives and we could collect some money.'

'You go, Gordonitzu. In all fairness, I am only a sleeping partner. Maybe we shouldn't take any money out now if you think it should be working for us on the streets instead. You go. You deserve a bit of a change, and I trust you, don't I?'

He couldn't believe his luck. The whole thing was too easy.

'Just get a little bit of money out,' the corporal said. 'I'll start with a small motorbike. You go see what you can do. The army will still be here when you get back. You can't get away from it unless it wants you to. If they want you out you fly out.'

He might as well have said deserters are shot.

The old man would know what to do .

'We'll arrange a pass for you,' the corporal said. 'You leave that to me. We'll have to wait until the company is back in barracks.'

They gave him forty-eight hours at first, and then he had another word with the corporal. He said it wasn't enough. The estate was far away. Just getting there would take up half that time. They extended his leave to four whole days.

They had arranged to see each other at the central railway station. He would bring some money then. Eight in the evening of the fourth day. Under the clock at the big hall.

'Like a couple of lovers,' the corporal said, and laughed.

★ ★ ★

Gordonitzu stopped in Bucharest to change trains for the west. He was not a stranger to the journey. He had made it many times, on his own, during his boarding-school days.

The station had not altered much, but the romantic hiss of steam was replaced by evil-smelling diesel locomotives. It was dirtier these days, and no one sold flowers or glossy magazines. There were no sandwich vendors, no fryers of meat balls, no purveyors of drinks. There used to be hundreds of urchins there, their hands looking for a coin. Now the beggars were gone too. The sweet, forbidden colour of private enterprise had vanished from the tarmac.

In the old days there was always someone from the estate to take him to the train. He hardly ever stopped in the big city unless his father happened to be there. He chuckled to himself as he remembered. The old man used to stay at the Athene Palace Hotel opposite the royal residence, and during the day he would walk the Boulevard with his son clad in his school uniform. In the evening he always went out on the town, dressed up in a tuxedo and patent leather shoes and a cape and black tie. He used to bend over him, the strong scent of French eau de cologne oozing from his clean-shaven face. He'd tuck the boy cosily inside the feather bed and kiss him goodnight. Sometimes he would stay a bit and tell him a little story.

These were the times when mornings became afternoons, and while the rest of the world had their first cocktail Baron Gordonitzu and his son Peter drank black coffee and ate hot, crisp croissants. They would lie together in the big bed and read the papers. Sometimes they went to an afternoon film-show. That was when young Gordonitzu was first introduced to Humphrey Bogart.

Funny, the young soldier thought as he waited for his train. The Germans had been defeated and King Carol was gone. The government had changed many times and then the communists took over and remained. Some of the Jews came back from the camps. The masses were being re-educated. There were new newspapers. New street names. New money. New uniforms and new emblems for everything. New stamps. Older people were confused. The world was falling away from right under their feet. This was a new way of life, yet in a way nothing had changed. Not for the old Baron, his father.

Even these days, his father still enjoyed himself. Once a month, as in the past, he would go to Bucharest and stay in that very same Athene Palace Hotel. He no longer had a room of his own there since he slept in the chef's quarters, but no one knew that. Saturday nights he went out on the town wrapped up in his velvet cape. The flower woman outside always had his red carnation and a toothless smile at the ready. Those people in town who remembered him from the old days thought he had fled the Red regime with the others. He was too colourful for the new order of things, and they believed he came back from the west once a month to visit his old hunting grounds. Most people thought that, except for the chef and a distant cousin who now worked as a night porter at the hotel and had kept the Baron's evening clothes in his locker. The other man who knew the truth was Mihai, their ancient manservant who still lived with the Baron on the estate. And, of course, Peter Gordonitzu, the Baron's son, who from the age of fourteen had been dealing in the black currency market and was now the provider.

The train rolled in slowly and the soldier walked along the carriages waiting for the doors to open. He was good at finding seats for himself, a talent he had developed in his schooldays. As he settled down on the soft, worn seat he thought of what had happened and how he was going to deal with the corporal. He also thought of his father and where he was living and how the heroes of his childhood had aged.

He was tired, and he slept most of the way up. The compartment was full of drab, ashen, unshaven people who ate out of newspapers and smoked cheap-smelling tobacco. Some tried to talk to him but he had much on his mind and pretended to be asleep when he was not. The visit was going to be a surprise and he would have to walk to the estate by himself. These days the train did not always stop at the village, and often he had to jump out of it as the valley of his childhood approached. The valley and the old village, and in the centre the church in which his father and his ancestors were christened, married and mostly buried.

The vineyards were now coming into view ahead. Long rows of familiar plants that curved with the countryside. He knew he was coming closer to the village. He himself had not lived there for years.

There was little for him to do up here because there were no foreign tourists or businessmen in these parts and no currency to buy. That existed only in the city where most of them stopped on the way to the coast. It was a risky business but the profits were fat. The official rate of exchange was much lower than that on the streets. It was illegal to hold foreign money, but there was never a shortage of takers. Would-be emigrants and often government officials preparing for an overseas visit to the West, whose currency allocation was too small for shopping. Human nature, Peter had learned, did not change with the man in the Palace. The foreign cash came from barmen, taxi drivers and prostitutes, who sought his youthful, handsome face for the transaction because they felt comfortable with him.

He had been living in Bucharest for four years, in a small but heated room. He had kept it after he was drafted into the army. He was used to a better life now, being quite rich under the circumstances. At any given time he had twenty or thirty thousand German marks circulating in the back streets. He was discreet and efficient and his rates were better than those of other dealers. He always knew where one could find an old icon or a painting or a piece of antique furniture. He knew where better-class women could be found. None were professional whores. Some were students or secretaries or daughters of impoverished families who had found their way to the city. Others were lonely or abused house-wives in need of company and a few luxuries. They all trusted him and his business flourished in spite of his absence. Had it not been for the draft he would have been richer, but no Gordonitzu ever avoided the call of the flag. One great-uncle of his father had made general and was decorated. Another was a famous aviator who ended up, uniform, plane and all, on a beach in Monte Carlo with his throat cut.

This was not going to last forever. Once he was out of uniform he could operate as he had before. His customers and his suppliers waited for him and all was well.

Except that now there was the corporal.

The train was slowing down. Gordonitzu put his greatcoat on, opened the door and stood there at the ready. The houses and the valley approached and the train assumed a snail's pace for the steep climb. It was not going to stop today, he reasoned, and he smiled as the air hit his face. He smiled at the surprised faces around him and jumped into the grass.

He walked along the path to the village and whistled 'As Time Goes By'. He had seen *Casablanca* after the war when anti-German films were popular. He always whistled when he walked in the fields by himself. It kept him warm, and he whistled faster as his steps overtook the tune.

'A kiss is just a kiss, tadam tadam tadam . . .' It was a good thing the corporal had declined his invitation. He would never have understood the situation up here. He would have expected things to have been the way they were before the war. Aristocrats lived in castles in that children's book that was his mind. Or in great houses with ornamented gardens and fountains and liveried footmen. He had said so when he'd handed the pass over.

The song ran out on him and he stopped. He tore a handful of grass out of the wet earth and the smell of freshly exposed soil came to him. He laughed out loud as he thought of the corporal. A nervous laugh loaded with uncertainty. What his face would tell if he knew the truth, saw how his father the Baron really lived.

In the old days Mihai would collect him from the station in the Bugatti and race it through the narrow cobblestoned streets to the estate. Sometimes his father was at the wheel himself.

In his memory it was always summer when his father came to collect him, dressed in tweeds, his good, broad face beaming under his English hunting hat with the pleasure of a reunion. The hat was a present from his uncle in England who was no longer his uncle because his mother had left.

These days Mihai was too old to drive and the Bugatti was gone. His father had lost it playing cards with a Luftwaffe officer during the last hours of the war. It would have been taken away in any case, he figured, as he resumed his walk. The communists did not allow private cars. Or any other cars, unless you were an official. There were no more private bankers or businessmen or aristocratic landowners. Yet his father, once known as Baron Gordonitzu by one and all, still lived in a place that used to bear that very name. God, the young man thought, moves in mysterious ways.

No one waved at him from the windows as he walked through the village. There used to be flower boxes that poured kaleidoscopes of colour down the old walls. Moss-covered old stones under freshly painted shutters that closed only in winter. He shrugged his shoulders. He must not malign. This was winter and the wrong season for flowers. In any case, he was not sure how much of his memory was fiction. Of course, it wasn't always summer when his father came to meet him. Church bells didn't ring at that time of morning, even in the old days.

He walked through the village quickly, then up the path that led to the estate. He was soon at the entrance. The large wrought-iron gate that once stood there was gone. All that remained were the two stone lions, one on each side of the entrance. They carried, he thought, the humiliation of their uselessness with pride. How many times had he crashed his bicycle into one or the other? He could not remember, nor was it important. The stone lions never scolded him for the damage and they took it all with the stoical calm of old age.

How he missed that old iron gate. It used to be such fun to sneak out in the night and roam the meadows in search of copulating young-sters from the village. Everybody knew what the place was called when he was a child, but these days the authorities played it safe. The name Gordonitzu was gone. Suspended over the lions, where the gate had once been, there was a red metal signpost that creaked with the wind. It read: 'People's Community Farm number 603'.

The same signpost, but smaller, was attached to the side of the large truck he was approaching. He walked round the wooden planks and came to the back of the vehicle. It was a long, Russian-built machine that was used to transport produce from Community Farm number 603 to the central market. The former landowner used to be a motor-racing enthusiast in his youth and the committee that now managed the estate agreed to allow him to occupy the position of assistant to the driver.

As such, the Baron sat with the driver when the truck was in motion to make sure the man did not fall asleep. Sometimes, very rarely, he was actually allowed to sit behind the wheel, but only when they were within the boundary of the farm. It was also the last available stage for his fa-ther's eccentricity. Since his old bedroom was now the farm's office, the old Baron used the truck as his sleeping quarters.

The mist was rising and there was the sound of chickens squabbling in the old stables. Other than that, it being Sunday and a day of rest, the place was as silent as the fields. The young soldier hoped he had got the date right. His father travelled into Bucharest on the fourth Sunday of each month and this was the second.

He lifted the thick canvas and climbed into the hold. Inside, in the dark, wrapped in his old sleeping-bag, lay the long shape of the man he had come to see. There were a few pictures and an icon, all strung along the sides of the structure. A kerosene lamp hung from the ceiling. There were flowers and a jug of water on a wooden box by his side. A few books were strewn around him, amongst which the young man recognised the leather-bound Bible and his father's black-rimmed reading glasses. He gave a sigh of relief as he approached. He could never be sure with the old man. This could have been anyone. He stood there for a minute and his heart warmed as rays of the winter sun streamed in from the back.

They lit the confined space he stood in, then his father's face. The older man stretched his arm out of the khaki rug. His eyes strained as they faced the sudden onslaught of light.

'Good morning, father.'

The Baron's knack of knowing exactly where he was the instant he woke had not deserted him with the years. A must for all gamblers, he used to say.

'What are you doing here? We didn't expect them to let you out that soon. Boy, the army has changed, eh? If this isn't a military secret, aren't you supposed to be in the middle of that dreadful basic training?'

'How are you, father?'

'Never better. Never better, my boy. Say, it's way past coffee time. I wonder what is keeping that old blackguard Mihai. Getting lazier by the hour he is.'

'Let me go to the kitchens and fix you something.'

'Nonsense. You just sit tight and tell me how things are amongst the comrades out there in the People's Army. The service in this place is appalling, I can tell you. Say, you couldn't let me have a few coins, could you, son?'

'I have a little problem, father ...'

'Yes ... I'm going into town earlier ... I'm off there next weekend. That's why I need the money now. I was going to write to you about it, in code, of course. But since you're here in person I thought I might mention the cash.'

'Don't worry about that, father. I'll see to it before I leave.'

'I hope you stay for coffee anyway. I wonder what that blighter Mihai thinks he's playing at. He's getting a bit past it, you know. It's good to see you, boy. Really good to see you. I did mention the money ... Yes, of course I did.'

From outside came a new voice that bawled at them.

'Get up,' it howled. 'You parasite. You're not in Versailles any more. The king has gone. This is a working day, you blood-sucking aristocrat.'

The Baron crawled out of his sleeping-bag. At the back of the truck, along with a series of groans, appeared the white head of a man. His face was wrinkled but his blue eyes shone with the vigour of youth. He looked over his shoulder. As if to make sure he was not followed.

'Forgive me, Your Excellency, it's after eleven.'

'I told you he's getting past it,' the Baron said to his son. 'It's Sunday, you fool. Day of rest. Even here and now, even for the communists. And it is nowhere near eleven yet. You'll bring the whole goddamned neighbourhood down on us with your screams ... And where the hell is my coffee?'

Mihai climbed in. He noticed the young man inside and was about to shout more abuse at the Baron when a fisted hand hit his shoulder.

'It's all right, Mihai. It's me. Peter.'

'Apologies, Master Peter,' Mihai said. 'You never know who is around. Officially there are no manservants any more. But as long as I shout at him now and again they leave us alone. You know I don't mean to be disrespectful.'

'Now that you have been introduced, Mihai, I would be grateful if you could manage a coffee,' the Baron said. 'And a bit of toast, if it isn't too much trouble.'

'Yes, Your Excellency. I'll see to it immediately.'

'I shall go with him,' said the young soldier.

They walked about what used to be the dining-room while the water came to the boil. On the walls there were blank squares where family portraits had hung in another age. Bare light-bulbs had replaced the chandeliers. All around them there were white-on-red slogans about the final victory of socialism and the merits of hard work.

'Who are they fooling,' Mihai said, shaking his head. 'Work is a thing of the past. All they do is talk and write about it. The system pays up whatever happens. They are a bunch of lazy dogs, if you ask me.'

'I don't know what my father would do without you, Mihai.'

'He worries me.'

'Why?'

'He keeps forgetting these are new times. I used to take him on inspection tours of the estate at night, to stop the others poking fun at him. Lately he has been demanding we make them in broad daylight. Always when he's supposed to be working. Yesterday he insisted he wanted to see the stables, would you believe. It took an hour to remind him all the horses are gone. I try to do what he says but sometimes he forgets even I can't bring the old days back. The others laugh at him, of course, but only behind his back. It could get nasty if they put their minds to it, Master Peter. Jealousy is not just ugly, it can be dangerous. But we've been lucky ... So far we've had no problems, but who knows?'

'You're a man in a million, Mihai ...'

'You know, Master Peter, perhaps the new order is not all that bad. It has made a survivor of you. His Excellency does not notice it much ... he was always far too sheltered. I don't know who is going to look after him when I kick the bucket.'

'You will be around forever.'

'It always rains on Sundays,' Baron Gordonitzu said.

'Naturally,' said Mihai the manservant. 'What better excuse for them to forget about feeding the chickens?'

'You keep your jokes to yourself,' the Baron said. 'It pours like mad; can you hear it, Peter? Sounds like a million can-can girls dancing on the canvas up there.'

'At least it doesn't leak, Your Excellency. We're dry in here ... Things could be worse.'

'One more crack out of you and I'll order you off this truck.'

Peter's face contorted in anger. He opened his mouth to protest but Mihai touched his arm and said:

'Yes, Your Excellency. I am sorry. I shall remember my place.'

'Can't help the margarine, son,' the Baron said. 'This isn't the Athene Palace Hotel.'

'This is 1956, father.'

'Of course it is. Do you remember the croissants? The butter? Oh, before I forget, you do have the money for me, don't you?'

'Of course I have, father. I may not be able to see you before next month. I have a spot of trouble ...' The soldier looked at the manservant, then at his father. 'I'd better give you two months' money. I'll leave it with your cousin at the Athene Palace Hotel. I haven't got enough on me ...'

'Make sure he knows it's for me. You can't trust anyone these days.'

'I will, father. You can count on that.'

'Good,' the Baron said. 'You do that. I hate handling this new money anyway. Doesn't quite feel like the real thing ... More like toy money. Are we going to inspect today, Mihai? I haven't seen the stables in weeks.'

'With respect, Your Excellency, may I suggest we wait a little? ... It's ...'

'It's raining like hell out there, father,' Peter said.

'I suppose you are right, son. I would much rather lie in today ... Some people have no idea the trouble you have when you own land. Come, give your father a kiss before you go. Mihai will take you to the station. Give him a treat, old man, take the Bugatti, but don't you dare scrape it.'

What had possessed him to think he could look to his father for help? Once, not too long ago, the Baron could muster a few words of advice. Must have been a bad day for him, that was all. What was he going to do about the corporal?

They walked to the village in silence. The rain smashed into their faces. The young man had asked Mihai to stay behind, but the manservant had insisted. They battled their way through the mud until they reached the paved road that led to the first row of houses. They walked through the narrow, deserted streets towards the old village inn that stood by the church. The rain had washed most of the dirt from their boots and they took their coats off and sat by the window. The place was empty.

'Some things never change, Master Peter. The old beggar never had any business. Not even when the king sat on his throne. Now he's better off. He gets paid whatever happens because the place belongs to the government. The villagers won't come in here. Never have.'

'Why not?'

'His wife is the biggest gossip in the land.'

The clock announced it was three o'clock. Mihai consulted his pocket watch.

'There's a train in an hour,' Peter said.

'They should stop here today. Unless they run out of fuel. Why don't you stay the night?'

'I've got things to do in Bucharest.'

'How's your business going?'

'It's ticking over. I haven't been able to attend to it much. Listen, Mihai, I am worried about him. You are right. He is losing touch. He seems worse.'

'Only on Sundays, my boy, because Sundays are difficult ... Lifetime habits die hard. In the old days he used to nurse his hangover until lunchtime every Sunday ... He didn't have too much last night but he still feels low. In the old days he had things to do ... on Sunday afternoons he was always out and about. People came over ... There were hunting parties, card games, picnics ...'

'That was years ago.'

'When a man gets into a habit he can't just shake it off. Not at his age. I wish you could see him when he goes off into town ... even nowadays. How he charms the stationmaster into stopping the train for him ... How he gets the ticket collector to give him the best seat without a ticket. He always tips them well, though, Master Peter ... He's a real gentleman. You should be proud of him. Sometimes he is as sober and articulate as a judge, but not always. Sometimes he is depressed and then he becomes forgetful ... He is not young any more ...'

'What about you, then, Mihai. You're no spring chicken either.'

'Never mind me, I'm a hardened peasant ... But you, Master Peter, you came up here for something else ... You'd better tell me what the trouble is. Something is bothering you.'

'Yes ... Something is.'

'You'd better talk about it,' Mihai said, and Peter nodded and started talking. The manservant listened attentively to what the soldier told him. All the while he sipped his drink in silence.

'This is serious,' he said.

'I thought so too.'

'Best get the corporal up here one weekend, when your father is away in town. We will think of something then. The countryside has a few tricks of its own, you know. The hills keep their secrets. Don't you worry, we too have our way of dishing out justice up here. Jealous husbands and horse thieves could tell you a thing or two, if spirits could talk.'

'Are you saying we shall have to kill him?'

'I said no such thing, Master Peter. People's fates depend mostly on themselves. Even if they're born in the wrong place. In the meantime, just give the corporal whatever he wants.'

'I'll have to think about that.'

'Don't think about it. Listen to me. You be nice to him ... agree with everything ... Give him whatever he wants for now.'

'All right, but we should get going. It's time.'

'Finish your drink first, Master Peter. Yes, I'll think some more about your problem, but make sure you let me know when you bring him up. I'd like to arrange a proper reception for your corporal when he comes.'

'What do you mean?'

'Nothing, my boy. Nothing of importance. You finish your drink now. Take your time. Maybe you should eat something. There's no hurry. The train will be late today.'

The innkeeper came to their table.

'Let me pay now,' the soldier said. 'I've got to get to the station.'

'Aren't you the Gordonitzu boy?'

'Yes.'

'You going to Bucharest?'

'Yes.'

'The train won't leave before evening. You can stay right where you are. Relax. Have another drink. Would you like some food?'

'Will the train stop here today?'

'It will stop here, young man, but it won't leave before evening.'

'Why?'

The innkeeper's wife shouted from the kitchen, 'The driver will stay here for more than an hour. He'll have his dinner in the village.'

'How do you know?'

'He's got a sister in the village,' she replied. 'She was here just before you came. She told me.'

'Know-all!' Mihai the manservant said, and they laughed. But a sadness came over the young soldier as he sipped his drink.

'What did happen to my mother, Mihai?'

The manservant's face fell.

'I think you'd better talk about that with His Excellency your father. It is a family matter and I cannot . . . I am . . . at the time I was only a manservant.'

'You know he's in no position to talk about anything at this moment.'

'He has his ups and his downs, like all of us. Perhaps you should wait until you see him again. You will be surprised how lucid he can be. In any case, I am sure you had occasion to talk about your mother with him before.'

'Yes. A long time ago. He said she went to England. Joined her brother there.'

'Well, then, there's your answer.'

'You do not sound too convinced. You see, Mihai, I get these moments sometimes . . . at night. Bad dreams. I can never remember them but I think it's as if we are in some danger . . . Mother and me . . . I don't know. I can't be sure.'

'You must be worried about the corporal. I told you, we'll solve that. You can count on me.'

'No, no. It's nothing to do with the corporal. I've had these dreams for years. At first they didn't come very often, but lately I get them almost every night . . . I have no idea what they are about . . . I hear voices. Noises . . . Then I wake up in a sweat . . . I don't remember any of it . . . I think they are frightening dreams . . .'

'Nightmares?'

'No. Yes. Yes, nightmares maybe. I don't know . . . Nightmares, yes, I think they are nightmares . . . I don't know. I don't remember.'

'Anxiety always brings fear, Peter. You lie there in your bed and you are frightened without knowing what you are frightened of. It happens when you grow older, too. Young people have fears of an exam or lack of money or love. Old people have the fear of bad health or death ... You think of death. Of punishment for things you have done.'

'Why should Mother be involved in nightmares, Mihai? She never suffered. It was I who was deserted.'

'Your mother? Do you think she has something to do with it?'

'Sometimes I think she has ... Maybe not. I don't know.'

'You cannot choose your dreams. In any case, I could not tell you much about that. In 1942 I was a soldier. I wasn't on the estate when your mother left.'

'You were in the army?'

'Only for a short time. Your father got me out of there pretty quickly. I was needed here, you see.'

'You still are ...'

'Being needed keeps you alive and fit, my boy. I suppose you know the Germans took your mother to a concentration camp. They were going to ship her away ...'

'But that would only have been after she left, right? I was not involved in that?'

'You used to spend time with her in Bucharest after she left here. They could have come for her while you were there.'

'I don't remember any of that.'

'She didn't stay in the camp too long. Your father had her released soon after they took her.'

'That's right. Of course he did. That's what I was told.'

'You see? You know the facts, then. Your father did tell you about it.'

'Yes. I am sorry. I don't know why I brought it up. But I don't know why, after her release from the camp, she did not come to see me. She left without a parting word. An explanation. I don't understand that. Anyway, I suppose my problems and my father's state of mind frustrate me.'

'I know what you mean, my boy. Believe me.'

Later, as the train crawled to a stop, the young man stood by the window talking to Mihai. The rain had ceased. The driver jumped off his locomotive. Walking past them, he disappeared into the village.

'Looks empty in there,' Mihai said. 'You might as well choose a good seat and lie down and get some sleep. The driver does have a sister here. I recognised him. Used to come to the village for the summer when he was a boy. Like you did.'

'You'd better go, Mihai. It's dark out there.'

'I have walked these parts for years, Master Peter. I know every tree. They have more rubbish dumps than trees here these days. Used to go into the village when I was young. Have myself a drink or two and a good time. I wasn't always old . . .'

'You'd better go all the same.'

'I suppose so. I'd better go see to your father.'

'Don't overdo it, Mihai.'

The old man shook his head.

'One day I'll have time and I'll tell you the whole truth. Perhaps you will understand me better then. Understand me and your father. You see, your father needs much care. Much encouragement. Much more than you know.'

'Are the others giving him a hard time?'

'No. It's not the Reds so much, nor his old age. His mind is tortured by the cards.'

'You mean he's still gambling? I thought that was against the law now. Where would he find a casino? Well, I suppose he's doing it on the quiet. Must have a group of his old cronies down in the town. Maybe some of the old-timers survived. No wonder he goes through money as fast as he does.'

'You've got it wrong, Master Peter. It's cards, but not now. He doesn't gamble any more. No, no. It's something else. Something that happened a very long time ago. It's yesterday's cards that trouble him. It's his inheritance. He does not own the estate any more.'

'We all know about that, Mihai. You don't need to tell me. No one owns anything. The communists took it. State Community Farm 603, I know.'

'No, Master Peter. That's not it. I mean before that. Before the communists took over.'

'What are you talking about?'

'Your father lost the estate many years ago. The communists did not take it away from him at all. When they came it was no longer his. He had lost it playing cards, just before the end of the war . . . These are the cards that torment him. That's why he escapes into a world of his own . . . He wants to forget. Forget he played away his birthright. Your birthright.'

'Who did my father lose the estate to?'

'That doesn't matter now. I only told you so you'll understand why he sometimes behaves as if he can't wait for you to leave. He's ashamed . . . Distressed . . . He feels he failed you, do you understand?'

'No,' Peter said. The compartment jerked and then the train started moving. The old man walked along the ramp. He said something but then the horn sounded and the accelerating motion pulled the wagon forward.

'What did you say?'

'They must have another driver on board.'

'What did you say before?' Peter shouted, and then they ran out of tarmac and the window passed the end of the fence. The old man was gone. Outside, the scant lights curved with the disappearing valley. Beyond, laden with fat, moonlit October grapes, the vineyards flew past into the dark. Then the rain came back and he moved away from the window.

CHAPTER FOUR

——■——

The pain throbbed inside his head but he remembered it all. Every last bit of it. He even remembered talking about the corporal to Annie a few years into their marriage. She had asked him why he had left Rumania and he told her but he did not tell her everything. All he said was that the corporal had suspected him and he had to leave in a hurry. He did not tell her what the end was. Perhaps he kept some of it back because he did not want her to know what he was capable of.

He lay there on the chesterfield and he watched the fireplace. The fire was going strong. He was not sure how long he had been asleep. Perhaps he had not been asleep at all. Just transported back to his father's old estate, the railway station with Mihai. He must have been unconscious. He looked at his watch. Annie had given the Rolex to him for his fortieth birthday, and now it told him that evening was close. They must have put something in the water. Yes, it had tasted bitter. Or maybe they had injected him with something while he was out cold. The woman? No. She had not given him anything. He looked at the carpet and searched for the little red spot. He was surprised at his own lucidity. The blood would have gone black by now but it was not there at all.

Had they served his lunch? Had they brought his cold dinner into the dining-room? He was too lazy to go and check. But one thing was certain. The carpet was as clean as new.

So they had paid him a visit. Or else the whole episode with the woman had never happened. A wishful-thinking exercise that did not come true.

He tried to think of the woman and what had happened between them but pictures of the central railway station in Bucharest started bursting into his mind. Vividly, in full colour they came. They were all new and crisp and with the pictures came the sound of a train arriving, and he heard announcements in a language he had not used for years. His head was getting heavier. He rested it on his arm and looked into his memory and he saw his young self again, walking towards the big clock for his meeting with his corporal.

'What the fuck do you mean there is no money?' the corporal fumed, twisting his lips. He was quite ugly when he was angry, Peter thought.

'It's all on the streets, and some is up on the estate. My father refuses to hand it over. He insists on meeting you in person.'

'Don't shit me, Gordonitzu. You mean he doesn't trust you?'

'Scouts' honour. That's what he told me up at the estate.'

'Scouts and estates do not exist here any more, smartass. You said we had thousands on the streets. Changing hands, you said. Working for us, you said. Making profits.'

'I do have a bit at my place. You're welcome to have that. But there's more on the streets and more up-country. And you'll get your share when you come up.'

'You think I am retarded? My place . . . No one's got a place. Your place is where mine is. The barracks. And there's no money there. I promise you. I've looked through every bit of shit you have by your bed. Nothing.'

'I have a little room right here in town. Come and see for yourself.'

'You bet your useless balls I will.'

It took them half an hour to walk to the room. He led the corporal through wet, misty back streets. The smell of poverty oozed out of shabby, cracked walls and mingled with petrol fumes and home cooking. He offered to stop for a drink first. A little place he knew nearby. Open all night. The corporal refused.

'I never drink on duty,' he said with a smirk. 'You must have nerves of steel.'

But his tone of voice and posture changed when they got to Peter's room and a wad of bills was put on the table. His eyes lit up as he touched the money. The landlady did not scold them for waking her up. She smiled and as they sat down she brought a bottle of brandy and peanuts. The room was warm and clean.

'You've got life pretty well organised, Gordonitzu,' the corporal said with unmistakable admiration. 'I am dying to meet your father. Must be a fascinating man. How many barons still live on their land?'

'It's not exactly what you think, Comrade Corporal.'

'Cut out the comrade bit when we're in town. When do we go up there?'

'We'll have to plan it. Say in two weeks or something. If we go back there right now he'd think I was in trouble. We'll need another pass.'

'You do the planning. Leave the passes to me.'

The corporal took a square printed form out of his pocket.

'You keep them handy, eh? That's against regulations, isn't it?'

'How do you spell you name, Gordonitzu?'

'I don't need it yet, Comrade Corporal.'

'Take it anyway. You can fill the date in later.'

'Shall we go out on the town for a bit?'

'You are a famous man,' the corporal said as they walked into the bar. 'Everyone knows you here. They greet you like you're everybody's brother.'

'This is my town.'

It was three o'clock in the morning but the smoke-filled place was crowded. Well-dressed, animated people sat at small tables and some ate while others waited. There were bottles of foreign alcohol everywhere. The happy chattering mingled with piped foreign music.

'I didn't know such places existed any more,' the corporal said.

'Yes. They do if you've got the money to pay for them. The chef's Hungarian. They give you the best goulash soup this side of the Danube. I don't know about you but I'm starving.'

'You're the boss. Where do they get the booze from?'

'They buy it on the black market.'

'Don't they get caught?'

'Half the customers are government officials. They have their connections.'

'Connections? Isn't everybody equal these days? This can't be our Rumania ...'

'It is, Corporal, it's the other side of our Rumania. The dark side.'

'Like in the old days, when people had money?'

'Yes. Just like that.'

'I like the dark side.'

When the waiter laid the two steaming plates on the table the chef came to see them.

'Can I see you for a minute back in the kitchen, Peter?'

'Sit down here with us. Have a drink ...'

'I need to talk privately.'

'The corporal is my partner. You can talk freely.'

'Partner? Things must be looking up.'

'You could say that. What's happening?'

'I have some Italian lire. Also a few Austrian schillings. Very little business these days. No tourists come in the winter. Got these off a couple of businessmen the other day. Do you know, they're not buying much local money here any more. You can get as much Rumanian money as you like in Vienna. At any bank. No hassle.'

'You should have told them they must never do that. It's easy to walk around with Rumanian money over in the West ... But if they get caught with it coming in they'll go to jail.'

'I did. I did. That's how I got the money from them.'

'Good man. We'll need to sell the lire quickly. The rate keeps changing. Italy's economy is not so hot.'

'So I hear,' the chef said.

'It's all way over my head,' the corporal said.

'How much will you charge me?'

'Twenty per cent over the bank. Is that OK, Peter? I would do it cheaper but I need some extra cash.'

'I'll give you thirty per cent over the bank.'

'You don't need to do that. Twenty is fine.'

'You waited for me, so I insist. It's thirty per cent over the bank or no deal.'

'Fine, but the stew is on the house.'

'Fair enough.'

'I'll go get it. Enjoy the food. The meat is fresh,' the chef said. 'I get it from a farmer who kills a bit of cattle here and there. Sells it on the quiet,' he added, and he winked and was gone.

'You're a clever bastard, partner,' the corporal said. 'Your talents are wasted in the army. Any women here?'

'I'll see what I can do.'

He sold the Italian lire within an hour. The buyer, a well-dressed young woman, had joined them at their table with an apology. She was alone, she said, because her husband was away. He was an engineer with the merchant navy and was at sea somewhere. He only received a very small allowance of foreign currency so he needed to buy more on the black market. She had heard about Peter from the chef here, she said. She'd been told his rates were good. She had been looking for him every day for a week. Then someone told her he was in town. She could use Italian lire. Her husband used the money to buy her things from Western Europe and they sold them here and were doing well. Good Italian shoes and American jeans and French perfume. English cigarettes, too. Last time he had bought an Omega watch but she was hoping to keep it for herself. She was a pretty girl and she kept covering her mouth as she spoke. She said her teeth were bad.

'Why don't you go and see about them? Medicine is free.'

'The dentists here are useless unless you go private,' she said after the money had changed hands. 'If you pay them under the table they're too expensive. You can't win, can you. God, I wish I could go to Italy with him one day. They won't let us both have a passport in case we don't come back. I don't really want to leave Rumania. With money you can live well here and, anyway, my whole family is here.'

'You got a sister?' the corporal asked. He reeked of alcohol.

'It's all a question of money. I am collecting enough currency to get him to buy a small television set. I figure we can make a bundle on that . . . to have my teeth fixed good.'

'You are a very attractive girl,' Peter said. 'I wouldn't worry too much.'

'It's the pain. I get it whenever I drink something. Hot or cold.'

'In that case you're right. You should really do something about it.'

'Can you get some more currency?'

'As much as you want. Fifty per cent above the bank.'

'I don't have any more on me . . .'

'I can let you have the currency anyway. You can pay me next time.'

'No, no. But thank you for your trust . . . When are you in town again? You're in the army now, I see.'

'He can come up here any time,' the corporal said, and he yawned.

'Any time he wants.'

'I'll be here Friday in two weeks.'

'That's fine. My husband will be back in ten days. He gets paid as soon as they reach Constanza. They never get enough foreign money, though. Not even for a sandwich. They have been in every port in Europe but they see nothing. Even when they are allowed off the ship they have no money to spend. Not even a beer or cigarettes. No one wants our money anywhere.'

'We are a poor country,' the corporal said, and yawned again. 'That's why they keep me and young Peter here in the army. They want to make sure no one steals the place. I wish you had a sister.'

'I wouldn't trust her with the likes of you if I did.'

The corporal fell asleep just then and Gordonitzu gave a sigh of relief.

He sold the Austrian schillings to a beautiful air hostess who came in just as they were about to leave. She said she lived out of town and Peter offered her a bed for the night.

'That's nice of you and I'll accept, but no funny business,' she said, and the young soldier laughed out loud.

'You have nothing to worry about,' he said. 'I am not interested and my friend here is in no condition to molest anyone.'

The three of them staggered out of the bar and hailed a taxi. The corporal leaned heavily on Gordonitzu's shoulder.

'It's just around the corner,' the driver said. 'Not worth my while. You walk.'

'I'll pay you double,' Peter said.

'Fine. Where would a national serviceman have money from?'

'Never you mind,' the corporal said. 'Some of us soldiers are rich. You drive or I'll have you shot.'

'Get out of my cab.'

'He's drunk,' the girl said. 'Don't worry about him. Please take us. We'll pay three times.'

On the short drive to the room she sulked. When they got there and laid the corporal on the carpet and covered him she looked at Gordonitzu across the sleeping figure.

'Don't you find me attractive?'

The corporal woke.

'I must be dreaming,' he moaned.

'You are,' the girl said. 'Go back to sleep.' She poured a little brandy into his parted lips. Soon he was snoring again.

'I am sorry,' Gordonitzu said.

'Don't worry about it. I am used to being accosted. You try to be nice to the passengers and you smile but in this business everybody thinks you're a whore. Believe me, there's no glory in being a flying waitress.'

'At least you get to see the world.'

'You must be joking. All we see are airports and sometimes, very rarely, a hotel bed. That's all. Oh, yes. We do get time off in Moscow or Sofia but there's nothing to do there. Nothing to buy.'

'How about Vienna?'

'They don't let us out of the terminal. Trip's too short. Or maybe they think we are all spies ... We load and leave.'

'When do you get to use the money?'

'There's enough time for duty-free shopping. Scotch whisky or brandy or something ... I buy it and then sell it here. But mostly I sell the money itself ... you know, to a passenger who wants to buy currency because the allowance is too small. You get asked for that all the time ... It's funny having money no one wants. You can't even use our money in other communist countries.'

'Would you like a cup of tea?'

'No, thank you,' she said. She looked at the floor and then at the bed. 'Where are you going to sleep?'

'Haven't thought about it,' he said, and smiled. 'Perhaps we could share my bed. I won't take my clothes off.'

'You're nice. You are the first man who hasn't made a pass at me.'

'Nothing personal. Just tired. I've had a long day.'

'Maybe some other time?'

'Maybe some other time.'

The corporal woke to find Peter making coffee. He looked at the sprawling girl on the bed and rubbed his eyes.

'She's out cold, isn't she?'

'Yes. Must be dog tired.'

'Who did that one, you or me?'

'I'm not sure,' Gordonitzu chuckled. 'I think it was you.'

The corporal smiled.

'Probably,' he said.

'Probably,' Peter said. 'But I wouldn't say anything about it.'

'How do you know she isn't working for the secret police?'

'I don't.'

'And you do business with her anyway? What if she tells on you?'

'I have protection now, haven't I?'

'What do you mean?'

'You'll look after me ... We're partners, no? If you don't we both go to jail.'

'I'll look after you. She's beautiful though, isn't she?'

'Yes. Even in her sleep.'

'Must have been me,' the corporal said, and he stretched.

'Must have. But say nothing.'

'What do you take me for? Say, partner, what's the plan for today? We have forty-eight hours left.'

'I thought of doing the hotels. See if we can buy some money off the cashiers.'

'Hotel cashiers? Christ, you must be walking around with a fortune ...'

'No. The money is already at the hotels ... I leave it with the cashiers.'

'You get a receipt?'

'Of course not.'

'Why not?'

'A receipt is evidence. Besides, this business is based on trust ...'

'Yes, but why do you have to keep the money with them?'

'Because they need it on the spot. Suppose they find a guest who is willing to sell them a few dollars. They must pay him right there and then ... They do not make enough to have that sort of cash on their own ... and that's where I come in. They offer the guest a better rate than the bank, say five or ten per cent. They make the exchange and I pay them ten per cent commission on everything. Buying or selling.'

'You're a fucking genius, Gordonitzu.'

'Thank you. Look at that girl. She'll be asleep for hours yet. I'm going to leave her a note. Tell her to show herself out when she gets up.'

'You trust her here on her own?'

'There is nothing in this room to implicate me ... that's why I don't keep any money on me unless I'm trading. Talking of trading, I'd like to get going as soon as I can.'

'What's your hurry?'

'It's best to get to the hotels before lunchtime. They have to straighten their books in the afternoon, and there are no inspections before then. I don't want our money confiscated. The cashiers expect me early. They take enough risks as it is.'

'What risks?'

'They are supposed to hand all foreign currency to the bank.'

'How do they know you're in town?'

'They know.'

'You deserve a medal, Gordonitzu.'

It turned out to be a successful day at the hotels. A lot of foreign currency had been purchased. While Peter talked to the cashiers and the porters and the head waiters, the corporal sat in the lobby admiring the furniture, the guests and their clothes.

'This is like being in the West,' he exclaimed when they walked out. 'I wonder if the government knows about this business.'

'Of course they do.'

'So why don't they do something to stop it?'

'They must see the positive side of it. Look, people out of jobs make money ... foreign goods are brought into the country and none of the official reserves are spent ... there's a lot of good in this.'

'But the National Bank is losing millions.'

'That's why it's against the law.'

'What happens if you get caught?'

'If *we* get caught, you mean, partner.'

'No, if *you* get caught. I'm a sleeping partner. I know nothing. I'm the simple guy from Ploesti, remember? Pure working class ... Salt of the earth. Pleasure is all mine, baby is all yours, that's how I operate.'

'Good to know how you feel.'

'Come on, what does happen?'

'I don't know. I haven't been caught yet. In Russia they shoot people for this.'

'They must have caught someone. I wonder what they do to them.'

'Couldn't tell you. I don't believe in looking for depressing news.'

'Have we made enough for a motorbike yet?'

'You must be joking.'

'I never joke when I'm on duty. You've got stacks of cash. Dollars, I see.'

'I need that for business ... I've told you. Unless my people have money they cannot work. Buyers and sellers do not wait. We'll get the motorbike money when we go and see my father.'

'Let's go today. I'm itching to get out of town. Watching all these rich people gets on my wick.'

'We cannot go up there during the week. We'll have to wait.'

'Let's go to the coast, then. We can have some fun there ... the sun ... foreign girls ...'

'You go. I have work to do.'

'I thought that's what you did this morning.'

'Now that I have all this foreign money I must sell it, understand? Money makes no money when it remains in your pocket.'

'Let's go to the coast tomorrow, then.'

'Why don't you take the train to Ploesti ... Visit your people.'

'I hate the place. Hate the people even more. I'll go to the coast. Give me some cash, then.'

'I gave you some yesterday.'

'That was for here. Not for the coast.'

'All right. I'll see you at the station the day after tomorrow.'

'Eight o'clock sharp,' the corporal said with authority. The younger man handed him a wad of notes under the table. The corporal felt the thickness of it and grinned. He looked at Gordonitzu and pointed a pistol-like finger at his face, got up and was gone.

CHAPTER FIVE

———■———

It must have been the old hate for the corporal that had cleared his head. That and anger. He could always think clearly when he was angry. It brought him back to where he was. In a room of a house on a cliff in Jamaica. On his own.

His fists clenched and his lips contorted and he sat up. I could break the fucker's neck, he thought to himself, and then he remembered. He looked about the room and at the fire that had died out. It was late in the afternoon but the outside world seemed to be going through a perpetual dawn. He got up and walked into the dining-room. The lunch tray and his dinner of cold cuts were there, untouched. He sat down and played with the meat. He was not hungry. The thought of the corporal brought about palpitations of anxiety in his chest. Nothing to worry about. No one knew and those who knew were all dead. Thinking about his security relaxed him and soon he felt strangely rested and fit. He

47

should put some food into his stomach. He could do that. He had lost some weight since he had been here. Better than all the fat-farms he had been to. Cheaper, too. Annie would like that, and then he remembered about her. Must not think of that now. He ate.

He mustn't hate the corporal that much. Mustn't hate him at all. Had it not been for him he would never have left Rumania to become an Englishman and a success.

Success, he thought bitterly. If this is success, how many floors down is failure?

He could feel the food entering his system. It was cold and hard and tasteless. But it was recharging him.

They should bring the woman in now. He could see her clearly, her rounded lips and long hair and her shapely back which had so excited him then, when she had tried to light the fire. She would have no problems with him now. When he was calm he was a tiger in bed. Didn't come for hours. He should pick up the phone and ask for her to be brought back. They granted all his wishes. He got up and started for the library and then he stopped and thought of what had happened to the woman. Had it happened? Had she been there at all? He was afraid to think about it. Afraid to ask and find out.

He sat down to resume his meal. Stick to the past for now, he told himself. He wasn't sure whether he had used words. It didn't matter. Stick to the past. Good or bad or sad or happy. It was safe. It could do him no more harm now. It was good for him. Why had he tried to avoid it for so long?

How Annie had enjoyed his stories about his currency-dealing days. About the people who had been his customers. The added colour in a drab communist world.

He had told her about the film director who had an insatiable need for German marks because he kept a mistress in Munich. He told her about the high-ranking secret police officer who had a passion for old cars. He had money to burn. He bought thousands of illicit German marks to buy spare parts for his 1930s Mercedes. He had become his protector. Helped him get business. Told him who was going abroad and how many tourists booked in and where. Finally they threw him into jail, but not for that. He got involved in a power struggle with his well-connected deputy. The deputy won, and on getting the job he continued buying currency from Peter. He had a wife who had a thing about Japanese photographic equipment. She was, Peter had told Annie, a gifted photographer who ended up leaving her husband and Rumania. She used her husband's position to get out of the country and never came back. These days she was living in Paris and worked for a fashion magazine. She was quite famous now.

'I'll introduce you to her when we're in Paris next,' he remembered telling Annie.

'You're a rogue,' Annie had said. 'No wonder you never got caught.'

It was the corporal's loose tongue that had brought the house down on him in the end. Otherwise the army would never have come looking for him. Made him flee the country. Change his name.

'I love the corporal,' Annie had said. 'Without him I would not have met you.'

'I suppose not.'

'You should write it all down one day. It will make a bestseller. A movie.'

'No one will believe it. Sometimes I can't believe it myself.'

'What did happen to the corporal in the end?'

'I'll tell you about it some other time.'

He never did tell Annie the whole truth. But he remembered it well.

That Sunday his father was in Bucharest. He had gone up to the estate with the corporal. They spent the day in the truck, playing cards and drinking.

Later, they all sat together in the village inn. Mihai the manservant, the corporal and himself. The corporal had been drinking heavily and needed to relieve himself often.

'He will have to disappear,' Mihai the manservant whispered while the corporal was out. 'There is no other way.'

'Why?'

'He will never tell on you, but he talks too much. I know the type. He's not used to having money. He will buy himself things and people will ask questions. He'll brag about your business to everybody and someone will pick up on it and come after you. He'll have to disappear.'

'I have never killed anyone before.'

'You won't need to, Master Peter.'

The corporal came limping back, and did his fly up in full sight of all.

'Pig,' the innkeeper murmured to his wife.

'Army people have bad manners,' she retorted.

The corporal sat down. He talked about the motorbike he was going to buy. A fast machine made in Czechoslovakia.

'It can do one hundred and twenty kilometres an hour,' he said, and hiccoughed. 'But I wouldn't have it at the base. I'm only going to use it riding up and down in town. There's a speed limit there. You can come too. It will be nice, eh, Gordonitzu? No more taxis.'

'You are going back to town tonight, Corporal,' Peter said, waving the ticket.

'You should have bought the ticket on board,' the innkeeper said. 'The ticket collectors run a private sideline on board. They are much cheaper.'

'I can pay the official price. My friend is rich,' the corporal grunted. He grabbed the ticket and waved it in the innkeeper's face. 'There, you see, he's rich, I tell you.'

'Not any more,' the innkeeper said. 'They used to own the village. But not any more. Gordonitzus are like everybody. No one is rich now.'

'Oh yes, he's rich. I am rich. We're all rich. And we'll be even richer.'

'Don't tell him that,' Peter said. 'You're going to Bucharest. You can take a look at the motorbike tomorrow. I'll bring the money down for you on Tuesday.'

'Motorbike? In this weather?' the innkeeper asked.

'My cousin had a motorbike before the war,' the innkeeper's wife said. 'He ran into a loaded bullwagon and killed himself. There were pumpkins all over the place for days. I am afraid of motorbikes. I hate them.'

'He likes motorbikes,' Peter said. 'That's why he's going back tonight.'

'What time is the train due?' the corporal asked.

'Nine o'clock,' the innkeeper's wife said.

They were the last to leave the inn.

'Have a good trip,' the innkeeper shouted after them.

'Busybody,' Mihai whispered to Peter.

It was a cold, starry night. The narrow cobblestoned streets were empty. They took the long route through the village to the station. Then they doubled back into the vineyards and the meadows. The icy wind had blown all the clouds away and the full moon lit the frost-covered fields as if it were daylight.

The commune had just finished excavating a new rubbish dump.

It was a very large, square hole. It was going to hide all the ungainly bits that cluttered the yards inside Community Farm 603. Twisted old metal barrels and barbed wire and hoses and the old German generator. Toxic chemicals and decomposed vegetables and empty cans and sanitary towels and hundreds of undesirable books. To start with the dump was a very popular spot. Children came up there in their eternal search for discarded junk to play with. Gypsies came to look for rotten food.

Central Committee hated it. So they had filled it to the brim with liquid gypsum. Now it was deserted. Not even the dogs came. No one understood why, but on clear nights one could see the ever-sinking white substance shine, many metres below. It used to be a shameful blot on the countryside and now it was left alone. The farm committee spent two evenings congratulating themselves on this success.

The three men walked towards the dump. All the way the young soldier fretted. The wind blew harder and it cut into his face. A thick, menacing carpet of black cloud returned. It covered the stars and the moon and they walked in darkness. They were coming close. Then, a few steps before the edge, the corporal said he was sick. He said he needed to put his finger down his throat.

They led him closer. A harsh, sharp smell of smoking gypsum came out of the hole. They brought him to the edge and held his shoulders as he retched. Then he slipped in. He let out a confused little scream before his bulk hit the surface and it cracked open with a splash. He sank into the white mash as a hissing sound came from below.

'Did you push him, Mihai?'

'I am too old for that, Master Peter. He slipped.'

'All by himself?'

'All by himself.'

They waited by the side for an hour. The white sheet-like gypsum screen closed over the mouth of the dump. There was no sound. Then it started to rain. The gypsum dump bubbled.

'Good God,' Peter said, 'he's trying to breathe.'

'No, no. It's the chemical reaction.'

'Are you sure?'

'Sure I'm sure. He must have gone to sleep,' Mihai said. 'By tomorrow there will be nothing left of him.'

They looked inside one more time.

'He didn't feel a thing.'

'We can never be sure.'

'He fell. No one pushed him. You saw. Anyway, Master Peter, he was bad news. I could have told you that the minute I laid eyes on him. People make too much of death. It's part of life you know ... I mean, it's the way all life ends and everybody has got to die some time, so what's the big deal? He was bad news and then he died.'

'You can't just get rid of bad news by killing it off.'

'Your ancestors have done it for generations.'

'That was in the Middle Ages.'

'Nothing changes in the killing department, Master Peter. What do you think the Reds do, eh? Even the great big famous ones. Stalin killed off thousands. Everybody knows that. Stalin's short arm got as far as Mexico to get rid of Trotsky. He could have lived with Trotsky, but you cannot live with the corporal. He was scum. It was either you or him. Anyway, it was God who killed him.'

'Come on, Mihai ...'

'He fell in, I tell you. Slipped and fell. He was drunk. He was thinking of his motorbike. He died happy. I promise you that.'

Later, as they approached his father's truck, the rain-drops thickened. They climbed in. Mihai lit the paraffin lamp.

'You'd better put something dry on yourself. You musn't catch cold now. I'll get you something out of your father's trunk there. You're more or less the same size now.'

'Thank you.'

'What is wrong, Master Peter?' Mihai asked. He looked at the young man's face. There was unfathomable sorrow in it. He bit his nails. He looked confused.

'You musn't think of it any more, my boy.'

'I can't help it.'

'Shall I tell you a story? The way I did when you were a child?'

'If you like.'

'Which one shall I tell you?'

'Tell me about that last card game my father played.'

'That is not a story.'

'I want to hear it, whatever it is.'

'It's long over and done with and really unimportant.'

'It is to me. It's my right. In any case, it will take my mind off the corporal.'

'If you insist.'

It was then, as they sat in the warm, dry place his father used for a bedroom, that Peter heard how the family estate had been lost.

⋆ ⋆ ⋆

'Your father was drunk and he kept on demanding that the game go on. He had been losing heavily all afternoon and all evening and by midnight all the players but one had left. Most of them were friends and neighbours, and there was one Luftwaffe officer, the one who owned your father's Bugatti. They were all in the throes of leaving the area. The Russians were coming closer and closer and those who could save themselves were going west to Austria. Roaring artillery battles filled the distant skies all evening.

'There was one other man left. He had not been playing with the others. He stood over your father's shoulder and suggested it was time to quit. They had a little money left and they could run west, towards the American lines.

' "The cards are still on the table," the Baron howled. "Must play."

'By that time there was nothing left to bet with. The paintings and the cutlery and the animals and the furniture were gone. There was only the estate itself.

' "If there's nothing else I'll play the estate," your father said. The other man tried to dissuade him from this madness. But the Baron, then as now, was a strong-willed man. That and the litres of wine in his veins made him more stubborn than ever.

' "If that's all I've got, I'll play for the estate," he insisted. "You do dice?"

' "Everyone does dice."

' "We'll throw dice, then," your father said. And they threw and your father lost the estate and all that was on it.'

That was the story Mihai the manservant told him. The corporal had flown clean out of his mind.

'Who the hell was that man? Who owns this place?'

'The communists own it, of course. Community Farm 603.'

'Don't play games, Mihai.'

'What difference does it make now, Master Peter? I'm going to fetch some coffee from the kitchen. I have an old thermos flask in good condition. His Excellency will be back in the morning. By then the others will have gobbled all the coffee up. I can make you a cup too, if you like.'

'Come on. Tell me.'

'It doesn't matter.'

'It matters to me.'

'It was only a game. He forgot all about it the next day.'

'He did not forget it at all. You said it tortures him still. It mars his judgement. His sense of time. Having lost his birthright, you said ... Come on ... who did he lose the estate to?'

'You swear you will never talk about it? Not to him, not to anybody?'

'I swear. Who did he lose the estate to?'

'He lost it to me, Master Peter. To me. To Mihai the manservant. You see, it was an accident. My family have waited on your family for generations. Don't get me wrong, we were all very happy here. Peasants were always treated like dirt in this country, but not on this estate. We were like a part of the family. And then, for one night and one day, I, a manservant of peasant stock, became the owner of the Gordonitzu estate. There was no one else there for him to lose it to. It could have been anyone because he was adamant about playing and sure to lose. It just happened to be me. It made no difference at all. It was an accident. But your father takes the class system seriously ... As I do, too. The whole thing didn't affect me because we have been servants for too long and had all that been real I wouldn't have known how to be a landowner . .. Tell you the truth, I wouldn't have wanted to. Still, you can imagine what His Excellency your father felt when he became sober ... What he feels every time he remembers that night.'

Peter Gordonitzu was lost for words.

'Your father is coming back in the morning. You swore you would not tell ... Remember, you must never reveal the naked truth to people you love. You'd best not think of it at all. Just forget it,' Mihai said as he climbed down for the coffee.

The toast and the coffee tasted especially good the next morning. The Baron complimented his man on his achievement. Mihai the manservant cooed like a pigeon in love at the sound of his master's approval.

They had to empty the truck out completely that day. Peter, with twenty-four hours' leave still available to him, helped them out. The truck was filled with the farm's refuse. It was tipped over into the large new rubbish dump out in the fields, where the corporal was. Someone dropped the long wooden ladder in by mistake. It was too difficult to retrieve it. It stuck out from the rest of the junk, like the two arms of a giant skeleton begging for mercy.

The loss of his father's estate that night at the end of the war had become entangled in his mind with the death of the corporal. He could not think of one without the other. He had sworn not to talk about it. Perhaps that was why he never told Annie.

One month later, on the last day of another furlough, just before lunch, the military police came up to the estate to see the young soldier. To talk about the disappearance of his corporal. The army knew, he said, that the corporal and private Gordonitzu were friends and that the corporal had visited the estate. They knew he had been spending heavily on the coast and was heard to say he was buying a motorbike. The army wanted to know where he might have obtained the money. It could have something to do with his disappearance. It was a preliminary investigation. Just collecting facts, they said.

Mihai the manservant took them all to the inn for a drink. They could, he had said, talk much better there.

Sure. The corporal had been up there with them. He had spent his last hour here in this very inn, making a general nuisance of himself. Everyone saw him. They couldn't tell the army where the money had come from. Up here in the country there were few places where you could spend money. In any case, the corporal had left. He was going to Bucharest to buy a motorbike. He had said that himself, and she had heard him.

It was a good thing he had taken the eleven o'clock train out of there, the innkeeper's wife told the military policeman. She had seen the ticket. She had seen them all leave. No, only the corporal boarded the train. She knew that because she had seen young Gordonitzu in the village the next day. The corporal went away on his own. Maybe he fell out of the train. He had drunk a lot.

The military policeman said he would check up on that and a number of other leads he had. As he got up to leave he thanked them all. Mihai the manservant did not like the situation one bit.

'The man's too clever by half,' he said. 'He wants to prove himself. Be a Sherlock Holmes or something. The corporal must have talked to people. The military police will be back. You can count on it.'

Later, as Peter boarded the train, Mihai the manservant said:

'You'd better come back up here as soon as you get another leave. In the meantime I'll think of something. You may have to get out of the country. You know a lot of people who travel. They surely have enough contacts to help you get away from here. It will be bad, because your father and I will miss you. But I'd rather miss you knowing you are a free man. Go to the West. Go to England. You have an uncle there, your mother's brother. He was always very clever and I believe he has become rich. He is a peculiar man but a blood relative. He is a Jew, and Jews take family connections very seriously. The military police will be back again, and if I'm right in my suspicions, next time they will take you with them. You'd better go, Master Peter. Come up here on your next leave and we'll see how we can arrange it. I am sure your father will agree with this. He sends his best regards to you. He couldn't see much of you today because he had very little sleep in Bucharest. You know how it is.'

Peter Gordon poured himself another glass of wine and raised it.

'To Mihai the manservant,' he said out loud. They were undoubtedly recording everything he was saying. This toast would puzzle them like hell. Let them work out who Mihai was.

As things turned out, Mihai the manservant had nothing to do with the way he left the country. All he did was tell him it was time to go.

It was the merchant seaman's wife who did it. The one who had bought all those Italian lire from him. She came to see him at the bar the night he came back from the estate. All he had for sale were German marks, but she bought them all the same.

'When is your husband coming back?' he had asked.

'Tomorrow morning. He's got two weeks off. They are sailing into Venice at the beginning of next month.'

'I'd love to meet him,' he said.

'I can arrange that. I'm sure the two of you can do business together. With your cash and his constant travels to Italy the sky is the limit.'

'You'll make enough money for the dentist,' he said, and he chuckled.

'I thought you said I looked good anyway.'

'I did, but I shouldn't say nice things to you the day before your husband comes off his ship.'

'We have all night,' she said, and she put her hand on his cheek. 'You're a good-looking boy, you know.'

In the morning, armed with the woman's address and blow-by-blow instructions on how to get on with her husband the sailor, Peter Gordonitzu kissed her goodbye and walked to the station to catch a train back to his barracks. While waiting, he wrote a note to Mihai the manservant at Community Farm 603. It was a long note and it was in code. In it, Peter asked the manservant to send him a cable a week later. Mention a death or a sickness or something. It must be good enough for a thirty-six-hour leave at least.

Annie had been particularly interested in that woman, the seaman's wife. She wasn't jealous on account of the night they had spent together. She was the saint who had helped him escape. Florence Nightingale.

'You are a romantic,' he had said.

'You are ungrateful. She could have got herself into an awful lot of trouble.'

'You are forgetting the money.'

'What money?'

'They didn't help me for nothing, you know. I had quite a lot of money put away by then ...'

'They deserved it. You are a rich man today. Giving a little of it away didn't harm you.'

'A little of it? Are you joking?'

'You've made it here anyway. So it's all for the good.'

He had made it and he was well on his way to making much more. He often wondered what had become of the sailor and his wife. They belonged to that classless, drifting section of communist society. The part no one admitted was there. The back-street, privateer survivors who could never enjoy their success because they couldn't show it off. The sailor knew how to survive. He might still be living in Rumania. Probably selling Japanese video games these days. Or maybe he'd managed to smuggle his wife out to the West.

He wondered whether she had ever had her teeth done.

Mihai the manservant was right. The military police did turn up again. They arrived on the estate the day he left his barracks. They knew he was coming and they sat outside his father's truck, waiting for him. But Peter Gordonitzu was on his way to the Black Sea port of Constanza.

His escape from Rumania had fascinated Annie more than anything else. It was, he had told her, the first time he had ever been on a ship.

'Surprising how you got to love the sea so much having first seen it from inside a crate.'

'It wasn't a long voyage. And they did bring me food.'

'My poor baby,' she said, and she stroked his head and massaged the back of his neck. 'You must have been scared.'

'Shitless,' he said.

He met the woman's husband at the harbour gates. He said he had to get out of the country there and then. They agreed on five hundred dollars and the young man paid in advance. His thick wad of bills was seen by all. It was a foggy, wet night and the seaman gave him a colleague's papers. He climbed the gangway with a bunch of other sailors. No one looked at his face or the photograph on the document and he boarded without a hitch. As soon as they got to the cabin, the papers were taken away from him, whisked back to the port and returned to their owner. He was given a parcel of food and led to the ship's damp hold. There, among jute, sackfuls of chemicals, bales of wax and barrels of motor oil, he was put inside a large crate loaded with knitwear. He was told to lie on top of the soft garments and given his routine.

Food would be brought to him each morning before the captain was up.

There was nothing to worry about because all hands were in on the deal. That was why it was so expensive. But he should avoid the officers.

He must not wander about the boat unless someone was with him.

He must not empty his bladder inside the crate.

Once they reached Venice the crate would be lifted out of the hold and dumped on the quayside. Once that happened he would be on his own.

They came late on the second night of the trip. Their voices woke him and before he knew what was happening they were all upon him. Five or six of them. They climbed in and undressed him and searched every bundle he possessed. They robbed him of all his savings. Every last Swiss franc and German mark, save a single one-hundred-dollar bill he'd managed to put in his mouth during the scuffle. There was nothing he could do and no one to complain to. For the rest of the night he stayed awake and he rubbed his painful skin. Could the woman have told her husband the sailor about the night they had spent together? Was that why he was beaten and robbed? No, he thought to himself. The man would have had to have told his mates about his wife's infidelity. He would never have admitted that. No. It was greed that made them do it.

The ship arrived in Venice long before the sun came up and the crate was lowered onto the quayside. When he got out there was no one about. He slipped out of the Customs area and into the ancient town. He was in pain still. He had no passport. No documents at all.

While having his first coffee he made friends with a group of Argentinian seamen. Soon he was selling smuggled American cigarettes.

He never did get a chance to see his father or Mihai the manservant. The Rumanian sailor had promised him he would go up to the estate and tell them what had happened. Only years later did he find out that he never went.

Mihai had died up at the estate and Gordon had his father move to Bucharest where he lived for a few years in the old room Peter used to rent. A trusted Austrian business associate brought him money each month.

For a few years the Baron lived as he had always done. Friday and Saturday nights he went out on the town. He sometimes took trips up to his old estate. He never wrote any letters.

He had died only a few years earlier. Fell at his table in a coffee house near the Boulevard. By then his son was rich and powerful and had become Peter Gordon.

'You will have to change your name,' his uncle had said. 'No one in England can pronounce Gordonitzu. If they can't pronounce it they won't remember it. I have been considering it and have come up with a few ideas. There is another thing. You will have to speak English perfectly if you want to work in the city with me. I'm sure you will have no problems with that. Your mother was good at languages. You look exactly like her, you know.'

No, he did not know. He did not remember what she had looked like. He wanted nothing to do with his mother.

Not after what she had done to him.

But he was smart enough and hungry enough to keep quiet. His uncle was his lottery ticket. This man was his mother's brother. Brains of a professor, his father had said of him. He had not exaggerated one bit. His uncle knew everybody and everything. He took him around all the churches and the palazzios and the galleries and the restaurants. He lectured him for hours. On how Venetian ships brought silk and design and spaghetti from China. How they mastered the silk route and how they had bought their enemies off with money to avoid wars. How they had encouraged the arts. How the great movement of the Renaissance was born there. How they blew the best glass and drew maps. How they perfected overseas payment methods and banking. And everything else they had invented, the commercial empire they had built. But mostly his uncle talked about the way his own business was operating. The empire Peter would one day inherit.

They were sitting in the Piazza San Marco sipping molten chocolate and watching the pigeons being fed by passers-by. They had been shopping for clothes all morning.

'You must change your name before you start,' his uncle said again.

'Gordonitzu is a noble old name. It has history . . .'

'So it has. But no one in England knows or cares about it.'

'But I like this name. It is a proud name . . .'

His uncle did not seem to be listening. 'Let me think about it,' he said.

There, sipping thick hot chocolate and listening to the band playing 'Spring in Portugal', the older man came up with his new name.

'It's easy enough, Peter. Your name will be Gordon. It doesn't sound too different and it's perfectly acceptable . . . It is Scottish in origin and no one will ask you where you came from or what Gordonitzu means. In any case, before you join the business you are going back to school. To learn how to speak proper English. You are going to have some time on your hands here in Venice. The papers will take a while. The man at the consulate knows someone right here who could start you off. A retired naval officer. I hear he's a bit eccentric . . . He might agree to give you elocution lessons while you sail with him on his little boat.'

That was how, Peter Gordon told Annie much later, he got to love the sea.

By the time his papers came through from London he was an expert in handling boats under sail. He was addicted to the breeze and the canvas. The ability to trick the elements and use the wind to go wherever he wanted intoxicated him. The fresh air and the endless stretches of water made him feel free. His English had become fluent enough for the consular official to comment on it.

'In a few months', he had said, 'no one will take you for a foreigner.'

'He was right,' Annie had said. 'I told you so myself, but then you are special, aren't you? I have never met anyone like you before.'

'You haven't met everybody.'

'I don't want to meet anyone else,' she had said.

His uncle had this thing about England. A sort of blind, grateful admiration for all things British. He lived and behaved as if he had no past at all before he got there, and he spoke the language beautifully. With his prominent nose, his chizzled features and his silvery hair and pinstriped suits he looked like an aristocrat. He had arrived in London in his twenties, but he did not talk much of his early days there. He had joined the British Army during the war. At first he was in the Pioneer Corps, but when they found out he was good at languages they moved him to Intelligence. He had a good five years there and ended the war with the rank of Major. He had charm, and with his ability to make friends and keep them he was soon able to revive his business. With his understanding of world markets he was a shrewd investor, and with the inevitable demand for goods after the war clients who deposited their money with him grew richer.

The fruits of his success – the Rolls, the country house in Hertfordshire and his Mayfair apartment – were there for all to see and admire. He had connections on both sides of the House of Commons. He had a place in the South of France. He kept horses. He hosted tea parties. He held string quartet concert dinners at home and had escorted many divas on his nights out on the town. He had a respectable collection of Impressionist paintings. He was considered a most eligible bachelor and was often mentioned in the gossip columns. He made generous gifts to the arts and funded university scholarships.

'I want to give some of it back because I owe all I've got to this country,' he used to say. 'This is a free, tolerant society. England has opened her gates to many. Huguenots and Indians and Africans and Jews. They all settled here and were allowed to thrive without being made to change their religion or culture. The sky is the limit here. You can be born in a mining village and die in the House of Lords.'

He yearned to be mentioned in the annual honours list and would have made it had he lived long enough. The police were convinced it was his lover, the tennis coach, who had killed him.

Annie did not believe it. Nor did anyone else in the company. Most of his friends thought it was an accident. There were con and pro arguments for weeks.

The police had the tennis coach under strict surveillance while enquiries were made. Lots of money was spent while detectives travelled to and from the Mediterranean where it happened.

They called the young man in and interrogated him for many hours but had to let him go in the end for lack of evidence.

CHAPTER SIX

He did not hear the car outside, nor the people as they came into the house. He listened only to the storm that was thundering past his part of the island. The waves below the precipice lashed punishing blows at the rocks while deafening heaps of rain water slammed onto the roof.

The first he knew of them was when they were upon him. He started to smile in anticipation and then he saw that something was different. It was the wrong time of day for a visit, and instead of the usual two there were four of them. For a moment they stood silently. They were dripping water.

'I have plenty of towels in there,' he managed to say before they grabbed him. They carried him into the bedroom and threw him onto the floor. One by one they kicked him, his screams lost to their laughter and the roaring elements outside. His body contracted. He covered his head with his hands. He managed to push his reading glasses under the bed. They pulled him to his feet and punched him in the stomach. Blows fell from all directions. He did not feel a thing at first. It could be that the drug they had given him earlier was a painkiller. Their wet rubber soles found his back and his shoulders and his arms and his legs. There was no blood. Someone pulled his head up by his hair and spat on his face. He was in great pain and he thought he heard himself scream, and he clenched his hands and groaned and the screaming stopped. He could still hear them laughing, but no one spoke. They took turns as deliberate blows covered him everywhere and suddenly, with a final barrage of hard-hitting feet, they stopped. He felt strong arms lift him onto the bed. He could smell their sweat and he heard heavy breathing somewhere close to his face. He kept his eyes closed and he knew they were watching him and then, as silently as they had come, they were gone.

He got up and limped to the bathroom and looked at his face. His skull hurt where his hair had been pulled and his chest was blue. He checked his thinning locks and sighed and sobbed a little and then he stopped. The bald patch had grown since he had seen it last. He noticed a slight limp in his walk as he went back to his bedroom.

This was a new tactic, he thought to himself as he lay down. A new turn in a six-week-old war someone was waging on him. Maybe they were frustrated. But no one had told him what they wanted with him. How was he to know what to tell them?

He looked out of the window. The night had calmed. The storm had blown the clouds away and a clear vision of sky stretched over the sea. He could make out the stars and, further down, above the horizon, a pale half-moon began its ascent. In the garden, the Rottweilers prowled about and he saw the glare of their eyes. The palms stood in majestic stillness as the song of the crickets invaded the bushes. He was in pain all over. He switched the light on and reached for his briefcase. He opened it and took Annie's passport out. Her pale face smiled at him from page three.

Annie E. Gordon, the signature said. A steady, rounded scribble, born of years of practice. He couldn't have forgotten her face. It had been there at the back of his mind all the time. Engraved on his memory ever since he saw her that first time. Yes. That first time. It was long ago but as clear and close as the night. It was the day the switchboard operator told him his secretary was off sick. He remembered.

'Send someone up this minute,' he had bellowed into the telephone. 'Get one of the girls from the typing-pool,' he added, and they said right away, sir. He didn't look up when he heard the girl come in.

'Sit down, will you,' he said. He spent a few more moments going through documents and then he looked up and saw her. He looked down at her long, crossed legs and then at the tight mini-skirt and her blouse. She had an oval, pale face and a pair of brown eyes that looked shyly at him from under her dry wheat-coloured hair. She sucked at her pencil as she waited for him to speak, then her gaze hit his desk. Her face was beautiful, like that of a Madonna. Her eyes had a distant look. He had never seen her before.

'How long have you been with us?' he asked softly as she pulled the pencil out of her mouth and straightened her hair.

'Two years, sir,' she said. The melodious ring of her strong Scottish accent was warm and her lips parted while she waited for him to say something. He asked her for her name.

'Annie,' she said. 'Annie Emily Sutherland, sir.' There was a hole in one of her stockings above her left knee, and he noticed her skin. It was soft and smooth, alabaster-coloured. He thought it was made for the night.

'How is your shorthand?' he asked.

'You'll have to find that out for yourself, sir,' she said, her eyes fixed fearlessly on his. She did not move, and then the brown gaze caressed him with a mischievous smile. He was taken aback. No one had dared speak to him that way.

'Beg your pardon?' he asked, his surprise concealing anger.

'I was only joking, sir,' she said, and her eyes dropped to her pad.

He dictated a large number of letters and when she brought them in for signature he had no comments to make. That night, sitting in his uncle's office, he looked out of the window and saw her leave the building. His eyes followed her until she reached the underground station and was lost in the crowd.

While his secretary was on holiday he had her in for dictation a few times. She was efficient and presentable, if a little forward, but he found he liked her directness. In the evenings, he caught himself searching for her in the corridors. When his secretary came back he started sending her out on errands to make sure that Annie would come instead. They did not talk much and once, when she commented on his style of writing, he told her to use her own words if she thought they made more sense.

'As long as they know what I mean,' he said, and they both smiled. He felt comfortable with her.

'This tie does not go with your suit,' was the first personal remark she offered. 'Green isn't happy with blue.' He got up and took the tie off and threw it into the waste-paper basket and she laughed. He laughed too, not knowing why.

'Are you all right?' she enquired one morning a few days later. 'You look a little lost.'

He tried to make out that he had not heard, but she was right. He did feel shattered that morning. It was the time he had found out about his uncle and the tennis coach. The time he saw them asleep together. The shock-waves that raced through his body must have shown. He strained to suppress the embarrassment and insecurity that fell on him and tried unsuccessfully to smile.

'Life at the top must be lonely sometimes,' she said. She looked so young and innocent and her kind eyes held compassion. As though she knew what he was going through. He found her supportive and later, when he needed help with his work, he started asking for her by name. He began to look forward to her being there with him, and he invented correspondence and other tasks for her to undertake.

'It's late-night shopping tonight,' he heard himself mumble one morning. 'I thought I might ask you to come and help me choose some shirts and ties. We could have dinner afterwards.'

She said she would be delighted. But would he mind meeting her somewhere out of the office? People talked. Especially in the general office. They had had little reason to talk about her thus far, she said.

'What does that mean?'

'It means I have kept my nose clean.'

'Aren't you allowed a boyfriend?' he asked.

'There's someone back in Edinburgh,' she said.

'Serious?'

'I'm not sure ... We have ... er ... a sort of understanding.'

'Do you see each other often?'

'Christmas and summer. He is a medical student. He has very little time.'

'Do you know anybody here? ... I mean, to go out with ...'

'Not really. People down south are different ... London can be a lonely city.'

'What do you do with yourself?'

'I work. I clean my flat. I cook ... I read. Sometimes I go to a film-show.'

'Why don't you go back to Scotland?'

'I came here to get away from my mother.'

Then the dictation was over and she left the room. Peter dialled his uncle's extension.

'About dinner ...' he said hesitantly.

'Yes. I'll see you tonight.'

'No ... I mean I can't make it tonight, Uncle ...'

'Another engagement?'

'No. I have a ... a date.'

'Business?'

'No. Private.'

'That's good. You are making friends at last. That's very good.'

They managed to keep it quiet from the others for a long while. They never met in the office, and in the corridors they greeted each other without a smile. He always called her 'Miss Sutherland'. She always called him 'sir'. She seemed fascinated by him, by everything he said or thought. Yet during their time together she was taking him over completely. He found her easy to talk to without his having to open up too much. She made no demands on him. And she made him laugh. He had not touched her and he wanted to and he knew he was falling in love with her. He did try to tell her about himself but always stopped short of things that might shock her. Like the corporal's fate and what happened to the woman who had been his landlady in Venice. The one he lived with while waiting for his papers to arrive. She had threatened to tell the police about the cigarettes he was smuggling from the boats in the port. He had given her a share of the profits but she was becoming greedy. He did not tell her he was going to England until the day before his departure.

She had made a big fuss. Accused him of having used her. Abused her hospitality and her innocence. Used her home as a warehouse. Treated her like a whore, a woman alone.

She said life was going to catch up with him one day. She said she would rejoice and dance on his grave.

She said he wasn't going to England or anywhere. She knew people. She was going to inform on him right away. The way he had come into the country illegally. How he had no papers. They would put him in jail and deport him on the next ship back to Rumania. She knew what happened there behind the Iron Curtain. People like him were shot or put in jail forever. Siberia. God only knew why he had left in the first place. God only knew what he had done before he became a refugee. Before she helped him.

She was only doing what was right, she had said, because he was a selfish son of a bitch. Then he said he was never ever going to leave her and she smiled and they made up. That night he took her out in his teacher's sailing boat and came back on his own. No one saw a thing. He was a survivor, Mihai had said. Survive and keep the family name going. That was all he was trying to do.

Annie did not see him like that. She said she knew him better than he knew himself. And yet sometimes she did say he was a rogue. But she always said it with a smile. He began to feel a need for her approval. Of his clothes, his methods of negotiating a deal, his letters and his sense of humour.

She was going to be his anchor.

They went out a few times and continued to meet only away from the office. The first time she came up to his flat they were going to go to a play and have a late dinner. He opened the door in his tuxedo and noticed she wasn't dressed for the theatre. She stood there smiling, holding two large packages of Chinese takeaway. The taxi driver waited behind her, carrying the wine.

'We'll stay in tonight,' she said, having insisted on paying for the meal herself. She brought flowers to decorate the table and she laid everything out beautifully and lit some candles. She put on a record of Rumanian gypsy music while they ate. Sweet and sour shrimps and Peking duck. Paper-thin beef and bamboo shoots in noodles. Heaps and heaps of steaming rice.

Until that evening he had always taken her out on the town. They went to the opera and the ballet and saw all the Humphrey Bogarts in the West End. She said he was making her fall in love with London, but she told him later she was falling in love with him instead.

That evening, before they began the meal, he took her in his arms and they kissed. He felt her body close and he thought she was eager. Later, as they ate, he knew she wanted him to go the whole way. She hinted at nothing but he knew she had intended to stay the night because she had a small bag with her. While she was in the kitchen he had looked inside and saw that it contained a change of clothes and her make-up kit. The expectation of things to come coursed through him. She had told him often how she was struggling with her commitment to her medical student. She could not have two lovers at the same time, she had said.

They ate the Chinese food and she talked about the medical student.

'You know, Peter,' she said, as if letting him in on a secret, 'last weekend, when you were in France with your uncle, I flew up to Scotland for a day. I saw him.'

'You saw him? How ... What did you ... What happened?'

'Nothing happened. Oh, he was kind and friendly and made time to see me. He's in the middle of exams just now. But the magic was gone ... We were like a brother and sister, you know ... I had to see him to find out what I felt about him ... He was sort of family ... the part that stayed home while I went away. You know what I mean.'

'Yes.'

'Look, he is sincere and he has a good strong character and he is committed but the excitement has gone, the attraction ... Maybe our friendship was too strong ... You can't have passion in friendship ...

At least I can't. I know it's my fault, but I met you. It isn't easy to explain ...'

'Then say nothing.'

'I have to. Perhaps there was nothing there that way. I don't know. We were neighbours. Friends ... We talked ... I mean I talked ...'

'Did you tell him ... About me?'

'Yes. I told him I had met someone. I told him the truth. I said we were not sleeping together. But I told him I wanted to ...'

'You do?'

'I do.' She came over to him and kissed him on the lips. A quick stolen kiss that tasted of soya. 'You know I do, you rogue.'

'No I don't ... You never said ...'

'I am a shy person.'

'You're a very decent girl.'

'Christ, that's boring.'

'No it isn't.'

'You get out of here now. Let me clear up.'

'No need. The maid will do that tomorrow.'

'Let me give the orders for a change. I talk strong but my knees feel weak.'

'Let me help you.'

'This is my party.'

'What do you want me to do while you're in the kitchen?'

She smiled. She beamed. She was enjoying this. She summoned up her courage and said:

'I want you to go into the bedroom. Warm the sheets up. I have waited a long time for this. I want it to be slow. I want the expectation to last.'

He could see the embarrassment in her face, but her eyes looked straight at him.

She was gone for ages. He did not know what she could be doing in the kitchen all this time. He took a lingering bath to help time pass. He looked at three different books but the excitement that hovered about the room took him over. He couldn't concentrate. He took a swig of whisky from the decanter. It calmed him a little. He turned the radio on. Then she came in and the telephone rang. It was his uncle.

'Can you come over first thing in the morning?'

'Of course. Is anything wrong?'

'I am going to the South of France for a week. We must talk before

I leave.'

'Shall I drive you to the airport?'

'No, thank you. That is sweet of you. No.'

'I'll be there.'

He did not hear her come in but then he felt her breasts on his shoulders. Her hands stroked the back of his neck.

'Sorry to bother you,' he heard his uncle say. 'You sound so relaxed. Were you asleep?'

'No, Uncle. I was reading.'

'That's good. That's very good.'

He felt his skin grow goose-pimples as he said goodbye to his uncle.

'Undress me, Peter,' she said. 'Undress me slowly.'

She was kissing him as he peeled her clothes off. She had a sweet scent about her that reminded him of cinnamon mixed with musk and vetiver. Her skin was soft and warm to his touch and he stroked her arms as her blouse came off. He kissed her legs as the stockings came off. She lay there naked and his lips crawled over her breasts and up and then down and her legs arrested his head as her body rose impatiently towards his.

'Take me now,' she said. 'Now.'

'You said you wanted me to be slow.'

'I've changed my mind . . .' she said. 'I can't wait. I . . . Come, take me now.'

He took his time still and she started to tear his shirt off, then his underwear. Her fingers dug ditches across his back. She rolled over on top of him and he felt her moistness hover along his hardness. She took it in her warm hand and rubbed it and guided it and then he pushed her over and mounted her and kissed her hard as his body plunged into hers. The whisky had slowed him up and he moved. Her hips were fast and her face urgent as her body came ever closer to his. Then her knees locked around his body and she said soon you'll be mine. My own, she said.

But he slipped away and came down to her and his mouth found her and he sucked at her until she screamed with the pleasure of it. He came plunging back and marvelled at the impossible bliss of his flesh lost in the throb of her. Tirelessly their bodies thumped into each other. Faster and faster they moved until she screamed and said I am dying and then he came down and they exploded together into a million pieces of spent ecstasy.

'I'll never let you go,' she said when her breath came back.

'I'm not going anywhere,' he said. 'My uncle is.'

She looked like a Madonna. Like the pale Holy Mother in the village church back in Rumania. He covered her body. They slept.

That was how it was the first time. Why do things change? he heard himself ask, and he sat up. His shoulder hit the bedside table. A stab of pain shot through him and he cried out. Quiet, he said to himself. He craved the memory of how it was between them but he kept being interrupted by other wrong, agonizing thoughts. There had been nothing painful about his first night with Annie. It was the sweet culmination of months of waiting. Of longing. Of tender thoughts and wild dreams and of love. It was magic.

Other views came into his mind. Pictures that had nothing to do with his predicament. He should be thinking of getting out of here. Were they controlling his mind too? They couldn't do that. The choice of memories was his. Must stay his. It was an assertion of his independence.

He was trying hard. There was confusion in the pictures. Bits and pieces of other times and other people kept creeping in, uninvited. If only he could have Annie with him now. She would soon put the whole thing into perspective. She had the most rational mind he had ever known. She always calmed him down. He was a complete man only when she was around. When she was not having a crisis or a mood.

He must not think of that now. The anger and the fights and her depressions came much later, when she began accusing him of every crime under the sun. Of insensitivity. Of selfishness. Yes, that came after the magic had gone, and he was not going to think of that. He was in enough pain now. But his brain was in no state to stop anything. The miserable moments kept coming anyway.

Stop it. Stop it now. He hadn't always been weak. He'd show the bastards. They held him in that house and he couldn't get out but they didn't know everything. They wouldn't have dared mess with him otherwise. The corporal and his uncle and that landlady in Venice had messed with him.

He was in pain but he wouldn't mention the beatings. He wouldn't sigh or groan. He wouldn't give them the satisfaction. He'd think of happier days. If they did not know everything they could not be in total control. That thought made him grin. He concentrated.

★ ★ ★

He thought of that first night again and then the other nights and the happy times they had. He summoned Annie's voice to him. It was slow in coming and then it did. Success. Success at last. He was in charge again, he thought, and he smiled to himself. It was Annie's voice before things turned sour. Her voice when it was soft and loving.

In the beginning, Annie called him on his private line every hour. She would whisper to him, praising his prowess. Sometimes she did so when he was in conference with customers, when discussing big projects.

'I know you have one of the biggest investors in there with you. I imagine you are telling the man how much money you'll be making for him this year. But I can feel you right here inside me,' she would whisper into the phone. 'You and he are talking of investment and money but what does he know of passion? I want you again and again and I want you to get the man out of there and carry me away and undress me and take this itch away from me, the way only you can. Right this minute. Now.'

That sort of talk made him feel good and secure and happy. She would go on and sometimes she would utter obscenities. He would listen and say yes and he would smile. His optimistic, gratified, beaming face would always put his clients at ease.

He loved it.

'Just had a bit of good news,' he would say when she was finished.

'What's good for you is good for us, right?'

'Right.'

'Aren't you seeing too much of that girl?' his uncle had asked him. 'You can do much better than that. I have a lady client who is keen for you to meet her daughter. A titled family. Bankers. Have a great estate in Berkshire. They have horses and famous people go to their shoots. Their house in Belgravia is something else.'

He agreed to meet the girl. He said she was a bit horsey and his uncle laughed.

'You will want many women in your life, like your father. Horsey women are supposed to be liberal with their husbands. Could suit you. Your girlfriend is too intelligent for a wife. Comes from nowhere. She pleases you the other way, yes?'

He did not react. He did not say yes or no. His uncle's vulgar sex-talk upset him. What did the old faggot know?

But he did meet the girl. They all went to Glyndebourne once, and she chatted incessantly during the performance. She talked about horses and lunches and clothes and she gobbled her strawberries on the lawn as if she had been starved all her life. His opera-loving uncle never mentioned her again. After that he accepted Peter's choice of Annie as if it had been his own.

His life and his work were complex and he needed Annie to balance things out. Hers were simple, home-made pleasures. A clean house, a made bed, a good meal. She seemed even-tempered, and to start with she was always happy. Occasionally she would fall into bouts of silence, but those were rare. At first he thought she was quiet because she was listening to what he had to say.

Whenever he gazed into her large brown eyes, he would talk of his aspirations. The plans he had for the company. With her doing his shopping and choosing his clothes and newspapers and guiding his selection of films, he would be free to do that. At that time she was the best listener in the world. In her silence and her care she became indispensable. A mixture of his father's love and Mihai the manservant's practicality.

'You should be a little more sociable with the others in the office,' she had said. 'They are jealous of you. But don't overdo it. They need to think of you as being better than they are . . . In this country they don't take you seriously unless you have class.'

She knew more about what motivated people than he did. She could always tell a fake. He listened to her opinions of people.

He got to be dependent on her.

Whenever she went up to Scotland he stayed in.

At the office their relationship was still a well-kept secret. No one knew.

CHAPTER SEVEN

■

He opened his eyes and looked out of the window. The moon dropped pale rays of light that splattered on the waves below like a million pearls. He heard someone breathing and he looked back and saw the two figures standing there in the shadows, staring at him. The room went dark and he shut his eyes and pulled his knees up to his stomach. He expected the blows to fall on him any minute now. They were back to hit him some more, he thought. Maybe not. One of them looked like a woman. But he was too scared to make sure. He turned his head away and waited. But they just stood there and they looked, and then they were gone.

Someone had left him a steaming cup of chocolate on his side table. His watch said it was midnight. He could almost hear the Roman numerals speaking to him. The small and the large hands were both stuck on the twelve. A long time to go before the dream. If he fell asleep, that was. He would make a special effort to listen and see and remember and understand what it was. Go deeper into the beyond. The other side. Find out what lay behind the voices and the pictures he was going to see. Stay half awake. Face them. Catch them unawares. Try and remember. He knew it was not going to be pretty, but he must face them some time. It was something no one else could do for him.

'I am going to give you more responsibility,' his uncle had said. They were sitting in the living-room and the tennis coach served coffee. His tanned knee touched his uncle's shoulder as he bent over to pour. They smiled at each other lovingly.

Peter had lifted his own cup but the coach's eyes were stern and said serve yourself.

'We ought to be talking privately,' he said to his uncle in Rumanian. They were discussing an impending takeover in the City. Inside information on which they stood to make a killing.

'Oh, don't mind the boy,' his uncle had said. 'He's naive. He knows nothing of business. He is safe.'

There was something in the young man's eyes he did not like. A sort of snarl that said you've got it made but you don't deserve it. You've got no class. Your uncle might be backing you up to the hilt but you aren't fooling me. Don't step on my toes or I'll tell.

'It's time you joined the board,' his uncle had said. 'We'll arrange that as soon as I get back from Switzerland. You're going to get the lot in any case, when I pop off. Until then I'll make you work. I want more time to enjoy myself.'

His nephew had wondered where the tennis coach fitted in. But two weeks after that conversation he was elected to the board. An announcement and a picture appeared in the *Financial Times*. Annie had chosen the suit for him. And the tie. She briefed him on what to say to the press in case they wanted an interview, but they did not.

He was to appear in the papers often. But that came later, and mostly in the gossip columns. Wealthy Peter Gordon seen at the Connaught with whomever. Annie was still a well-kept secret.

He sat up and looked into space. No one was coming back to beat him. He warmed to the memory of his successes. He felt sufficiently safe to summon the unpleasant bits.

'It wasn't all roses,' he said out loud, knowing she could not hear him. He could hear her, though. She was speaking to him. Repeating something she had said once, he did not remember when.

'What do you know about humility? About shame. You have never been forced to parade, dressed up so ludicrously you felt you were naked. Made to walk up and down in front of an assortment of old ladies who were supposed to admire you but were ridiculing you whenever your mother looked the other way.'

When was it she had said that?

Maybe before she left him the first time.

'When I was little and badly in need of support she took pleasure in denying me. She looked the other way, too, when my father needed a wife. You've had it all too easy in your life, Peter. It's been one big adventure, a game. Yes, even the money-changing business and breaking the law and all that junk you call danger. You had great fun. You were having the time of your life. You were happy.'

It was best to let her go on ranting and raving until she cooled off. It did not take long. Half an hour at most. And then she would leave the room and cry into her pillow a little and come out again with a brave smile as if nothing had happened.

Maybe she had been right. Maybe it had been easy for him. But why did she turn her anger on him every time she talked of her childhood? He was not to blame. He hadn't been there.

'When something is ugly or hard to digest you simply ignore it. You eradicate it from your mind as if it didn't exist. That is what you would like to do with me sometimes ... I know ... You're lucky you can ...

Most people cannot do that,' she used to say. She was right there, too. The dreams were ugly. He knew that much. Was it self-defence that always made him forget what he saw?

When things were bad he immersed himself in work, but she started on him as soon as he came in. Her moods and her anger fell on him almost daily.

God, at such times Annie was the accuser and the judge and the jury all in one.

And now that she was gone he missed her so much it hurt. Her advice and encouragement. Her voice, her soft skin, the touch of her hands soothing his pain away. The way she urged him to undress her and the sweet moistness of her wild sexuality. The virgin forest that surrounded her bitter-sweet scent.

No use thinking of that now. Annie had been taken out of his life and, even if it was his fault, this was not the time.

No time was the time. Nothing was going to bring her back.

We are, all of us, our own worst enemies, she had said.

Why did he keep hitting at those who had helped him?

Everybody does that. It's impossible to admit you haven't done it yourself. It is hard to accept you needed help. He was no exception.

Why shouldn't he have it easy?

Annie's mother was bad for her but she had not deserted her. Not the way his mother had.

He was jumping about again, he thought as he drank the chocolate. It was cold inside the house but out in the garden and all over the island it was warm. The sea was rough. White foam raced over the swell. It reminded him of some old pirate movie. He expected Paul Henreid to appear on some moonlit deck kissing Maureen O'Hara. Two cigarettes in his mouth, lighting them together. No, that couldn't be the one. He was getting things muddled up. That was Bette Davis and not aboard a pirate ship. He had actually seen Maureen O'Hara in a fashionable restaurant and had pointed her out to Annie. He said he used to be in love with her.

'Before my time,' Annie said, and she laughed. 'Some gambler you are. You didn't win a movie star but you got the hair colour right.'

He made a face and she said: 'Only joking.' She always tried so hard not to hurt him. At least in the early days.

* * *

The pain was still acute and he got up and went to the bathroom. He'd take an aspirin. The bastards had really done their job. Back on his bed he saw the elegant little shape of his uncle. It materialised in the room. He knew where it had been and when but he did not want to think about it just then. But his mind did not give him a choice.

It was the evening his uncle had talked about his mother. Told him his version of the story. Of all the lies he had heard this was the thickest.

How could a bright man like his uncle, a man who possessed the brains of a professor, believe such crap? Or think anyone else would?

And yet he had told him of his mother by way of a revelation. A great personal secret. Like telling a thief where the family jewels are hidden. Giving him the code for the safe. The key. The lot. And all along there is nothing in there.

Maybe his uncle thought it didn't matter because he was telling lies to a liar.

But at least they were alone. The tennis coach was not there, for a change. His uncle was keeping his fabrications strictly in the family.

'Towards the end of your parents' marriage she was going through hell. I cannot forgive your father for that. He was ruthless. He more or less pointed his finger at her as if she were a common criminal. They wouldn't accept him for the fascist Iron Guard until he got rid of her. He had tried to certify her. As if a divorce was not enough. I know you were very young but you must have noticed that. You know, you were living with her at the time.'

'I don't remember any of it, Uncle.'

'You do not want to remember, and I cannot blame you. I wish I didn't know. But the brain never forgets a thing, my boy. It stores every second of your life somewhere and releases it when you least expect it to. Like a computer out of control. One day, when you're tired or ill or in pain or old, you'll remember. For the moment your brain is protecting you. It stops you from thinking of it. But it will fail you one day and you will have no escape. You won't be able to hide because it will come at you from inside. It's better to be ready for that, hard as it is. You must have suffered, my poor Peter, but your mother suffered more.'

He had grimaced as he looked at the old fox.

'Why are you telling me this now?'

His uncle put his hand on his arm.

'I couldn't bear to hurt you when we first met. You were so young. So vulnerable and frightened and sensitive. All refugees are that way when they first come out of hell. I was one myself, and just about your age. I couldn't do that to you. You are my sister's son. My flesh and blood. My only flesh and blood. But you are older now, and I feel strange every time I board a plane. What if I die? Who will tell you then? I have to tell you. I am sorry.'

There were tears in the old man's eyes. But he wasn't fooling him. He was hiding his mother somewhere. He was trying to discredit his father. Make him hate him. Hate himself.

Sensitive, vulnerable refugee, he had called him. Bullshit. Young Gordonitzu, when he fled Rumania, was not afraid of a thing. He fell right on his feet.

His face hardened and he fought to keep the surging hate inside. He kept silent. He nodded.

'Good thing you are accepting it, my boy. It would have been impossible to have comprehended this when you first came out. I remember what you were like there in Venice. You know, your mother was not even thirty when they took her. She could have survived. Maybe she didn't want to. But I knew her well. Better than any other human being on earth. We were twins and we were close. She could not have faced herself after being messed up the way she was. She wasn't hard enough. She knew she would never come out. But across all that distance she made me swear I'd look after you. This I did and will always do. And may the Lord forgive me for the pain I am causing you today. This is why I insisted on seeing you alone.'

Insisted on being alone, huh? Just then the tennis coach came in. As if he had been listening outside and knew when to crash in. He was dressed in long white slacks and a matching polo-neck sweater. His sun-tanned face revealed a set of perfect white non-smoker's teeth. He held a briefcase in his strong arms.

'Is this the one you want to take?'

'Yes,' his uncle said with a smile as bright as the sun. His tears had disappeared as if by magic. His eyes shone. 'Whatever would I do without you, Sunshine?'

He motioned the coach to sit down and the boy looked through him as if he wasn't there.

Now he knew for sure the old man was lying.

He sat up in bed. He wanted to say something to his uncle but the dapper figure had gone. He was sure he had seen it there on the bed a few seconds before. He looked at the sea and switched the light on and remembered where he was. It had all been an illusion. A figment of his imagination. The conversation had taken place but long ago and far from here. It was not imagination, but a part of his past. Real and true and stuck in the slow lanes of the mind which never forget a thing.

Brains of a professor, his father had said. His uncle was right. He did not forget a thing.

He yawned and stretched his arms and felt sleep coming close as the pain in his body subsided. They might have put something in the chocolate.

That was it. A hallucinatory drug. That was the reason for the voices and the woman and the vision of his uncle. And the nightmares. And Annie's voice. He was about to feel relief when he remembered. Not the nightmares. They had been there before. Five years. Maybe ten. Long before he ever came here. The nightmares had been there ever since he could remember. Even at boarding-school.

Annie knew about them and had asked him to describe them but he never could because he did not remember.

There was a good side to all that. On days when he had dreams he would sleep late and get up and go to a gym in the City. He wouldn't show up at the office before eleven. But his mind was as clear as a bell. As if the nightmares had cleansed his brain. He would work out the best deals after such nights. And he ran the business like clockwork.

He knew all the investors and the banks and the lawyers personally. Knew every member of his staff by their first name.

Like Napoleon, Annie had said, proudly. So legend had it.

And after his uncle's demise he made the company five times bigger.

He was going to go public shortly after this trip. The institutions and the pension funds were going to back him. They were going to buy large chunks of shares.

It was going to be the flotation event of the year. For all he knew it might still be. If only he could get in touch with someone at the office. They were probably looking for him frantically. They must have hired private detectives.

The thought of the business brought the adrenalin into his system and it fought hard to keep him alert.

But his eyes were moist and tired and he yawned and took another sip of the chocolate and turned off the light.

He'd ask them tomorrow. He needed to know what was going on. A company going public was a serious thing. They would surely let him call the office. He must make that call. They could cut him off as soon as he said something they didn't like. It would be strictly a business call.

Annie would know how to do that, he thought. She always knew what to do. When all the food shops in town were closed, she always found somewhere. When something electrical broke down she knew how to fix it. On their honeymoon she found a money-changer at midnight when he needed cash. She'd know how to get him a call to London. To-morrow, not now. He was too tired to talk to anyone now. His eyes became unbearably heavy. Tons of strain lay on his lashes and his chest as he breathed in and then out. Breathe through your stomach. It will relax you, Annie's voice said.

Out in the garden one of the Rottweilers came to the window and looked inside. Alert and shiny and wet with the sweat of an aimless run. The dog's breath steamed over the glass. But Peter Gordon's eyes were shut to the world as he slept and the dog did not frighten him at all.

CHAPTER EIGHT

■

The old man made out he knew everything about his mother.

'She was in love with your father, oh yes, I'll admit that,' he said. 'More than that. She was crazy about him. Much more than he deserved, the way things turned out. Oh, it was all roses to start with. Music and dances and moonlight parties in high places. Society dinners. We were not rich, your grandfather having been a medical man, but we were all sent to private schools and were going to university. It was a large family, the way families used to be in those days. Only you and I are left of it now. There were uncles and cousins with whom we spent long summers at the seaside. We went for winter sports in the mountains. We kept ourselves to ourselves and learned to like each other. Until your mother got to know the Baron the family was the centre of our existence. It was a good life, if traditional. As for the rest of the people, we were doomed to remain foreigners forever. That was because we did not celebrate Christmas or take part in the parades at Easter like the others.

'Your mother was interested in history. Yes, that's why she was so good at languages. She wanted to read about countries through what their own nationals had to say. By the time she was twenty she was fluent in German, French and Italian. She was planning a trip to England when she met him, the Baron Gordonitzu. He lived up in the country, but one weekend each month he'd go down to town to live it up. He cut a dashing figure. He drove fast, elegant cars and always had a carnation on his lapel. He smoked Turkish cigarettes and used the best French cologne. He turned up at all the best night-spots in town. He was a good-time boy. He laughed a lot and drank a lot and threw the dice on the tables as if there were no tomorrow. She was totally different. Frugal almost. She wouldn't let anyone help her and always insisted on paying her own way. She worked as a librarian while she was a student. Summers she worked as an interpreter in a private bank. It belonged to a distant cousin of ours with whom no one spoke because he had converted to Christianity. The joke was that the Iron Guard did not take that into account when they took him away, and neither did the Germans. He ended up gassed and burned. Still, while we were young he was by way of a big-shot and I think I might have modelled myself on him. Your mother helped him out during the summer since he had a lot of foreigners to deal with. She did so well he offered her a permanent job.

'I think she met your father there. Yes, that's right. He always lived on credit. On other people's money. He came into the bank to arrange for a loan. Our cousin the banker was only too happy to oblige an aristocrat. Your father, as usual, had gambling debts, and in the end the family bailed him out, but the damage was done. They had met.

I remember how excited she was about him. We were close. She told me almost everything. We were twins, you know. They say twins are closer than most.

'She went the whole hog for him. She stopped studying and in the end she joined the Church. That was shortly after your grandfather had passed away. At least he was spared that humiliation. Mother never found out. Or maybe she did and kept it to herself. But then, my mother was special. Very special. A woman in a million.

'Hard as I try to detect a resemblance, you look nothing like your mother. You may have inherited her talent for languages, her seriousness and naivety perhaps. Good thing you've been in the military. Otherwise I'd worry about you. People might take advantage of your easy nature, my boy. That was her trouble, you see. The Baron needed her and he used her and when things got tough he dropped her like a sack of rotten apples.

'When the Nazis came to power and the rightists rose, I was living abroad. We kept in touch by letter. I have kept those letters and one day I will give them to you because they are a treasure. A source of information for a historian. Your mother could have been a writer, you know. Her descriptive powers were immense. Immense. Sensitive and good and gullible as she was, you could read her letters and know exactly what was going on. She saw only the good side of people, and even after your father had left her she believed in him. She thought he was weak and couldn't help it. She knew he was going to divorce her, but she said he had to. He could look after himself very well, I tell you. He fooled everybody, including you. And me, too. I used to cash cheques for him in the old days. You know, discount them and give him the money. Guarantee him in a way, and I lost the lot. Used to send him presents from here, and do you know why? Because your mother had asked me to.

'The last time I actually saw her in the flesh was in Nice. They had gone there for a short holiday, and while he gambled your mother and I visited galleries and museums. Funny, but I lent him some cash that time too. He stayed at the Negresco while I was shacked up in a small *pension* in the back streets to save money.

Then he had a bout of good luck and he paid me back. It was the first time he'd ever done that. They left and the next thing I knew she moved to Bucharest with you. I have a photograph of the two of you somewhere. He gave her little money and came to see her only rarely. But she kept her face clean for him. I am using her words. She kept calm and brave and hopeful for a long time. God, how she suffered. I am not sure I would have had the courage to go through what she had to endure. And yet she behaved as if all was well. She did not want to worry anyone.

She asked me to tell Mother she had left the country. The old lady never knew what finally happened to her. No one knew. Only me and, obviously, for all he cared, your father.

Your face looks hard and disturbed, my boy. I am sorry.'

And again, just when things were getting a little heavy, the tennis coach came into the room. As always, he sneaked in unannounced. As suddenly as a chameleon changing colour, his uncle's face would lose the tragic expression it had worn. Gone was that false grief, the sad lowering of the eye, the soft, reminiscing voice. His eyes lit up as he greeted the bright, godlike figure. He offered him a seat. A smile suffused his face.

'Am I in the way?' the young man would ask.

'Not at all, Sunshine. We've just finished our business discussion,' his uncle would always say.

Insensitive, lying bastard that he was.

Most embarrassing of all were the times his uncle talked of his own mother. He would get shamefully sentimental. He would cry. What a woman my mother was, he'd lament. He'd spend hours describing her classical beauty. Her strength of character. Her love of music. Her knowledge of art and the way she had played the piano. Whenever the old man started to talk of her, Peter knew it was going to be an all-night session.

'Ever since I can remember – yes, even when your mother and I were small children – she watched over us. She knew how to make us feel self-reliant, how to help us with things without ever reminding us of it. She learned maths just so that she could supervise my homework, and in anticipation of your mother's projected trip to England, she took secret lessons in the language herself. What do you think of that?

'I suspect she used to meet your mother on the quiet. Yes, even after your mother married your father. They mostly met in Bucharest. That was because at the start of the marriage they lived up at the estate most of the time and they travelled a lot. They visited every casino on the European map, although I believe your father did not lose quite as much while they were together. Maybe your mother brought him luck. I hope he had none when he kicked her out. I don't know if he ever mentioned me to you, but when they first married and travelled I used to see him whenever I came to meet your mother. We talked. In his way he was an amusing man and I admit he was extremely handsome. We were never friends, but for her sake I kept the relationship going as long as I lived in Rumania.

'The Fascists and the Iron Guards were gaining power. In the streets and the coffee houses and other public places. Foreigners were made to feel insecure. Things were unstable. You never knew who was wielding power behind the King's back. It was then that I started to make arrangements to emigrate. There were rumours about your mother because she was living on her own and everybody knew she was going out with the Baron. At family gatherings her name was never mentioned.

But I distinctly remember one time, when someone said something derogatory about her. Called her a traitor to the faith or something. It happened just as we sat down for dinner. No one reacted because most of the people present agreed. Then your grandmother got up and issued a silent command in my direction, and we left the others and made for the door. It was our own house we were leaving, remember.

'Before she left the dining-room she looked at the person who had talked about your mother and said:

' "I am going for a walk with my son. When I return I do not want to see you here."

'You know, of course, that I had her brought over here. She managed house for me in the early years. She looked after the books, too. She always stayed in the kitchen when I was entertaining. She did not wish to embarrass me in front of my guests. Only once did she come out with the coffee, when she introduced herself as my housekeeper.

'Make them think you are rich, she used to say. Rich people have housekeepers and cooks and their mothers never live with them. Never.

'And so no one ever knew her, or who she was, and I have lived to regret it.'

In his office his uncle kept an enlargement of an old photograph of her. As a young woman, dressed in lace. She had jet-black hair and she smiled sadly. Another photograph of her stood atop an antique French desk displayed in his bedroom. Peter had been in that bedroom only once while his uncle was alive. The morning he came in to find him asleep with the coach. What he had seen gave him a great shock, and as he slipped out he noticed the picture there. His uncle's mother again, but as an older lady. It was retouched, as if the old fox couldn't take the imperfections of age. Someone had added colour to it. It was a little smaller than the one in the office and, right by it, was shattering testimony to his uncle's perverted nature. Beside the old lady's proud image there was a full-frontal nude picture of the tennis coach, flashing his suntanned smile.

'To my own big mouse,' it said. 'From your ever-adoring Sunshine.'

That picture was moved out of the apartment later. It was put in the old man's desk drawer. He saw it once more when he moved into the big office after his uncle's death. He put his lighter to it as soon as he was alone.

Homosexual. Queer. Pansy. Annie was the only one who spoke to him of his uncle's way with men. There was a lot of it about, but in those days it was against the law. In his youth in Rumania he had known there was something bad about men loving other men. He was not sure why, but his father had once mentioned it. Some fellow in his old regiment who got caught out and had shot himself or was shot or something. He wasn't very sure what it was but it was bad and in his memory there was a bad word to describe it. Annie was much more accommodating. When he told her about it for the first time he was in a state of outrage. He thought her clement attitude to his uncle's weakness was meant to ease his own agony, but she had meant it then and had continued to defend them ever since. She treated and spoke of it as though love between men was natural.

'They look sweet,' she had said. 'There is something touching about the way your uncle looks at him. Depending, yearning. Protecting ... true, pure love, I would say.'

Dirt, he would have said, but she went on about Oscar Wilde and Lord Douglas and the beauty and purity of love. He was too nauseated to comment.

'Don't ever think he is being used,' she had said on another occasion, after they had finally been invited together for tea at his uncle's flat. 'The boy loves him very deeply. Maybe it's a father-figure he is looking for, or an older brother or a teacher he admired and has lost. I tell you it's love.'

Well, she ought to know, having spent entire afternoons chatting to the tennis coach.

He often saw her talking to him at the office. They had tea together.

'What do you see in that ham?' he had asked.

She hoped he was jealous.

'Oh, you'd be surprised. The boy is very sensitive. And intelligent. And well brought-up too. He went to one of the best schools in the country. He is a lawyer by profession and was an officer in some famous regiment. The sort that only takes the best ... you know ... classy people.'

'He's a queen.'

'And he fought in Korea. Was mentioned in dispatches. I can show you what they wrote about him in *Who's Who*.'

'I am not interested in layabouts.'

'But he makes your uncle happy. That's a full-time job, you know. Your uncle is not an easy man. He used to suffer depressions. He used to go to an analyst before the young man came into his life.'

'How do you know?'

'I came across some bills in the file the other day. Can't be very easy for him, this pretence ... having lost everybody, having survived.'

'The man is after money.'

'Far from it. He is not poor at all. No. It's love, and more than love. In your uncle's mind he is standing in for something or someone.'

'Yes. His mother.'

* * *

He trained himself not to mind his uncle speaking of the old lady. It was always a monologue. He didn't need to listen or comment or nod, and as long as he looked interested the old man was happy to carry on. It was the way his uncle spoke of his own mother, and thus of his father the Baron, that incensed him. But he kept his mouth shut and bided his time. The Baron was a gambler and he drank sometimes, but he was a warm, loving man who had cared for him and who needed protection. He must have been a good man or else Mihai the manservant would not have stayed with him all that time. Loyal above and beyond the call of reason and duty. His father had allowed him to make money for him. That proved he loved him, too. The Baron was a proud man, Mihai had said so himself, and so had his uncle. His uncle must have known how his father got his mother out of the concentration camp ... Anyway, the concentration camp story was a lie.

He for one did not remember a thing about it, hard as he tried.

His uncle must be hiding her somewhere, but why should he care?

Now that he had Annie he had lost all his curiosity about his mother. Annie made him forget his past.

Anyway, why should he feel sorry for his mother?

It was his father who had suffered. Living in a community farm that was his birthright. Having lost it to a servant. God, how he must have suffered.

That's why he drank and gambled. To forget.

His uncle and his young stud knew nothing of pain.

Sunshine. That was the name they had all given the tennis coach.

'I promise you it's love,' Annie used to say. She said it each time she had been with the young man. 'Hopeless, fruitless love that leads nowhere and ends in tragedy. But it is as sweet and all-consuming as any other love, maybe more . . . It is as selfless as love can ever be . . . David and Jonathan . . .'

'Rubbish. It's immoral. It's against nature. He's taking my uncle to the cleaners.'

'You know as well as I do that Sunshine is paying his own way. It's not the money. Sunshine is rich, for God's sake. The way those two care for each other is so touching you forget they could go to jail.'

'And where does that leave me?'

'Different, Peter. Different. In your uncle's world you are his flesh and blood. You are his obligation . . .'

'That's it. I am his obligation, huh? What a thing to say . . .'

'Look, you are his house. Sunshine is his garden.'

'His bedroom.'

'You are vulgar.'

'He screws him. Sucks his cock, that's what he does. He's his whore.'

'I do that too, Peter . . . Am I your whore? Is that what you think of sex? Something only whores do?'

She had to talk about herself. She could never discuss something calmly without bringing her own troubles up. She took everything he said personally.

It was funny how long it had taken him to notice that. He noticed it but he never understood it.

To start with he'd say nothing and he'd take her in his arms but later on he did react.

'Don't feel sorry for yourself, Annie,' he'd say.

'You just don't care, do you?' was the answer. 'You are too involved with yourself, you can't see things clearly.'

'I suppose clearly means seeing things your way.'

'You don't even know what I'm talking about.'

It was a waste of time.

And yet, depressions or no depressions, Annie and Sunshine became intimate friends. Every time he showed up or called, her moods evaporated as if that dark side of her was strictly reserved for him, her husband. She'd sit with Sunshine and talk and gossip and laugh. Later she would argue for him and fight tooth and nail for him and that true love of his.

She never tired of giving him examples of the boy's loyalty and devotion. His giving the old man a reason to live beyond office hours. Everyone knew how lonely his uncle had been before Sunshine came into his life. How his socializing was a fake to cover his unhappiness. All that changed when Sunshine appeared.

The young man never tried to hide the relationship. The admiring way in which he looked at his uncle in the company of others was discomforting. In Peter's eyes he was flaunting it for all to see, but Annie insisted he did it because he was proud of it. Not showing off. It takes guts to do that, she'd say. People sit in jail for it.

And yet, through all the years since Venice, until the last week of his life, his uncle went to great lengths to make his nephew believe there was nothing out of the ordinary in the association. Nothing sordid.

He made out that Sunshine was a Man Friday turned friend. His tennis coach, housekeeper, private secretary, companion and chauffeur.

Well, his uncle was a coward.

The boy did something for him. That was distressingly evident. He was happy and he hummed songs and he was generous and understanding. He told funny stories and was playful. He was a different man when Sunshine was not about. At such times he was reserved and morose. He talked only about business or his mother. He did not go out on the town and did not travel. As soon as Sunshine reappeared, life came back to him. He became socially visible. He would entertain lavishly, escort ladies to the theatre and the opera and exhibitions, and leave the office right after lunch.

On all these outings, Sunshine was noticeably absent.

'He is here all the same,' Annie used to say.

'Where?'

'He's represented by the rose on your uncle's lapel.'

Once, when Peter and his uncle were alone in his office, the old man talked of his will. It was common knowledge that Peter would be the sole beneficiary.

'The purpose of this talk is presents ...'

'What presents?'

'You know, gifts I wish to make to people. You'll have to see to that because you're the executor.'

'You're not dying.'

'I know that, but I like order.'

'Do you want me to do something about him?'

'Him who?'

'Your tennis ... your ... you know, Sunshine.'

That was the first time his uncle lost his temper with him.

'You leave Sunshine to me, do you hear?' the old man shouted. His eyes burned as he hit the desk with his fist. The blue veins on his temple filled out. 'Sunshine is not "him" ... Not a dog or a pig ... Never say "him". He is a human being. A very dear human being, and he is nothing to do with you, understand? Nothing.'

Perhaps his uncle could not imagine life without Sunshine, Peter thought. But he would have to accept death without him. The man was only twenty-five. Soon the old charm came back and, with a smile as large and as false as the stuffed barracuda on the wall behind him, his uncle said he was sorry for losing his temper.

'I should apologise, not you, Uncle ... But I asked because I am your executioner. I should know what to do.'

'Not executioner, I hope. Executor, dear boy, executor.'

Slip of the tongue, Peter thought.

Having seen his uncle's last will and testament for himself, Peter concluded that the document gave him full protection. He was doing well, as it was. He had access to everything even then. He could never be seen to have a motive. Not even if there were twelve thousand just men on the jury.

After that they sat there and looked at each other and the old man smiled and apologised again. Why am I in such a hurry always? Peter asked himself. There was no call to kill the old man. He ran the place all on his own now. His uncle hardly interfered with him now that he was managing director. He was signing all the cheques and vetting all new investors. It looked like his uncle's time was up anyway. He had lost a lot of weight lately and his skin had become almost transparent. His hands took to shaking more and the lustre had gone from his eyes. There were rumours he had a terminal illness.

It could be a temporary state of affairs, Peter thought. Sunshine was away for a month on a trip to Peru. He was visiting Machu Picchu and Cuzco. Places he had dreamed of since his schooldays, his uncle said with a proud if wintry smile.

Poor old sod, Peter thought. Why not let time take its course?

Because it had nothing to do with money.

No. His uncle had stained the family honour. His father's proud old name was at stake, and it fell to him to be the defender. He could not accept what the old man had said. His father would never have let his mother die in a camp. It was all an invention. His uncle knew he loved his father and he was jealous. He was jealous of all the care his nephew had lavished on the Baron. Peter had been looking after his father for a long time now.

He had found ingenious ways of continuing to send him money, almost as soon as he arrived in the West.

Even from Venice, where, on the second day, he had stolen a carton of American cigarettes and sold them for twenty dollars in the Piazza. Later his Argentinian sailors found him a steady supply.

There was a Rumanian ship in the port and he made friends with a man from the boiler room. A fellow from below decks who saw more soot than fresh sea air. He asked him to take some Italian lire back with him. He could change it and make a profit on the deal. He knew that only some of the money was going to reach his father. He had even told the boilerman he could keep half for himself. Later there were other ships and other crews. But by then he had the means to make sure.

He took care to have himself photographed with the crew member every time money changed hands. Armed with a copy of the picture, he used pure blackmail. If the money does not reach my father, this picture is going to the consulate. You will never be allowed out of Rumania again, he would say. Or out of jail.

You just make sure my father gets this and the picture will never reach the secret police back home.

Maybe it was crude but it worked.

Once he was established in London things became easier. The company had an office in Vienna. From there, for a small commission, anything was possible. One could always find a way of getting money to the Baron.

And then he became an important man, and all doors opened. There was a Middle Eastern country that had close ties with Rumania. They saw to it.

Money begets money.

There might not be much justice in this world but he was going to make sure the old Baron got his. Make sure his father ended his life the way he had started it. In comfort.

He could never go back to Rumania and never saw his father in the flesh again. He could have tried to bring him out or meet him in a third country, but he did not make the effort. The Arab courier said he could fix that for him. Get the old man on a Black Sea cruise and disembark in Istanbul. Then get him on a plane.

Annie said she would gladly go to Bucharest and bring him out. Or at least visit him.

That was impossible. Peter knew his proud father would never consent to receive his daughter-in-law under squalid circumstances. Not while he lived in a truck. Not even later when he moved to his son's old room in Bucharest.

She understood that. In the first few years she showed much perception.

He could have tried to see his father somehow. He wasn't sure why he didn't.

Did he secretly believe his uncle's stories?

Never.

Annie had guessed he was gunning for his uncle and often she tried to dissuade him. But never directly. She used to tell him how lucky he had been to have found his uncle. How his uncle loved him. How proud he was every time he made a killing on the market. The will was proof enough, she said.

It was not proof he was after, but revenge. He could not tell her about the concentration camp and what his uncle had said about his father.

No, he couldn't tell her. It was a lie anyway, and she was too fond of his uncle to believe he was a liar. As her friendship with Sunshine deepened she began to see his uncle through his lover's eyes. It was best to say nothing.

Oh, what a simple-minded girl she was. Once, when they told the old man about the depth of their love, he advised her to marry him quick.

'He'll need you when I'm gone, Annie,' he had told her. God's word would not have impressed her as much. How happy she was when she heard that.

Why did she need recognition? She was no refugee.

The old man's confidence in her was flattery. He knew that. He never told her how, at first, his uncle had objected to her. How he had said Peter could do much better. How he made him go and meet that horsey girl.

Then, when she talked to his uncle herself, she came under his spell.

He must have charmed her off her working-class feet.

OK, she admired his uncle, but that was not what had started the rift in the marriage. Nor was it her attitude to his working habits. She had worked in the office herself and she understood it well.

No. What had started it was a simple matter. A mere difference in preference. His love of the sun and her fear of it. That and other stupid little things had started it. Such as his going to bed early while she read well into the night. All sorts of books about finding one's happiness and asserting oneself.

In later years he would look at Annie and think to himself that it was the wedding ring that had changed her.

Yes, she had told him she thought she was pregnant. Six or eight months after they had met.

'Well,' he had said, 'I suppose I'll have to marry you.'

He was crazy about her and had meant it as a joke, but later on she kept reminding him of it. In any case, it was a false alarm and months had passed since his remark and the ceremony.

The wedding was a small, private affair and news of it hit the staff like a bombshell. Until the selected invitations were delivered no one knew a thing.

The reactions were varied. Some said he deserved better. After all, who was she? Just a long-legged nobody from the general office who got to grab the almighty by the balls.

She could have done better, said others. What did she see in that foreign bastard, except a meal ticket for life?

But at the luncheon after the register office there was jubilation. Well done, Annie, they said one and all, and wished them both happiness.

His uncle gave a speech.

He could never remember what the hypocrite had said. They honeymooned in Florida. She stayed in during the day and read and read and painted her nails while he sailed and swam and lay in the sun. They ate clams and visited the Seaquarium and Key Largo. He half expected to meet Humphrey Bogart there. They walked on the beach in the cool of the night and she poured calamine lotion on his darkening skin to ease the pain. She said he was the most considerate man in the world. They made love until it hurt.

She said he had saved her from self-destruction.

He had no idea what she meant.

Why now? Why now that it was all over and had been buried for years did he recognise how important she had been in his life? How he needed her. How her words and her touch had stretched out from the abyss to help him, even now that she was no more.

He could hear her words every time he was in pain.

'Let me massage the back of your neck.'

'I'll rub some cream on your shoulder for you.'

'They will not hurt you again now that I am here.'

Or other things she said and did to make him feel better.

Of course, he was daydreaming, but the mere sound of her voice soothed the pain. He smiled a smile of satisfaction and turned over.

Someone else was sitting on the edge of the bed. He was too weary to look. Best not to in case it was a dream. If it was he would be disappointed. He stretched, looking away, and thought how he had plenty of time for everything. He was not going anywhere.

And then he stole a glance and saw his uncle sitting there. Sunshine, broad-shouldered and tanned, stood behind him. Must be a dream. But it couldn't be. He was not asleep. The room was as hot as a furnace. He was sweating like a pig. It couldn't be his uncle. His uncle had never sat by his bed in his life. Anyway, his uncle was dead.

There were two women there. Or three. All dressed in decrepit old cotton dresses. He stole another glance. There was a man, too. He did not know who he was. A cold hand touched his forehead and he heard someone say:

'His temperature is sky-high. He is boiling.'

He must be sick or something. The voice sounded familiar. He thought it was Annie's voice because only Annie cared, but Annie never wore rags. She was fastidious about her clothes. Nothing but the best always. But Annie was dead too. His mother, that was right. It must be his mother sitting there touching his forehead. She always did that when he was sick. He opened his eyes and saw her face. God, how beautiful she was – alabaster skin and green eyes, thick black hair assembled over her oval head like a Spanish dancer. Aquiline nose and the face of a siren. Why did she look so poor and desolate and lost? She always knew what to say, but now she was sitting there with her hand on his forehead, shaking her head and saying nothing.

Big, soothing hand. Long fingers. The hand nearly covered the whole of him. Maybe he was small. Maybe he was still a child. He was not afraid and he did not want her to go so he pretended to sleep. Looked at her from under closed lashes. Waited.

It had all been a dream of his future.

Everything.

Yes. He was still a child and he had been given a glimpse of what was to come. He was warm and snug and smug and safe. Yet his mother's hand shivered a little. If he lay there very quietly and slept like a good boy he might never grow up to become what he had become. Never lose her or have to kill the corporal or walk the streets in search of money for his father. Never lose Annie.

All that had never happened. Not yet. It was going to happen but right now it was a crazy bit of imagination. Had to be. Could one change the future?

What would a Rumanian boy be doing dreaming in English? He knew it was English because he could hear words. His mother's voice came closer and then it became the voice of his uncle. Then it became Annie's voice. Then Sunshine. They were whispering. Slow, careful words. Weighed one by one before being allowed to exit those unseen lips. Non-committal, sophisticated. What was his uncle doing there? He had not met him yet. Or maybe he had. He was his mother's twin. He could be mixing them up.

He was having two dreams at the same time. That was it. A life within another life. He was dreaming of being a man but he was still a child. When he was a child it was his mother sitting there. When he was a grown man it was his uncle. He listened to what was said. He was not sure whether the words came to him now or were from the past. Fact or memory.

You must learn from future mistakes, his uncle's voice said. No one gets a chance like this. Now that he had the chance to change things he must make sure all that had happened would never happen.

Someone gave him two tablets and he gulped them down with a glass of freezing water. He soon felt better.

'Give him two more in a couple of hours,' someone said.

'I was locked up in some house,' he heard his voice say. 'Dreamt about it.' He started to tell his mother and the familiar sound of his own voice woke him. The figures were slipping away. He sat up and looked into the dark. They were gone. They had never been there. His captors must be stuffing him with drugs, but he was up and alert.

Outside the sea was in turmoil as white stretches of foam ran across the wet, dark surface all the way to the horizon.

Night reigned supreme. A storm was brewing somewhere far off.

Cold. He pulled the cover up and willed himself to stop the thoughts that raced through him. His body ached and he tried to remember who had hit him and why. The Rottweilers out in the garden howled a serenade of warning. He did not look but he imagined their teeth and eyes and saw them shine in the night.

They were all still to come. Annie, his uncle and Sunshine. England lay in the future, her warm, inviting arms stretched towards him. Tolerant, forgiving and full of opportunity. Grateful. Even the dogs were still to come, if he let them. He must try to stop the future.

Think well of the past, he heard his uncle say. It will teach you. Yesterday is a tired friend. But if you get the chance to see the future you'll be perfect. You will know what not to do. Can you imagine that? To know which shares will go up and which down? You'd make a fortune. You'd do better than me, his uncle said.

Christ, he was hallucinating again. He must be high on something.

Just then, unexpectedly, a desire to sleep came to him. He saw nothing and thought of nothing. Tiredness settled on him and he yawned and lay back and let total exhaustion cover him. He floated between the sheets as though he had never been awake in his life.

He slept and then the voices came out of some corner and entered his space and frightened him.

Something in him cried NO NOT NOW but the invasion had started. Drifting between awareness and slumber he shook his head but they came anyway.

There was something he was struggling to remember, something he had promised himself he was going to do. He must stop the nightmare.

But the avalanche of voices and faces and scenes came rushing in and he forgot them almost as soon as they came.

They were upon him. Hard and harsh and painful.

Must think of Annie now. She'd make it all go away. Not now. He couldn't. He'd think of her tomorrow. Or the next day. Whenever he woke.

He slept.

CHAPTER NINE

———■———

Annie's anxieties and breakdown had come as a shock to him. Especially since he saw her as the anchor that could secure his life and give it stability. He did not understand what her distress was and why she blamed her mother for it. Annie said she had only come to London to get away from her mother. He had tried to make a joke of it. He said he ought to send her mother flowers every day because they would never have met otherwise. But she did not think it funny. She said her mother was the original cause of all her troubles. She said she would never have needed the help of a psychoanalyst had it not been for her mother. He could never quite see what the problem was or the reason for it. He had met Annie's mother and she seemed a pleasant enough lady who talked a lot and giggled and laughed at her own jokes. One never knew when she was serious and when she was making fun.

She was fond of saying how she loved children. How she should really not have had any children because of her frail health. How she nearly died when Annie was born, and had to spend months in bed after that, in agony. How it was only her sense of humour that had saved her. How she had looked after her own daughter, in spite of what had happened. How she dressed her as best she could, fed her and made sure she did her homework every day. How she could not help Annie with school-work because she had not been lucky enough to have had an education. Not lucky like her daughter.

She was so proud of Annie, she always said. Proud because she had had her regardless of the doctor's warning. Only to please her husband. Annie was lucky, he thought, to have a mother like that. Someone who loved her that much. Who sacrificed her health and still laughed about it. How could that simple soul play such a negative part in her life?

Annie had told him she was made to change schools. As soon as she got to know the teacher and made a friend or two and mastered the bus route she was told the school was not good enough. It usually followed a parent's evening in which the teachers were subjected to her mother's venomous tongue. She could always tell a change was afoot from the way the teacher looked at her the next day. A mixture of surprise and pity, she thought.

She was always presented to her mother's lady friends who came to

Sunday afternoon teas. On such parades, as she called these occasions, she was made to model her skirts and pullovers and dresses and shoes. She was made to recite a poem and sometimes she'd be forced to sing. Her mother used to have her photograph taken and would send copies off to Hollywood stars and receive signed prints in return. She made her friends watch the way Annie nibbled at her cake, used her knife and fork and spoon, and would boast of her immaculate table manners. Everyone knew how she stopped wetting her bed before she was two years old.

Her father, Annie had told Peter, hardly ever said a word in the house and spent every free moment he had in the pub, avoiding his wife. He gave her his weekly wages, he gave in to everything she demanded of him. He crawled, he never insisted on anything, and all in order to keep the peace. He was a big, strong man who was well liked by his friends.

Often, in her teens, Annie shared his humiliation. She did not understand why he never stood up to her mother's chattering nonsense. He was forever being sent on errands. Even as they sat down to meals she would make him get up for the salt or the mustard. She was constantly testing her authority and his patience. Especially when there were people in the house.

Once, when Annie stayed out all night at a beach party, she was made to stay in her room for a whole week. No note was sent to school because her mother said she'd have to explain it herself. On the first night she heard her mother scream at her father.

'The girl nearly killed me when she was born. I could have become a cripple. And all because you wanted children. I gave her my life and looked after her and what do I get in return? Nothing but shame.'

Later on, when there were boyfriends, her mother used to tell them how beautiful and clever and talented Annie was. How she was going to be a big star. How no one was good enough for her. The man who ended up marrying her would have to be special. Everybody knew she was a robust girl because she had taken all her mother's health into her body when she was born. Child-bearing will come easy to her, she would add, and invariably embarrass them away.

Annie had come to live and work in London as soon as she could. Her mother never came down because she was, she said, only able to sleep in her own bed. She wrote to her daily and advised her on every step she was taking. She read Annie's replies to anyone who was not too bored to listen. The whole street knew everything Annie did or said, where she worked and what she ate.

Having failed to obtain a place in any of the dramatic circles, Annie took a shorthand typing course and worked in various offices until she settled for Peter's uncle's company. Her mother kept sending her parcels of fruit cake and sausage and haggis. Sometimes she sent smoked salmon.

'I can't see anything bad about that,' he had said.

'You wouldn't.'

'She really cared for you.'

'She told people everything about me. Where I was and what I did and what she sent me. She made me feel naked. She was a monster.'

He had tried to calm her.

'Maybe she was a little childish ... That's no crime. She was interested in you ...'

'She wasn't interested in me at all. She just wanted to know what I was doing so that she'd have something to talk about ... Something to be pitied for ...'

'She tried to give ... didn't she?'

'She gave but she took it right back. She made me pay ... She gave me things only to make me feel sorry for her. She craved sympathy. She demanded it.'

'She wasn't very happy, maybe, but I always found her very funny.'

'Funny is one thing ... she was funny to others but not to me. A child needs someone reliable. Someone to look up to. Not to laugh about or feel sorry for ... You did not live with her. You did not have to listen to what she said ...'

'The poor soul had no one to talk to ...'

'Of course she didn't ... No one wanted to listen to her. I had to.'

Two years after Annie moved to London her father went to live with the widow of a friend who had owned the local pub he frequented. Her mother said he was mad and was going through the menopause and couldn't face getting older. She said he would soon come back home to her, where he belonged. After all, she had looked after him all these years and he would never survive without her. She had sacrificed her health for him. That other woman was pushy and had dyed her hair and everybody knew she had killed her own husband by driving him to drink. When you next come up here, she wrote, he'll be back. Her father's pay still came to her mother every week and his clothes were still in the house. Her mother showed them off to prove he had not gone for good.

He came down to London to see Annie two or three times a year.

As time passed they both realised how happy he was now. He had changed a lot since leaving the house. The widow's pub, where he now worked, had become very popular. He was drinking less and had taken up fishing and playing golf. He was talkative and supportive and their friends liked him. His laugh made her think of her mother sometimes, but he never mentioned her.

He came down for her wedding and with the pub-owner's widow presented her with a dinner-set for twelve. He got on well with Peter. His inner joy and strength and the common sense that beamed out of him reminded Peter of Mihai the manservant. Within an hour of meeting Peter he was hugging him openly and saying that Annie would be happy with him.

He was a handyman who could repair things. He stayed in London to look after their flat when they went on their honeymoon. He was waiting for them at the airport when they returned. He was an easy man to please and be with, and sometimes he'd cook a simple meal and often he'd clean their car without being asked. That latent friendship between father and daughter did not go down well with her mother.

Having found out that he had been at the wedding with 'that woman', she wrote Annie a long letter. In it she accused her of enticing her father away. She said Annie was an ungrateful girl who did not appreciate what her mother had sacrificed for her. She said Annie repaid her goodness by inflicting pain and public humiliation on the only person who ever truly cared for her.

The letter was never posted and was found on the table four years later, after her mother had shot herself. She did so with the old shotgun that had hung over the fireplace. A passing gamekeeper who had lodged with them when Annie was little had left it there.

There was another note addressed to Annie in which she said:

'You sucked my blood when you where a small girl. All I ever wanted was to see you successful and happy. I gave you what I could. Now help yourself to the rest of me.'

No one understood why her mother waited that long and why she chose to commit suicide four years after the wedding. Peter was away on a long business trip when it happened. By the time he got back the funeral had taken place and Annie was back in London. Her words and demeanour betrayed nothing. He only found out about it at the office the next day. At home in the evening he broached the subject gently, but Annie exploded. She said he was insensitive and aloof. She said he was never there when she needed him.

He tried to talk to her all week but she did not open up at all.

'You are under pressure,' he had said, 'and if you cannot talk to me perhaps you should see someone. You can get help for bereavement, you know.'

'You wouldn't know what bereavement is,' she had snapped. She refused a drink or a sedative and told him that if he was not happy he was welcome to leave.

It was he who suggested an analyst in the first place. Boy, was he going to regret that.

She never mentioned her mother again, or her schooldays. She tore up all the old photos in which her mother was present. She gave away all the books her mother had sent her over the years. She gave away a vase and a Spanish painting her mother had bought for her on her one and only holiday abroad.

It was as though the woman had never existed at all.

Annie's father moved back to the family home a few weeks later. He lived there on his own and Peter made sure he was never short of money. He did not see the pub-owner's widow again and had taken to going to another watering-hole. A telephone was installed in the house and father and daughter talked to each other daily. Sunshine, who had once spent the night with Annie's father on his way to a fishing holiday, remarked that the old man never called anyone else. He must think, Sunshine said, that the damned thing only works when connected to you.

After her mother's death, Annie's friendship with Sunshine became absolute. She could talk to him about everything. They became inseparable.

At first, when Peter made snide remarks about it, she used to say she was safe with him. Later, when she wanted to hurt him, she'd say it was a pity he did not like women because she could express herself better with him.

In truth, she was helping him cope with his own emotions. After his lover's death, Sunshine kept falling in and out of meaningless liaisons. But she did not admit that to Peter. Girl-talk, she called their lunches, and when she was in a good mood she repeated Sunshine's amusing gossip to her husband.

The three of them often sat together. Peter was silent but Annie and

Sunshine never ran out of things to say to each other. More than anything, Peter agonised over the way Sunshine could make her laugh. He kept coming, unannounced, and spent hours with them as if he were trying to keep in tangible touch with a spirit. It seemed the young man never left their orbit once Peter's uncle was gone.

A screwed-up ménage we are, Peter would think to himself. A husband, a wife, and a dead man's lover.

Later still they started ignoring him. He pretended he did not care but it was hurting him.

Sunshine's trim tennis figure had filled out with the years. Having taken over his family's wine and spirit business, he had thrived. He inherited his lover's passion for music and the arts. He took Annie out whenever she was alone or wanted to go somewhere. The opera, films, the theatre, and even shopping. He always treated Peter with polite, if intimidated, respect. There was a courteous rejection in his posture and voice whenever the two men met on their own.

'He doesn't like me much, does he?' Peter commented.

'Maybe he is scared of you,' Annie said.

Maybe he was. But he could not prove a thing, Peter thought.

It was Sunshine who had first mentioned Jamaica to them. He had a distant cousin there who lived on a sugar plantation. He knew the island well, having spent the war years at school there. He could imitate the local accent like a native.

His Jamaican antics never failed to make Annie laugh.

'You simply must go and take a look at Jamaica,' he had said. 'Your uncle loved it. The food is fresh and the music is out of this world and there you will see the most beautiful scenery God has created. White sandy beaches, green mountains, humming-birds and fern-strewn valleys. The people are a treat. They have a great sense of humour. There is no winter in Jamaica.'

'Annie can't take the sun,' Peter had retorted.

In any case, by then he had found other things to be amused by.

'Sunshine says you are screwing around,' she said one day out of the blue. Just as they sat down to dinner.

'He does? Well, I suppose Sunshine knows best.'

'He's reliable enough for me.'

'Is he good at predicting market movements too?'

'Spare me your stupid jokes.'

'Sunshine doesn't like me much, does he?'

'You've said that before.'

'Yes, I have. Do you know what he's got against me?'

'He thinks you killed your uncle.'

'Yes, so you keep telling me. Do you think I killed my uncle?'

'I don't know. I don't know any more.'

'If Sunshine is wrong about that, he might be wrong about other things too. What will you do with your theories then?'

'I didn't say he was wrong. I said I didn't know.'

'Do you trust me, Annie?'

'I used to. I used to think you were the sun and the moon and the stars. You were everything to me, Peter. You saved me from ... I will never forget that ... If I were sure about you I'd be much happier. If I ever came to distrust you completely I would leave. There is no room for distrust in a marriage.'

'People never change, Annie. You know that as well as I do. They accommodate, they bend, they move with the road, but they do not change. You've always known me. I am the same man I was when we first met. A little older, yes. More tired, yes. But that's all.'

'Money. Money could have changed you.'

'I was never poor, Annie. A little in Venice, but not for long. I have always made money. Even in the army. I am the same man.'

'I might have read you wrong from the beginning.'

'What if you see things wrong right now? What if the way you see me comes from inside of you ... The way you see yourself maybe ...'

'That is what my analyst says sometimes.'

'Well, maybe you should listen ... What if he is right? Ugliness, too, is in the eye of the beholder. You look at me and see me not as I really am ... you see me the way you feel inside ... If you see black when you feel black inside, regardless of the facts, what then? Your treatment of me then would be unfair, right? Did the analyst tell you that too?'

'You always say my analyst talks shit.'

'I was angry when I said that. Paying him thirty pounds a shot makes me angry. I am sometimes jealous of the way you can talk to him while you close up tight whenever I'm around. But what if he's right? What if you keep blaming me for your own faults?'

'Then I would get out, if I were you.'

'You keep threatening me. Don't do that.'

'Or what?'

'Or nothing. Just don't do it.'

'You must be a masochist, living with a mess like me.'

He wanted to tell her she was making sense at last. But her face looked drawn and there were dark circles under her eyes. Her mouth contracted in pain as she sucked at her cigarette.

'I am not complaining,' he said with a big smile. 'The chicken was sublime. I don't know where you get the patience to produce such miracles in that hot little kitchen.'

'I see we're complimenting the house-help, are we? ...'

'No, not the house-help ... I don't take the house-help to bed ... Between the sheets you are a marvel ...'

She went all silent. She stubbed her cigarette out and her face relaxed.

'You're so vulgar,' she said, and he thought there was a smile in the making somewhere. Her eyes and her lips softened and she straightened her hair. He got up and touched her shoulder and said:

'Maybe, but it's the truth ... I can never have enough of you.'

'I am good for something, at least ...'

'You are great at everything. I can't live without you,' he said, and he gently pulled her up and hugged her and led her into the bedroom.

He should encourage her to do something with all that time. Go back to school or get a job. Even see more of Sunshine if that made her happy.

His uncle used to tell him to make sure she always felt needed.

'You are a talented boy. She looks up to you, but one day you might hurt her by virtue of your success. By being a winner you may make her feel she is a loser. A nothing. She will feel she has wasted her life. She'll be unhappy then and that will make her do things she'll regret. She must feel useful ... needed ... Make sure you watch that, my boy.'

That was what he used to think too, but then doubts started to creep in and confuse him. What did that old pansy know about women? Or about him? ... or the way things stood between himself and Annie? Make sure she was needed? Was he joking or just blind? He was the one who needed. Needed her more than anything. He could not function without her. She was indispensable to him, not the other way round. His uncle was a conceited old fool. He was wrong. But so was every other man in the office. They all thought she was lucky to have hooked a winner like himself. She never had it so good. Everyone was jealous of her.

He loved her and wanted only the best for her, so where had he gone wrong? Was she right to say she was unhappy because of him?

He began to think of going to see her analyst. Finding out how the man succeeded where he had failed. She was always composed and tolerant and often happy when she came back from one of her sessions. Not for long. Just for a day or two, yet, still, the man must know how she worked. Yes. He was paid plenty for that. Enough to have some answers. He'd put his side of the story. Let the man see who he really was. He'd got nothing to be scared of. He'd go speak to him.

He went.

CHAPTER TEN

'You ought to see someone,' the analyst had said. The man seemed reluctant to talk to him. He was grey-haired, with thick horn-rimmed glasses and a tweed jacket. All parked inside a dark room in Hampstead. The place smelled of stale tobacco and freshly opened sardine cans. Heaps and heaps of books and ink-splattered notepads. Empty milk bottles strewn all over the carpet. A huge slant-eyed cat floated silently around the room.

'How about you? I could come and talk to you.'

'It's your wife who is my patient. You will need to see someone of your own. I could recommend you to a colleague if you wish. We can then work together. On a regular basis . . .'

'I don't need that. I just want to talk to you about Annie.'

'A relationship is to do with two people. You will have to understand yourself to understand your relationship with your wife. Analyse . . .'

'You don't understand. I'm not looking for treatment. I did not come here for analysis. I just want to know how to handle Annie.'

'Annie is a person. Surely you don't mean handle . . .'

'You know what I mean . . . I mean how do I get on with her the way it was?'

'If something went wrong, it is to do with both of you, isn't it? You must learn about yourself first . . . Analysis is not easy, Mr Gordon. It's not easy to open up completely, to expose things that bother you. Things you are ashamed of ... Things that stem from your childhood.'

'I had a great childhood ...'

'You could have had some traumatic experiences ... bad moments.'

'None at all.'

'You may not be aware of everything. We often hide things from ourselves.'

'You people insist on finding stuff that isn't there. I had a great childhood, but I'm having a rough time now.'

'What do you think is the reason for that?'

'I feel I'm made to pay other people's debts. Cover up for other people's mistakes. Whatever her parents did wrong falls straight on my shoulders. Every time she comes back from here she seems better for a couple of days and then the old problems are back. She gets depressed. Stays in bed for days. She loses her temper for nothing. I can't talk to her any more. I have to be so careful. She is always angry with me. I'm walking in a minefield. Everything I say makes her start a war. I am, she says, the source of all the trouble in the world.'

'Surely you exaggerate, Mr Gordon.'

'You should be there. You'd hear for yourself. Doesn't she tell you what a shit I am?'

'On the contrary. She has great admiration for you.'

'I wish she'd show it sometimes.'

'Some people find it hard ... to be demonstrative ...'

'Oh, she can if she wants to ... She used to show plenty of it ... There's none of it now, though ... it's like living with a stranger.'

'Come, come, Mr Gordon ...'

'I'm telling you she blames me for everything. Am I paying for her parents' mistakes?'

'Could be. We all do sometimes. But Annie is like a flower. A gentle, dainty flower that needs much love and care. She is a sensitive woman, Mr Gordon. Her childhood is still with her. Sometimes it is very much alive. She has a lot of anger inside her ... about her mother and her schooldays ... things she cannot quarrel with because they are not there any more. You are, and perhaps she directs her anger at you. It will take time. There is no short-cut here.'

He felt envious of the man. He knew her more intimately. She was open with him. She talked of everything with him. He made her feel better. How he wished he could do the same.

'She never fights with Sunshine. If he was interested in women she'd run off with him.'

'I shouldn't think it's that at all.'

'Then why is she so good to him?'

'That may be because he needs her.'

'I need her, too. I'm her husband.'

'Do you ever show her you need her?'

'How can I? She's always angry with me.'

'You might trigger her off, Mr Gordon. You are a very strong man.'

'How do you know?'

'Your wife knows you. We talk.'

'I can't help being the way I am. She knew this anyway.'

'She did not know how it would affect her. Perhaps she does not know how to deal with it. When you are young and in love things move fast, you know that. You jump into things. It could be that she was not aware of what was bothering her. How your character would affect her. Perhaps she was too happy to notice. It is a difficult time for you, I know. I promise you it is harder for her than it is for you. These things take time. Years.'

'What do I do in the meantime?'

'You must admit she is better. Much better. You see, she looks up to you and that sometimes makes her feel worthless. She will get over that in time, because she is learning to like herself. When she's down she feels she does not amount to much. And her inactivity does not help matters.'

'My uncle said the same thing.'

'He was a wise man. You should . . .'

'I'm not stopping her. She can do whatever she wants. Go back to school, anything.'

'That would be wonderful. She is a very intelligent woman. And a very strong one. For people like her, who are used to an active life, sitting around is stupefying.'

'Why doesn't she do something with herself, then. I'm not stopping her . . .'

'She will do that one day but she hasn't got the confidence yet.'

'Confidence? Annie is a very capable woman. She can do anything. You should have known her when we first met. There is nothing she cannot do. She's a great organiser, she knows about people, she . . . she is very confident, I assure you.'

'She might have lost it somewhere along the road. These things happen.'

'How is she going to gain confidence when the marriage is in trouble ... when we don't get on ... when the atmosphere at home is full of anger and tension?'

'I promise you she is aware of what is happening. You must know that. She cares for you, Mr Gordon. She cares a lot. She's having bouts of anxiety. Of fear.'

'Fear of me?'

'Could be. In part ... You have a very strong personality.'

'I wouldn't be where I am if I didn't.'

'That is true.'

'What can I do to help?'

'You must be patient. This is very difficult for you, I know. Her moods come and go without warning. That happens when her anxieties overwhelm her. I imagine you never know where you stand. I do understand, Mr Gordon, but I'm afraid you'll have to live with it until she gets better. It's a slow process, like growing up all over again. It's not easy to do that once you're an adult. But I do feel we are making progress.'

'Why is she always angry?'

'The alternative to that is depression. When anger cannot be expressed people often sink into depression. It's a good thing to let her get it out.'

'She has no reason to be angry with me. Is she angry with herself?'

'Could be.'

'Or her mother ...'

'I have told you. It could be.'

'Can be, could be, may be ... Can't you tell me something more definite?'

'Not yet. These things take time, Mr Gordon.'

'And meanwhile I sit there and get shot at every day?'

'It hasn't always been like that, has it?'

'No. At the beginning, for a few years, it was incredible. No anger, no bitterness. What happened? Why? ...'

'At the beginning she felt she was of value to you. She tried to help you. She felt you needed her. Perhaps you stopped needing her, stopped showing her you need her ...'

'I can't believe that.'

'You may not be aware of it, Mr Gordon. Perhaps you wanted to prove things to her. Your own worth. Show her you could manage things on your own. It could be that you were growing up yourself. You have a strong personality ... You have charisma. You are used to giving orders. Sometimes impressing others can lead to anger in this way. Look. You listen to her. You take her advice. Then you begin to want to show her how great you are and then you stop listening. You make her feel useless. She gets angry with herself because she cannot do a thing for you. She is afraid to lose her temper so the anger stays inside. As I've said, frustrated anger can lead to depression ...'

'What happened in the old days? I mean, people were married and wives sat at home while their husbands built empires ... How come they got no depressions then?'

'Oh, they did. In every family there was some aunt or a grandmother or someone, usually a woman, who one day took to her bed for a year. They brought the family doctor in or took her to the seaside but nothing changed. There are letters about things like that. No one understood. Sometimes you read about such a woman ... you know, in some nineteenth-century Russian novels ... Aunt Anya spent two years in bed, that sort of thing. Aunt Anya was not ill. She was depressed, but people did not know she was.'

'I don't believe that for a moment. In the old days people were too busy to have depressions. They had ten kids to bring up ...'

'I'm afraid you are wrong.'

'All right, all right. How long will all this last?'

'Difficult to say.'

Why should the bastard hurry it up. He wouldn't give him any answers. The longer it took the better it was for him. He was making a living out of it. The visit was getting him nowhere. The man cared for Annie, not him. He had said so.

'Maybe I should come along with her some time?'

'We could work on this but I shall have to ask her. You are not in the country very often. It would be difficult to do this haphazardly. Perhaps you should see someone on a regular basis. To help you in the meantime.'

'I'm fed up with answering for others. I can manage my own life.'

'You may be surprised. You too may have things that eat at you. You may be making her pay for your problems too.'

'You people always think everybody's got problems. You look for them even when they aren't there.'

'Everybody has problems.'

'I haven't got that sort of problem.'

'Don't you have nightmares sometimes?'

'What of it? I operate ... I function ... I don't take it out on her. I can handle my problems, Doctor.'

'With respect, Mr Gordon, if you could you wouldn't be here.'

'I didn't come here to cry about my problems. I can handle those. I came because I'm having trouble with Annie's problems. Business problems are rational. You are either too cheap or too expensive. You sell too soon or too late. You either make the right decision or you don't. Your customers pay or they don't pay.'

He didn't like the tone of his own voice when he said that. The man was paying him no attention at all. He was not interested in him.

Go get some help elsewhere, he had said. Annie was his patient.

I hope you two will be very happy together, he thought as the analyst showed him to the door. She would enjoy coming here that afternoon.

The stuffy smell of the place, the sight of that eerie cat and the books and the heavy curtains did not leave him all week.

His other life at the office proceeded, swift and crowded. He was too busy. People, men and women alike, had become sources of information or connections or ideas that were helpful in advancing his business. He was an impressive man who talked well but had found it unnecessary to form long-lasting friendships. His world moved too fast, across many continents. Deals, once consummated, were over for him, and so was the contact with the people he had concluded them with. The contact was alive while the mutual usefulness was there, never afterwards.

'You are afraid of rejection,' Annie had said. 'You don't know how to have a relationship with others. Someone must have rejected you once. When you were a child maybe.'

She talked of relationships. She used big words. Communication. Projection.

She said he knew nothing and understood nothing. All he was good at was making money.

He had taken it in his stride because he knew she had picked all that garbage up from her analyst. Or those know-all books she always read. She used to bring them home and they piled up all over the flat. She used them on him without fully understanding what she was about.

His career made the globe grow smaller. His investors were impressed by his boundless energy and those endless new ideas that made fortunes for them. They were content to leave the thinking and the planning to him and watch their coffers grow, and demanded no more than the usual statement just before the festive season. They gave him power of attorney. At the end of each financial year they read the results of his efforts and they rubbed their hands in satisfaction. He made it possible for them to be generous with themselves and their loved ones. Move to larger houses and buy bigger boats. Have second homes in the sun and a mistress. And they loved him for his success and left him alone to get on with it.

There was one exception. He fell into that woman's arms almost by accident. He wasn't really interested in other women. She was the newly wedded wife of a very rich client who had taken it upon herself to prove to her husband that the company was taking advantage of his trust. She used to come to the office twice a week and demand to be shown an in-depth picture of how their money was being spent. At first, Peter took her attitude to be motivated by a genuine interest in the financial world. He took great pains to go into the minutest details with her. He spent hours with her.

'You are having an affair with my husband,' Annie accused her one day when they met at the hairdresser's.

'I suppose he told you,' the woman retorted with an amused smile. 'It's the first I've heard of it. You'd better find out some more and let me know. I like hearing things about myself.'

How dare she talk to me like that? Annie ranted. She sulked for a week. She cooked food he hated. She threatened to buy an Alsatian for a pet before he promised he would stop seeing the lady.

When she came to the office next he told her he could not work with her any more. He would arrange for another member of the company to deal with her.

'Are you afraid of what I might find?'

'Of course not. You will be dealing with someone who's got more time, that's all.'

'Do you not find me attractive?'

'I haven't given it much thought.'

'Your wife has.'

'She finds you attractive? My God, you do learn new things every day.'

She laughed.

They both laughed.

* * *

'Get off my back,' he told Annie angrily. 'I have nothing to do with the woman.'

'Not in the office, I know. You are meeting her outside.'

'Where, for instance ... When?'

'I don't know that yet. You must have an apartment stashed away somewhere in town. All tycoons have.'

'I thought you were into more useful things now. Have you run out of books about bettering yourself? About being your own woman? Maybe you've been watching too much television. Why don't you hire a private detective? He'll soon tell you what an angel you are married to. If I'm not here I'm at the office. I don't drink, I smoke a few cigars and I go to bed early.'

'You think you are so clever. So articulate. You enjoy putting me down because you think I'm weak. One day I'll be able to think clearly and I'll know how to stand up to you. You are cruel, Peter, you are inconsiderate and selfish. Somewhere inside that conceited head of yours there lurks a frightened coward. I'll be ready for him when he finally bursts out. I'll hound you and your lady friend until I catch you.'

'I'm a good boy. I don't deal with her any more. Someone else does.'

And then he ran into the woman in question at Heathrow Airport. They were both going to Paris. At first he tried to avoid her eyes but they were the only passengers in the first-class compartment. She came up to him and sat down by his side as soon as they were airborne.

'It seems your wife is willing us to fall into bed together,' she said. 'Any minute now she'll come through from the cockpit. Or be on to my husband. Luckily he spends most of his time in the South of France these days. Thanks to the money your brains are making for him, I might add.'

'I'm sorry about that. She is going through a phase, that's all.'

'I'm staying in Paris for a few days before going down to Nice.'

He did not comment.

'You are the first man who ever played it cool with me. Funny. Not so funny, really. Gives a girl a complex. I suppose I owe you a lot. In a way we live off you. May I buy you dinner tonight?'

'My wife will ...'

'Your wife is convinced we are way past dinners. Who am I to stop her?'

It was the worry of his busy, fast-disappearing youth and the frustration of his inability to make Annie out that made him a tiger-like lover during their short affair. He was truly tired in the evening, and when he rang Annie he lied but did not feel remorse. Her intensity did not anger him.

Within months of Annie's words, her prophecy of an apartment stashed away in town had materialised. It was a small service flat in Park Street, Mayfair. It was discreet and impersonal and his infidelities took off in earnest. He had met a lot of women. They liked him and were attracted by his charm and power. One or two fell in love with him. In spite of his successes he could not wait to go home to Annie. If only things could have been as they were. He still wanted her. More than ever. But being with other women made it easier for him to cope with her anger.

He was careful.

He did not buy himself fancy clothes. He did not go into massage parlours.

He accepted no gifts and gave none. There were no notes or secret post-office boxes.

He did worry about his thinning hairline and sometimes he took to falling asleep while Annie read or watched the television.

'I think he is finally settling down,' Annie confided to a sceptical Sunshine.

CHAPTER ELEVEN

———■———

Outside, the morning sun came and wheeled the garden shadows into the sea. The room was alight with glare, and he opened his eyes. A splash of colour came streaming at him from the flower-beds around the green lawn. The grass was dry and he knew he had overslept because the dew had gone with the dawn. His head felt light and he thought no voices had come to him during the night, or else he would have been up and alert hours ago.

He heard the car stop outside and the dogs barked and then the door opened and they came in and laid the table in the dining-room.

'Breakfast, Mr Gordon, sir' came piping into his ears and he tried to get up, but his back and his chest were hurting him still.

What the hell, he thought, he'd stay in bed today. The room was cool, while outside the automatic sprayers came on to water the lawns. He imagined walking on the grass, feeling his bare feet sink into the wet surface. The way they did at winter-time around his father's estate.

The aroma of freshly ground coffee wafted into his nostrils and he tried to get up. A sharp sting of pain kept him down. He would wait until they'd left. He wouldn't give them the satisfaction of witnessing the blue marks on him. Nor his weakness or the soreness they had inflicted on him. He whistled. He whistled 'As Time Goes By', even though he didn't feel happy. The tune would take the ache away.

He now knew where he was. He was almost sure of it. None of it was a dream. He was living his future for the first time, and for real.

He heard them go and he pulled himself away from the sheets and limped to the dining-table. He didn't stop in the bathroom to brush his teeth or look at himself. He wouldn't shave. He'd take it easy today. Nice and calm. Like those middle years of his married life.

What calm?

The bitterness of that time struck him as he took a sip of coffee. The liquid burned his throat and for a moment he lost all vision while the memory of it lingered.

No. Not that. He must not think of that again. He might not survive it this time. Why think of that now? Because he could not control himself, he thought as the old misery came back. That accursed day was to rule the middle years of his marriage.

Before the explosion she had been acting strangely cheerful for weeks. Something was wrong, he had thought. Crazy. Why should he think that? Why get all hepped up just because she seemed happy for a change? Her exuberance did not turn into hysteria and she did not argue about his choice of television programme. She'd come and go and chat and in the kitchen he heard her sing. She seemed happy to see him every time he came through the door. Did not accuse him of anything. She'd serve the meal and ask about the day and give advice. She was almost her old self in the way she cared for him, but when he went to bed she stayed in the living-room with a book. She often fell asleep there. He would find her during the night when he woke, and he'd lead her into bed without a word.

Once, as he carried her into the bedroom, she put her arms around his neck and kissed him. They did not make love but there was a smile on her face all night.

Flash in the pan, he thought in the morning. That time she did not get up to make his breakfast. She was still asleep when he walked out of the door.

There was a bizarre new bliss in the house all that month. He had come in late on two occasions and on both she did not sulk. She got up with a smile and handed him a drink. She told him about the book she was reading. About some film she had seen with Sunshine. She made small-talk. There were no arguments. He said he had a headache and she made him sit down and massaged the back of his neck as she used to years before. She said he was overworked. She said he should go somewhere in the sun and have some fun. He deserved it, she said. He did not understand what she meant because she had never suggested that before. Why would she want him to go by himself? Was she still looking for that famous space she'd been talking about when she was angry? Didn't she have enough space all day when he was in the office? He tried to reason with himself. He was being childish. There must be a simple explanation for this. Had he forgotten what she was like before she became angry? Did he begrudge her being contented?

Her current silence was different. Not the serene stillness she had projected when they were first married. When she was at peace. No. That was not how she had been before. There was more. Could it be she was really better for good?

He had thought of calling the analyst but the beggar would only congratulate himself on his success. Better wait and see how long this lasted.

And then, on the fifth week of her new demeanour, she said she wanted to talk.

'Sure,' he said, and he sat down. She handed him a drink.

'I have been having an affair. I think I am in love.'

Her words were a bomb that fell on the glass-topped coffee table and exploded in his face. He laughed nervously and shook his head and took his glasses off to wipe the steam.

'I don't think you believe me.'

'You're right. I don't.'

'I haven't been so happy in years. You are my friend. I have always been open with you ... I wanted to share ...'

'Who was it?'

'Not was.'

'Who is it?'

'I don't want him to end up in a morgue. I know what you are capable of.'

Her voice was strong and her gaze steady as she looked him straight in the eye. He felt his heart palpitate and thump and swell. He thought it would break out of his chest. He could not breathe.

'Why tell me at all?' he said, trying to be calm.

'I told you, we are friends. I said I wouldn't always be down. You've been having your fun for years while I grovelled in pain here.'

'Revenge? Is that what it is?'

'No. Not revenge at all, Peter. You don't really love me. You don't need me. If you care for me at all I am sure you won't mind if I live a little.'

She must be mad. She knew exactly how he felt about her. She must be trying something on. He looked at her and tried to find some signal. Some sign. Maybe he was dreaming. He must tell her exactly how he felt about her. How much he loved her. How he would always love her.

'What now?' he managed to say.

'What do you mean, what now? I never asked you what now when you were ...'

'Yes. It's revenge. You're paying me back.'

'No, Peter. I am growing strong. I am standing on my own feet, that's all. I have met someone who likes me ... maybe loves me. Someone who thinks I am intelligent, who thinks my jokes are witty ... A man who does not use sarcasm or power. A man ...'

'Tell your analyst.'

'I have.'

'He must be laughing at my expense. All the way to the bank.'

'You are wrong.'

'I suppose he approves.'

'He does not approve and he does not disapprove. He does not sit in judgement over me or give me advice. He listens, that's all. Something you never did.'

He thought he would faint. He though he would kill her. He was surprised at his own silence. His face went pale and he took a cigar out of the box and clipped it on the wrong side.

'Let me do that for you,' Annie said.

She must be out of her mind. How could she offer to help him after what she had said? He needed time to think. He must talk to someone. That was what the analyst had said. To hell with what the analyst had said. He'd sort it out by himself. Not talk about it to anyone. She was right. He'd take himself off on a long holiday somewhere in the sun. Screw himself to death. Eat. Get a boat and take a cruise. There was no one he could talk to anyway. He was too powerful and distant for that. What was he so surprised about? Had he thought she would never do it? They all did it. Most of the women he knew had husbands. But he was young and strong and ... So what? Women never cheated on weaklings. That was what they liked their men to be. They cheated on a macho. To show they were just as good. To be equal. All that crossed his mind, but he yearned for her to deny everything. To wake him up from this nightmare. He wanted to cry.

'He is only out to use you.'

'Who?'

'Your lover. You'll see. He's after your money or your contacts or something. He'll drop you like a tray of bad eggs afterwards.'

'Is that what you think of me? A tray of bad eggs? Can you not believe someone likes me? Loves me maybe? Can't you be my friend? Do you have to ruin this for me too?'

The woman was crazy. She wanted his approval. She was blind. Couldn't she see the agony he was in? Couldn't she see he was only trying to protect her? Maybe she was only pulling his leg, to see how he reacted. Make him jealous. But her eyes said she was telling the truth. The hurt in them confirmed it.

'He can't be much of anything, your Romeo.'

'You don't believe I could do better for myself, do you? Why do you have to put me down all the time?'

'I am putting you down? You've just told me you have a lover.'

'And you just said he must be a nobody.'

'He must be. He doesn't have the guts to take you away from here. To face it with you.'

'He wanted to. I talked him out of it. I want him alive.'

'What does that mean?'

'You know what it means. Once you know who he is you'll ...'

'I'll what?'

'Never mind. In any case, he's not taking me away. He wants me to be sure.'

'You must not let him manipulate you, Annie.'

'That's a laugh, coming from you.'

'I am your husband.'

'We are not in the Balkans, you know. You can't tell me anything. You don't own me. I have a mind of my own, even if you haven't noticed.'

She was not shouting. She was not angry. Behind her words there was strength and conviction. God, she was so contented underneath it all. The beggar must be a marvel in bed, he thought as the pain hit him. Perhaps he should have her followed.

No. He was better off not knowing.

'You don't give a damn, do you? You're only upset because someone has been playing with your toy.'

After that he stayed at home and sat around like a puppy, knowing he was not wanted. She was kind and polite and oh so happy, but whenever he tried to touch her she froze. His pride was non-existent. The humiliation interfered with his thoughts and killed his concentration.

Little things like telephone calls or signatures tired him. She began to take courses. Art and languages and cookery. She was always out somewhere and there was little talk. As though she was preparing herself for some other life. A life without him.

One night she packed her bags and left the house while he slept.

In the note she said she'd arranged to have her mail collected once a week. Would he make sure the porter had it. She didn't want a thing from him. She never wanted to see him or hear from him.

'I want to remember only our yesterdays,' she wrote. 'You have killed the present and the future stone dead. I must forget the hurt before we talk again. I am sorry it had to end like this, but you cannot be a friend to me. I know that now. Don't try to look for me.'

He went through hell but her analyst refused to give him an appointment.

The bloody prima donna agreed to talk on the phone but not for long. He listened and then he said:

'All I can say is Annie is going through a phase. She is bound to make mistakes. She may well come back.'

'I don't want her back.'

'That is what you are saying now, but I read otherwise. Why else would you want to see me? Perhaps you ought to see someone else. I can recommend ...'

'I can handle this, thank you.'

'She must learn to stand on her own two feet before she gets better.'

'Fucking another man . . . does that mean she's standing on her own two feet?'

'I only listen. I do not tell her what to do. She needs time to find herself.'

'This has nothing to do with me.'

'I am sorry,' the analyst said with a final, closing-down tone of voice. 'She is my patient and I cannot talk to you without her permission.'

While she was gone from the house he was devastated. He did not go out at all. All thoughts of flirtation and sex vanished from him. He saw no other women. Ate junk food. Could not concentrate on anything. Could not read more than three lines of any written document or book. He'd let the telephone in his office ring for a long time before he'd answer. He had to force himself to talk to people who were known to him. New callers were not put through at all. The urge to live and the quest for success seemed to have deserted him. He crawled, uninterested, through his work and his life as though there were a thousand hours in each day.

She called him one night a few weeks later. She sounded urgent and hoarse.

He had taken a sleeping-pill and felt groggy. He took some time to wake up. At first he did not recognise her voice. When he did he nearly fell off the bed.

'Annie?'

'Yes.'

'Is that you, Annie?'

'He has humiliated me, Peter.'

'Who? What is it?'

'Are you there?'

'Let me put the light on.'

'Are you alone, Peter?'

'What is it you want?'

There was silence on the line. He said:

'Why are you calling me?'

'I need your support. I have no one else.'

'What about your . . . what about him?'

'There's no him now.'

'What do you mean, no him?'

'I don't want to talk about it.'

'What has he done?'

'He told me we were through. He said there was someone else. There always was but she walked out on him just before we met. He said he had me on the rebound ... And now she's coming back to him. Oh, he said it was great and I was good for him and he thanked me for what I've done and the help I've ... God, what a fool I was. Gullible, naive ... to be in love with a man who never thought of me ... Never really wanted me.'

She was going to burst into tears.

'Why don't you go up to Scotland ... stay with your father for a bit ...'

'He doesn't know.'

'What do you want of me?'

'I want to come home.'

'Well, come if you like. I can't stop you.'

'Thank you,' she said, and she hung up.

He thought he would die of joy. The effect of the sleeping-pill evaporated. He was as fresh and alert as a boy. He jumped out of bed and got dressed and washed the dishes and cleaned the house. He raced down to the corner shop and woke the owner and stocked up the refrigerator. He shaved and sprayed himself with Guerlain all over. He put on her favourite suit and tie. He waited for her most of the night. She came in just after dawn. She looked like a beaten animal. Her face was ashen and drawn and her hair was in a mess. She smoked roll-your-own cigarettes. She wore a pair of faded jeans and an anorak and no make-up. She carried all her belongings in two plastic supermarket bags. There wasn't much left of her clothes, and when she saw he had noticed she said she had sold them all. He ran a bath for her. He made her hot chocolate and put her to bed.

Later that morning, on the way to the office, he vowed he would never mention it.

But these were tough times at work. There was a recession and he had to concentrate on repairing the damage his long absence had caused. Of course, it was all her fault. He would have been well able to deal with problems had she not walked out on him just as things became difficult. Now that she was back his confidence was returning. He worked like a horse and he threw her failure at her every time he was in a temper. He'd mock her and her defeat and regret it as soon as he saw her face.

She did not answer back. She'd lower her eyes and nod.

She worked like a slave and took his constant abuse without a murmur. She didn't leave the house for weeks. She did not see Sunshine all that time.

Her analyst called him at the office.

'Would it be possible for you to come and see me?'

'Sure.'

'Today?'

'Right now, if you like.'

'That is very good of you, Mr Gordon.'

'I bear no grudges.'

The analyst said Annie was in a bad way. She had experienced something that had confirmed her own feeling of being a failure. Her self-esteem was gone. Smashed to pieces. She might damage herself if this was allowed to go on. She needed constant care. She might be better off in a hospital. He knew of a discreet little clinic out of town. They would take care of her there.

'Why do you need me for that?'

'You'll have to convince her to go.'

'Why?'

'She feels that what is happening to her is a punishment. She riddles herself with guilt. She doesn't believe there is anything wrong with her, but there is. Believe me, there is. She must not be left on her own at all.'

'Why would she listen to me?'

'At this moment she will do anything you ask.'

'What makes you think that?'

'Many reasons. Guilt. Love. Her recognition of her dependence on you. Her regret at causing you pain ... Her fear of losing you ... Her identification of you with success and herself with failure. Many things. I can't say ...'

'If you can't say, who can? Aren't you the analyst?'

'Are you going to talk to her?'

'I'll talk to her.'

'I know what you are going through. If ever you need ... I can recommend someone for you to see.'

'You keep saying that and I keep telling you I can handle this. Don't concern yourself with me. I'll talk to her.'

'Thank you.'

She did not put up an argument. She just looked at him vacantly and said:

'If you think it's for the best, I'll go.'

But the clinic was full and they had to wait a week before she could be admitted.

His business difficulties continued. The currency market was in havoc. The recession was biting deeper into people's pockets and nerves. They were losing money and were quick to forget the good days. They threatened to invest elsewhere. They wanted their money back instantly. He tried to explain. To tell them that selling now would cause further losses. He preached patience. Only a few listened. He had to force himself to remain composed while he talked to them. But the tensions that simmered inside him during the day threatened to burst out each evening. He held on.

Then one night she spilt some coffee on his knee after dinner and he snapped. He cursed her and her family and her childhood. He accused her of everything under the sun. He told her she was responsible for the mess he was in. He said she was useless.

'You're no good at anything at all. No one will have you. You can't even keep one lousy little lover.'

He did not wait to hear her reply. He repeated what he had said and stormed out of the house.

At midnight, when he came back, he found Sunshine in the living-room.

'What the hell are you doing here?'

'I am waiting for you.'

'I thought you and Annie were not on speaking terms.'

'We are now.'

'Where is Annie?'

'She took an overdose, Mr Gordon.'

'She what?'

'She tried to kill herself.'

'Are you mad?'

'No, I am not mad.'

'How did you get in?'

'She left the door open for me.'

'Good God.'

'Quite.'

'I am sorry.'

'So you should be.'

'How come you're here?'

'She phoned and told me what you said. It was a very cruel thing to do, Mr Gordon. Kicking someone when they are down ... when they crawl back to you for help. It would have been kinder to have thrown her out. You should have been here with her. She needed you ...'

'She didn't call me.'

'Maybe you were too busy.'

There was accusation and hate and anger in Sunshine's face but his voice remained calm and even. Peter did not know the sissy had it in him. He did not answer. Sunshine said:

'She'll be all right, if you're interested. They managed to pump it all out of her in time.'

At the hospital she was too drugged to make much sense. In between falling asleep she kept saying she was sorry. She was pale and her lips were dry and her closed eyes sank deep into her face. Her hair looked ratty.

At the office the turbulence continued. He buried his shock in work. It was the end of his financial year and he could never stay with her for longer than a few minutes. They did not talk because she was incoherent most of the time. The analyst said she was going through a full-blown depression. She might try it again at any time. It was best to keep her away from the flat. Make sure she was never alone. The clinic said they were able to take her in. The analyst and Sunshine drove her there.

He had to make an unexpected overseas trip and got back to England after she had settled in. On his first visit she seemed happy to see him and did not mention his absence. They did not talk of her suicide attempt. He took her for tea in the village before going back to London. She did not say much and her lip movements seemed as stiff as her walk. He'd have to talk to them about it next time.

As he stood by her door she said:

'Come and see me every day. Or call.'

'I will ... Of course I will.'

'I know you are busy and I am grateful. All this is my fault. You know it was always you I wanted. I was looking for you that time. Your attention. Your love. Your arms.'

He was so happy hearing that he could have cried.

'I'll come as often as I can,' he said. He walked back towards her and kissed her cold cheek.

Her mouth sketched a brief smile but her eyes were dark and lost and sad. The nurse told him not to worry. She wouldn't get her hands on any pills. They were watching her like hawks. He left with a heavy heart and drove himself to London.

The police were waiting for him with the porter when he got back to the flat.

CHAPTER TWELVE

He sat, the paper sprawled over his knees, and he stared at the dead fireplace. He felt revived and his appetite was back. It was ten o'clock in the morning. Breakfast would be cold. Might as well wait a couple of hours more and enjoy his lunch.

Should he shower and shave now? There was the sound of an engine outside. Someone was coming, but surely they were early. He'd surprise them. Show them the lethargy was over.

He got up and went into the entrance hall. He heard someone ring the bell and he chuckled. You'll have to stay right there, he said to himself, whoever you are. That door only opens from the outside. There was another ring and then he heard the tyres screech as the car sped out along the driveway. In the letter-box there was a parcel.

The postman always rings twice, he said out loud. A name of a book or a film or something he had enjoyed in the past. That book was in the house somewhere. He remembered it. Short, crisp sentences and exquisitely raw, two-line sketches depicting situations, thoughts and characters. Yes. James M. Cain.

There was a white label on the package and he stared at his name, typed in big red letters. Peter Gordon Esq. No address. No date. No postage stamp. He weighed the parcel in his hand. It felt like a video cassette. Strange. He opened the parcel. Inside, the cassette was gift-wrapped. Shiny golden metallic paper with flowers. Maybe they had sent him another film. They had never done that before. He usually asked for one, then found the requested video by the television in the morning. Maybe they had found a new release or something. He was bound to like it.

They knew him well. He chuckled. He tore the gift paper off. On the cassette was a label: 'View as soon as you receive.'

Couldn't be the title. Must be a message.

He went into the library and switched the set on. From the screen, a dusty Western street snaked between two wooden houses. A saloon. Horses. An undertaker's yard and four open, empty coffins. Clint Eastwood's cold, commanding eyes looked at him. From under an oily leather apron he pulled out a gun. He stopped the film and ejected it. Clint was going to get them all. He'd go back to that later. He slotted the new tape in and sat down to watch.

At first there were numbers and lines in colour and crosses and numbers again and then the screen came alive. It filled with a close-up shot of a face. It took him some time to put a name to it. It was puffed and there were blue and red veins under the eyes and black shadows. But the tan was still there and then a smile and suddenly, just as he recognised him, the voice came. Precise and aloof and collected.

'Sunshine, Peter Gordon, this is Sunshine speaking. I thought I'd let you take a long look at me first. See how the ravages of time and age have treated me. But as the saying goes, I have promises to keep, and time, as always, races on and won't wait. Not even for you, so here goes.

'I am not sure where this message will reach you or when. No one knows where you are but your secretary says someone collects the mail for you each week. She won't divulge a thing. I suppose you are having one of your naughty weekend flings, if a somewhat extended version.

'It seems you have now been gone for a long time. I suppose someone, somewhere, might want you back. I can almost hear your short fused voice telling me to get on with it. But as you are having a holiday I am sure you won't mind me waffling on a bit, will you?'

Sunshine started laughing. An uncontrollable youthful laugh came bursting from the screen. He laughed so hard it brought tears to his eyes.

'Sorry,' the television said, 'I couldn't help myself. D'you know what I was thinking about? I was thinking that in a different world, with a different set of habits and morals and rules, I would have been a relative of yours. Yes. I would have been your auntie, Peter Gordon. Your auntie Sunshine. I would have been that sunny, pleasant, gift-bearing relative such childless aunties usually are. Make no mistake, Gordon. I would have been the greatest. I would have spoilt you rotten.

'Funny, what? I laughed because the thought made me think of that French film *La Cage aux Folles*. The one about the two gays running a nightclub in the South of France. Had to laugh. There are, I suppose, places where two men are allowed to bring up a child, but then you have never been a child. You must have been born cynical and pragmatic. Without any illusions or dreams. Instead of baby-talk you probably blabbered sarcastic words of command. Still, who am I to tell you about yourself? You know all about that.

'I wanted to tell you about my friend Annie. Your wife. One of those who, against my advice, would like you back again. Must be love, I suppose, and if this is what heterosexual love is about I can only tell you we gays are just the same. That's right, Gordon. Not pansies or sissies or queens or poofs. Gays. We're almost legal now, you know. Anyway, Annie wants you back.'

Sunshine's face disappeared, and in its place there appeared on the screen an Alpine view he instantly recognised. It was from a metal box of chocolates his uncle was fond of. He used to keep his cuff-links in it.

You bet I need a pause now, he thought to himself as the snow-covered cottages quivered on the screen. Annie does not want me back. She doesn't want anyone back. She is in no condition. Annie is dead.

'Annie is dead,' he shouted at the screen. 'She's dead.' And then Sunshine's face came back.

'I must have given you a shock just now, having told you Annie wants you back. That is why I went off screen for a few seconds. To give you a chance to gather your thoughts. I hope you are alone, Gordon. I do not want to embarrass you. Did you like the pretty Swiss picture? Do you remember it? Yes, she wants you back, and I can imagine what you're thinking. Maybe you are saying it, but I assure you she is not dead. Annie is very much alive.'

Sunshine's voice sounded menacing and near.

He looked about him, but there was no one there.

'Don't bother,' Sunshine said. 'I cannot hear you but I know your reactions. I know you well, Gordon. I have made a study of you over the years. The kind of study lovers make about their rivals. I wanted to find out what it was they saw in you. First your uncle and then Annie. In his case it was family. A sort of obligation ... You know, blood is thicker than whatever ...

'You were, he used to say, all that was left of his much-adored sister, and he was hell-bent on giving you all he had. But he knew you wanted more than that. He said once you were going to kill him. What you don't know is that he didn't mind that.

'He was dying, Gordon. He was a very sick man. He said he wanted me out of the way when it happened. He was afraid of becoming shrivelled and thin and ugly. He said he didn't mind you killing him as long as it was quick. He much preferred to die by your hand because his illness was a nightmare. He knew you were going to finish him off. Your method would be quicker, he said. So you did him a favour and murdered him and if he could speak to you now he would thank you for that.

'You and I know you killed him, but then you were lucky to get off. Well, maybe not lucky, maybe just clever ... I don't want to talk about your uncle just now. This is not the time to get emotional.

'I wish to talk about Annie. What she saw in you is way beyond me. You know what a talented woman she is ... She could have been anything she wanted to be. The poor darling still loves you, but I am working on it. In your absence, behind your back, I have been maligning you like a thief. Like a snake, a coward, a cheat ... In short, like you.

'After all, we live in the same town and soon we will meet again and then ... no ... it's better you don't hear too much of how I feel about you. I have been trying to find clues, but then you have been very clever. And yet you have made mistakes. I suppose that makes you human. And your mistakes and vanity gave me the opportunity to get back at you.

'Maybe you will give me a call once this film-show is over and the screen goes dark. Had I known where you were I would have called you or even come to see you in the flesh. It's been a good year in the wine trade and I came into some private money last month. An old aunt died. Natural causes, I assure you. I wonder whether you ever gave it any thought, but there is really no need to kill anybody, because death comes to us all. You need patience. I suppose the lack of it was your mistake.

'I make mistakes too, lots of them. Maybe because I have not been able to get my act together ever since I lost your uncle. Like any auntie, what?

'He was a father, a lover, a brother, a world to me. Air and blood and water. I loved him more than life. I still do. I have never learned to live without him and I have taken to fantasising. I dream of him by night and talk to and of him by day. Annie kept me alive. Enough said.

'Do you remember the time the police were waiting for you at the flat? It was I who fixed that and I was pleased they came because I needed to get you out of the way. I needed to get into the flat. Annie had given me a set of keys when I went to see her at the clinic, just before you arrived there. We had a plan for you. Nothing sinister. Educational, rather, even if it was going to be a surprise. I can assure you it was harmless.

'The police asked you to go down to the station with them and that served my purpose. You agreed without asking for a lawyer. Thanks. I needed to steal some papers you had in your desk. Stuff your uncle left you. I know you had never looked at these because they were still sealed when I got inside. He very much wanted you to look at these papers. Had you done so there might have been some remorse. You might have felt a little sorry for yourself, too. Above all, and most important, you would have eaten some humble pie while you suffered the pain of reading your uncle's papers. You might have had regrets. You might have become a human being for a bit.

'Anyway, while you were gone with the police I removed the papers and have kept them until today. I have taken the liberty of sending you that parcel. This, my little excursion into show business, or live television, if you will, is by way of introducing you to your uncle's real legacy. The stuff he really wanted you to have and look at. The stuff he bequeathed to you. Your own past. You haven't looked at it. You didn't even miss it after I took it away from you that day. I am sending it to you. You should receive it soon.

'Go through these papers, you poor bastard.

'I am calling you that because I have come to pity you. I hated you for what you did to your uncle and your wife and all the others. I hated you for making me a suspect when my loved one died. I have sought to have you found out and brought to justice. You will laugh because you do not believe this is possible. I have heard you tell Annie that thieves and murderers are never caught. Only on television by Hollywood detectives. Only Kojak gets his man, you said.

'You may be right. Read the papers, Gordon. You will find what really lurks behind that big macho success of yours. Underneath Annie's servility, the tormented, confused soul you have tried to dominate feels sorry for you, too. Maybe she mistakes that for love.

'Maybe she doesn't know you yet.

'Your uncle certainly thought you were a pathetic figure. That was what he thought of you after he saw you in Venice. The time he came to arrange for your immigration papers.

'He must have changed his mind later, poor darling, but then he was a gentleman and would not have admitted it.

'You are a slave who became a king, Peter Gordon. There are many like you.

'Some are my best customers.

'Some run the biggest enterprises in the land.

'Some are ministers and leaders and men of letters.

'Most are never found out, but they can be forgiven because they have not forgotten who they were when they were born. They repent, even if only when on their own. But not you.

Well, this recording is coming to an end and so I shall have to talk to you some more when you finally decide to come back. Contact me any time, Gordon. Don't fret. I am not a violent man. And remember, Annie is not dead. I shall give you tangible proof. And she wants you back. Other people's love can be confusing. You don't deserve her, you know. God, how I hate playing hide and seek, but this is the game you know best. You don't believe a word I say, but I'll prove it to you.'

There were a few numbers and a few crosses and then he saw Annie on the screen, smiling and waving at the camera. She wore a thin, transparent summery dress and she was happy. She walked up and down and touched the hem of her dress like a model. She straightened her hair and she smiled and then she waved one more time and the picture blurred and died. The tape clicked and rewound itself, and the machine switched itself off.

He sat there quietly. He thought of running the tape again. Not to listen to what Sunshine had said, for he remembered every cynical word. Just to hear another voice, see another face. Someone from his world. The world he had been forced to leave behind. The real world. A face and a voice from what used to be his life.

Sunshine's mockery of him made him feel strangely fulfilled. He had not been dreaming at all. The pictures and the conversations and his actions were all fact. Sunshine was there, stored in the cassette to prove it. He was not going mad, and Sunshine's timely appearance on the dead little screen was going to keep him sane for a long time. He wondered why it was that he felt so good. He was hungry. A piece of toast would do him fine, he thought, and he got up.

On his way to the kitchen he almost danced. The man had brought him a real connection. A contact with himself and the way his life used to be. A direct line to reality.

What the man had said had no significance at all.

He had lied, anyway. Annie was dead.

Or was she?

Sunshine had said she was alive. Dare he believe him?

He must think of something else to deter the evil eye. In case she was alive. He was strong enough to do that now.

He sat and chewed the hard white bread and he remembered the day the police came for him at the flat.

They looked the way the police are supposed to look. Just like in those old black and white movies. Two of them, one in a tatty grey raincoat and the other in tweeds, notebook at the ready. They waited downstairs with the porter. They were reserved and their movements polite. They gave him a chance to look at his letter-box before they approached him. Only one spoke. The one in tweeds.

'Mr Gordon?' he asked. A silent, steady voice that was courteous but expected an answer. The voice of the law.

'Yes.'

The porter shrugged his shoulders. 'I told them you were out, sir,' he said, his voice masking an embarrassed apology.

'That's all right,' Peter said. 'And what can I do for you?'

'Sorry to bother you at this hour, sir, but we would like to ask you a few questions.'

'Shall we go up to my flat?'

'Would you mind coming down to the station, sir? This won't take long.'

'Certainly, Sergeant. Your car or mine?'

'The station is only around the corner, sir. We'll walk if it's OK with you.'

'The exercise will do me good,' he said, and handed his car keys to the porter.

The policemen exchanged a 'how the other half lives' glance on the way out.

They told him that some new material relating to his uncle's death had surfaced. They were trying to find out how authentic it was. They were apologetic and asked him whether he was comfortable and offered him tea.

'You were on a trip to the South of France when the gentleman died?'

'We went out there together but I came back earlier. There is ample evidence to back that up. Telex from the office asking me to come back ... Flight number, booking ... the exit stamp on my passport the day I left Nice ...'

'This is only an enquiry, sir. We know all that. It came out at the inquest.'

'Then why are you asking me all these questions?'

'It's routine, sir. Now, how long did you stay in Nice?'

'We didn't stay in Nice. My uncle had a house in Antibes.'

'Of course ... well, how long did you stay in Antibes?'

'Three days.'

'Your uncle was well, was he?'

'Under the circumstances he was. He was a sick man, Sergeant. But at that time he was in remission and seemed very fit. We had a big dinner the night before I returned. There were a lot of people there.'

'You didn't notice anything unusual about your uncle? He wasn't depressed or upset or anything, was he, sir?'

'Why should he have been? The people we were with were close and trusted friends. He was in his element. We were dining at his favourite restaurant and the wine was superb. My uncle knew his wine.'

'Yes, quite. Tell me, Mr Gordon, was your uncle surprised by your sudden departure?'

'Not at all. A problem cropped up in London and I told him about it. He said, "I suppose you'll have to go back" ... The others all heard it.'

'So they did. That came up at the inquest too.'

'May I ask what new material you are checking?'

'We cannot tell you that right now. No doubt we will do so once it's all cleared up. You see, sir, in confidence, we are still very much in the dark ... we're not sure about the source of this new material. We were hoping you'd give us some clue.'

'How can I give you a clue about something or someone I know nothing about?'

'That will come out in the course of this enquiry, sir. Now, you were at the restaurant having dinner. How did you get back to the house in Antibes?'

'We were driven there. My uncle employed a chauffeur in Antibes. Whenever he went out and was expecting to have a drink. On other occasions he used that E-type Jaguar which he loved ... he said it was a luxury he couldn't indulge back in London. People would have said he was having a second childhood. The chauffeur doubled as a gardener.

He looked after the pool too. His wife did the cooking and the cleaning.'

'Was the chauffeur a handyman?'

'No. As a matter of fact he was quite clumsy . . . But he was a good driver and because of his affinity to plants he was a superb gardener. My uncle called him "Green Fingers".'

'You keep referring to him in the past. Is he dead?'

'I wouldn't know. The couple left our employ when I took the house over.'

'Did they have any animosity towards you or your uncle?'

'I don't think so, but you never know, do you? Anyway, they had been with him for years.'

'Did your uncle keep a lot of cash in the house?'

'My uncle never kept any cash at all. He used credit cards. The couple were paid directly by the bank. Salaries, expenses, food, repairs . . . that sort of thing.'

Both nodded and the one in tweeds wrote things down. They kept him for the best part of two hours and then they apologised and thanked him and told him he could go. Not once did they ask him where his wife was. He got up to leave and they offered him a lift but he declined. As he walked back to the flat that night he thought about how the interview had been a waste of time and he wondered what the new evidence was and who might have given it to them and why.

And now, as he sat and ate the cold toast, he knew. It was Sunshine who had arranged it all. That was why the police had come. Just to get him out of the house while Sunshine sneaked in. The bastard had admitted it in his video. Nothing had come out of that visit and the police did not bother him again. It was never meant to amount to anything. He was in the clear. It didn't matter much any more.

What mattered was Sunshine and what he had said. How he got into the flat and fished those papers out.

He expected to be angry, but he remained calm. He must be getting old.

What of Annie? The man was off his head. Of course she was dead. She had died violently while he was on a sailing boat off Majorca and totally out of reach. No one waited for him. They made all the arrangements without him. Only her father was present at the cremation. Her father and, yes, Sunshine, of course.

How they were sorry. The whole thing was a mystery since she was getting so much better. They did not forget to enclose the bill.

They were heartless bastards, so Sunshine had said afterwards.

And now he said she was alive.

Did Sunshine take him for an idiot?

Annie had been dead for almost six months now, and it was his fault.

It had all started when she had been admitted to the clinic. She was there for the seventh or eighth time in three years. She had taken to going there of her own accord. Every time she felt low she'd say she needed to get some of the muck out of her head and would book herself in. Sometimes she'd not even tell him. Just leave him a note to say she'd gone.

She seemed happy there and he felt he could go sailing while she was away.

He went to see her and told her he was tired of looking at walls. Tired of being on his own. He told her he was going away. All she did was scream at him.

You should stay here, close to me, she had said.

The bloody boat is just an excuse.

You should supervise and support and care more. You bring out the worst in me.

You are the cause of it all.

I wish you were dead, she had said.

He had tried to reason with her. To tell her he needed to go. He said he had checked with her analyst and the man had told him he could. But she did not let him get a word in. They had to give her a sedative when her screams reached the corridor.

All through the drive back to London he thought of his marriage. He'd had enough.

So he wrote her a letter which he posted from the port of Palma. That night he was sailing north, to Minorca. He posted the letter to his office and instructed his secretary to deliver it to Annie at the clinic in person.

He said he was lonely living with her. He said they were through. He said she could stay in the flat and pack his things but if she wanted to leave he expected her to be gone when he was back. He did not expect to remain single for the rest of his life. He said if she did not want to stay in the flat she could take anything she wanted. He would settle up financially with her later. Her account was well in credit.

He wrote and said he would continue to pay all her bills for ten years. Married or unmarried.

She could buy herself a new place, he wrote. Start again like he was going to do.

He said maybe she should look for that lover again now that she was truly free. Maybe she could lure him into divorcing his wife.

Or go back to Scotland and look after her father. Anything. If he had made her unhappy it was best for them to part. He, too, deserved a decent, uncomplicated home life.

He had felt sorry for himself and was angry and had ended by saying she had little to worry about. Someone would surely want her.

No one knew about the letter except his secretary, and she did not know what was in it. She did not like Annie very much. He was the only mug that did. Barring Sunshine.

Maybe he shouldn't have put it quite like he had. Why not? She didn't mince words with him when she was angry. He was a human being too. How many times had she told him to leave the house and leave her if he wasn't happy? How many times had she told him to drop dead?

Well, he was going to start a new life right then. He was going to start it with a sailing holiday, and he was happy. Or thought so at the time. The woman he was cruising with was wrong for him. They were both wrong for each other. But when he wrote the letter he was sure she was it.

They did not leave for Minorca as planned. He had to stay in port for three more days to fix a leak in the gearbox. They hired a car and toured while the work was being done.

When he finally got back from the cruise there was a cable waiting for him. Call the office urgently, it said. He was told Annie was dead and buried.

Strange how he never questioned the speed at which they had done things. Maybe he was too shocked to have noticed.

And now Sunshine shattered him. He claimed she was alive.

CHAPTER THIRTEEN
------■------

He went down on his knees and clasped his hands. Like he was made to do as a child, when he went to church with Mihai the manservant. He had been to church many times then, dressed in his sailor's suit. He knew how to pray.

Oh God, sweet God, make Sunshine right for once. Make her live. She must live, please, dear God. I will be good. I will be so good you wouldn't recognise me, God. Good like I have never been before. Good like nobody has ever been. I shall come to church and pray to you every Sunday. I shall donate. I shall give a quarter of my income away. No, a half.

Keep me here forever if you want. Have me beaten up and tortured every day, only please, dear God, make her live.

Make the message from Sunshine be true, please, great God. Best God. Bless you, God. I will build you a church right here on this cliff. Make her come to me on a cloud. I will repent. I know I have been a great sinner. I know I have never been caught. But I know you knew all the time, dear God. Oh, how I will repent. I will ask her forgiveness and give her happiness she has never known.

Adopt a child maybe.

His lips were moving at great speed and he looked up and thought he saw a stained-glass window above the fireplace and in it a large stone cross. On the cross he saw himself, arms stretched and blood coming out of his hands and ankles. If that is what you want, God, I'll do it. I'll ask them to nail me to the wall for you. Just make sure she's alive.

Make sure she knows what happened to me and maybe make her see me on the cross. Just before I die, God. Make Annie see.

Into his mind's eye came a scene from a film. Kirk Douglas hanging on a cross and Jean Simmons, with a baby in her arms, looking up at him. Kirk was smiling his tough smile and she was tender and she called his name.

Spartacus, that was it. King of the slaves. The hero.

If Annie saw him and heard him and knew what he had been through she would know he was a hero too. Not just a sinner and a rogue and a killer. He would make himself known as a giver from now on.

He would never say a bad word again. Never steal, never cheat, never kill, never whore around again. Give money to any beggar he came across. Tears were streaming from his eyes and he felt a caressing relief spreading all over him.

Outside, the car was pulling up and his watch told him it was time for them to bring his lunch. They must not see him like this on his knees. His repenting had nothing to do with them. They might think they had succeeded in breaking him.

He'd go into the bathroom and shave and shower and hide. The water was hot and it stung his skin where they had beaten him but he did not turn the cold tap on. He stood there and felt himself being cleansed and he rubbed himself with the fine soap and watched the steam collect on the thick glass shower door.

Somewhere there was a memory of another shower somewhere. Soap bubbles on some distant floor. But no picture materialised. It had never happened. Maybe he'd seen it in some movie.

He came out of the shower and waited for the water to run down to the floor before he wiped himself dry. He cleaned the mirror and looked at his face. He had gone pale and his hair had receded some more and a dark grey growth covered his chin and his cheeks.

The last time he had shaved a woman had died in this house. No. No one died. It was a dream or a hallucination or one of the horror films they showed on the box.

The woman had never existed. Or had she?

He dried his face and stood on the towel before switching the Remington on.

The current could kill him if his feet were wet. He must not die now. Not yet. Not before he had served God. Not before he had found out about Annie.

He would be faithful from now on.

And to think he nearly got hooked by that other woman on the boat. They had had such a good time circling Majorca and Minorca. They anchored in small deserted coves and swam and made love. They rowed the dinghy to small quayside restaurants and feasted and drank. They had so much in common. She seemed to be so energetic and intelligent and understanding. She was pretty and long-legged and agreeable and smiled a lot until they got back. What she did then had shocked him.

She had turned out to be a coward. Panicked when they got back and heard what had happened.

What will people say? she asked. They might blame me for her death. I cannot be involved in any scandal.

I am not really interested in you, she said. Just came for a bit of a sail. It was all a big mistake. It wasn't even fun.

The woman came out with many offensive things. He didn't mind any of it. But all that was after the holiday was over.

It was a good thing she had left. He would have married her on the rebound. It had been a narrow escape. With Annie being alive after all he could have committed bigamy. Annie was a saint.

If it all turned out OK he'd even make it up with Sunshine. To please her.

Sunshine was God's messenger. A bearer of good news. Sunshine was Hermes.

Damn right God moves in mysterious ways.

Lunch was on the table. A favourite dish of his. Steak and kidney pie. Yorkshire pudding. God had heard him and was giving him a reward. He once told Annie that steak and kidney pie was the best dish in the world. The very reason why he had remained in England. He had not had any for a long time and the familiar beefy smell filled the room as he took the silver cover off the tray.

He was going to enjoy this meal, he said to himself. Good thing they were gone. He hated eating with them standing over him, watching him from the sidelines.

He could eat with his fingers and lick them clean, but he remembered he was going to be good and he used the napkin and held the knife with his right hand, *comme il faut*. He wasn't going to put a foot wrong after his confrontation with the Creator. He felt a presence in the place, hovering over him and inside of him all at the same time. Must be the presence of God. Must be. This house spelt nothing but fear before today. Now it would be a temple.

People who believe are lucky, Mihai the manservant had said to him once when he was a child. I am a sinner but I know about luck, he had said.

He could remember precisely where and when that was. On the train coming back from school for an Easter vacation.

It was definitely Easter. Mihai had said something about the procession.

His father the Baron was not going to be there. He was on a Bucharest weekend binge that started on Good Friday. How he managed to find someone to play with on that holy day was a mystery. He would be missed because one member of the family was expected to be at the service. There was no one else around. He'd have to do it, Mihai had said. He'd have to greet the people as they passed the estate on their way to the church. A Gordonitzu was always there every Easter for the service. It was an ancient custom. *Noblesse oblige.*

You will have to go and pray, too, Mihai had said. Believers are happy people.

On his way in everyone welcomed him and saluted and bowed. He liked that.

He even remembered what the priest had said. He could hear that well because he was sitting where his family always sat. On the first row, only him and Mihai and two of the women. They were spinster aunts of his father who lived on the estate. He remembered that it was a little chilly for his sailor's suit. He was dressed like a prince in his best velvet jacket.

The priest said God will reveal himself to you one day and then you will remember your sins and He will remember your prayers and attendance. He could have been speaking to him alone. He was a holy man and would have known what the future held in store.

Now he had seen God and had felt him. It had taken a long time to happen, but now it finally had. It had happened to him today.

Just a few minutes ago, here in the house on the cliff where they had locked him up.

He would be a believer from now on. That meant he would be happy from now on.

Sunshine was a sinner. He practised godless sex. Sodomy. And yet he had been chosen to be God's messenger. Maybe he knew he was being used by heaven. Maybe he always knew. That was why he had been so conceited all the time. A budding tennis star. A has-been that never was. He used to get tickets for Wimbledon. Knew someone who had reached the semi-finals. His uncle bragged about going there.

That was no big deal. Anyone can go, he had sniggered. Plenty of tickets on the black market. All you need is money.

His uncle had said that in England money didn't really count. Class counted. If you walked into a bank with the right accent and the right school tie and the right name and family connections they didn't dare ask you for collateral. Bullshit. His uncle used to hire public schoolboys as pathfinders. They knew people but knew nothing about business. They were members of all the best clubs and they knew how to spend money. They filled a few decorative positions in the company and he got rid of all of them after his uncle died. Of all his uncle's useless hangers-on only Sunshine remained. But he mustn't dwell on dark thoughts now.

And then he noticed the parcel at the edge of the table. It was wrapped in thick brown corrugated paper. It had a white label affixed to it and on it was his name. He had seen the parcel somewhere else, and then he noticed the company logo on the sticker. It was his uncle's handwriting.

Next thing they'd tell him the old bugger was alive too.

He looked up and crossed himself and said he didn't mean it. Of course the old man was dead. That he knew for sure. And the parcel was no mystery. It had been among the papers that were delivered to him after the funeral. The papers Sunshine stole from his desk while he was with the police.

Sunshine was right. He had never looked inside. He hadn't even noticed it was gone.

'Go on, open it,' Annie had said when it arrived with the rest of his uncle's papers.

As if it were a Christmas present or something. Her face lit up in anticipation before he said he wasn't going to. She had felt its outlines and had said:

'There are papers and photographs. Maybe documents from the family past. Your uncle wanted you to have it. You should really find out what it is.'

'I'll do it when the time comes,' he said decisively.

'When will that be?'

'When I'm ready.'

'Don't you think you owe it to him?'

'I am not ready.'

She was silent after that.

It had nothing to do with her, he thought. What his uncle had to tell him after his death could wait. He had things to do.

And yet, sometimes at night, when he sat at his desk at home looking at papers, he would glance at the parcel and often he was tempted to open it.

He always found an excuse. Perhaps he was afraid.

Maybe the papers contained a threat. What could happen to him now? The company was his, lock, stock and barrel, and after the recession it thrived like it never had before. Dark secrets? He knew his past well. Including the lies about his mother. Maybe the papers were going to tell him what was in store for him.

Maybe he was scared.

Still, it didn't matter a damn. His uncle had been punished anyway. Just like the family code of honour had demanded.

He must not sin now. Must not think of sins. Must not remember sins. His soul must be filled with pure, charitable, noble thoughts.

'I love you,' he shouted at the house. He ran to the library and picked up the phone and said: 'You too. I love you too.'

No one answered.

'I love this whole beautiful world. The sea and the sky and the flowers. I even love the fucking dogs in the garden.'

He danced around the house and felt light-hearted and free and in his ears there was the sweet reverberation of organ music and psalms. The sound of the village choir led by the nuns from the convent had come back to him. Mihai had taught him the words and he sang along while God looked down on both of them from his icon. He was going to make an icon too. As soon as they got back to the house he would ask for wood and paints and a carpenter's knife. He could see God's face on the icon, a gaunt, bony face with shining eyes and a beard. No. That was Christ, not God. They were one, Mihai had said once when he asked what the difference between God and Christ was. He would make an icon and paint the face on it. And God's broad face and large beard too. If God and Christ were one it didn't matter. He'd find a way to paint them both on the icon. He'd keep it with him all the time. He would pray to it even away from the church. He had good thoughts then too. But as soon as they got home he was shown a new bicycle his father had bought him and forgot all about the icon and God and the church.

He had forgotten then but he would not forget now.

Maybe he should open the parcel immediately, he thought. No. Have dessert first in case it was going to upset him. It was a pineapple pudding with a soggy slice of fruit cake inside. A split, fried banana adorned the top. A trifle heavy for midday but he was hungry.

After his lunch he took the parcel into the library. Somehow, his uncle's elegant shape appeared to be there with him. He thought he could see the dapper figure sitting on the chesterfield, and he looked at himself and decided to dress up before going through the papers. His uncle was always smart and had frowned upon casual dress in the office. The rule did not embrace Sunshine, Gordon remembered bitterly as he looked through his clothes. The dark grey pin-stripe would do. The one he had worn on the flight from New York. His last flight. The flight that brought him to Kingston and here. A blue shirt and a plain red tie.

Annie had chosen that tie for him. It had the old-fashioned broad cut but still looked good. His uncle would approve.

He checked himself in the mirror before going back to the couch. He put his glasses on and, raising his eyes above the rim, he went back into the library and sat down. Might as well look at it now. Funny how Sunshine had mentioned the parcel in his television show. How he had made it the centre of everything. Perhaps he did not know what was in it. Maybe they'd kept the whole thing from him. Sure they had. That parcel was between him and his uncle and Sunshine was out of it. But he had told him to open it and look inside. He had said all that. He had almost commanded him to read the papers, only he did not know they were with him now.

He was not curious at all, and he took his time. He opened the parcel slowly. He did not tear the paper the way he would usually have done.

Why were they keeping him here, without any human contact at all?

Never mind. They were sinners but they could be forgiven. He must remember to say a prayer for them.

He'd say a special one for the soul of the corporal. He had not thought of the corporal for days. He'd do it as soon as he had looked at what his uncle had wanted him to see. God had sent the corporal to him. To make him leave and come to England and then here.

He should not be angry with whoever kept him here. He should be grateful to them because they had made him see God.

First there was a bunch of ribbon-wrapped yellowing photographs. The largest, in the front, was that of a pale young woman who directed a generous brown smile at him. She had short-cropped hair, clipped eyebrows and the palest skin he had ever seen. She wore a pearl necklace that disappeared where the photograph ended. He couldn't see how long it was. The eyes were melancholy and intelligent and virginal, and he recognised his mother. He had forgotten how beautiful she was. It was signed and dedicated to his uncle. In French. The year was 1935.

'To my dearest, only darling twin.'

He spent some time looking at his mother's face.

She was undoubtedly pretty. Young in an old-fashioned way. Serene, devoid of any spirit of mischief. A set of white non-smoker's teeth. The clear non-drinker's skin of a decent girl. He tried to remember her voice and he put Rumanian words into her full lips and listened to himself in the silence. He was not sure whether she was tall or short. Tall, he decided, and he pulled the other photographs out and looked.

There were many pictures. One of her and the Baron walking the streets of some city. It must be Bucharest. A better, clean, elegant part of town. His father was wearing a hunter's hat and she wore fur. The fur was open, revealing a plain woollen skirt and a marvellous shape. No, she was not tall, he decided. At least a head shorter than his father. Her foot, frozen in mid air by the shutter, was flying forward as if to catch up with his father. There was another picture of herself with the Baron, and on her knee there was a child in a sailor's suit. How he had hated the cap, he remembered, but he was a cute child nonetheless. It was a large studio picture and again dedicated to her brother in French. It said, 'Darling brother, here's the son and heir, your only nephew. Don't worry about us. So far no one is invading the country.' The date was November 1939. The handwriting was expansive and generous and happier than on the first picture. She, too, looked happy.

There were other photos of street scenes and one of the big house in the country. The one that became a community farm. Taken right in front of the gate with the two stone lions. Parked behind her was the elongated, graceful shape of the Bugatti. She was dressed in a light summer dress which clung to her thighs in the wind. Her hand held on to her hat. It seemed a happy picture and was not dated.

The caption read 'Life in the country'. The writing was flat and impersonal.

Perhaps someone else had written it.

There was a whole batch of pictures of himself as a child in various places, attires and poses. He must have been fond of posing, he thought. Boots, riding-breeches, cap and a whip and a cocky little smile that made him cringe. Christ, what a little show-off. He covered the picture with his hand and looked up at the ceiling.

Maybe God hadn't noticed.

He couldn't be everywhere at the same time.

A helicopter flew overhead with a deafening noise that stayed in his head.

It was surely a sign, but what did it mean?

He put the pictures down and touched the letters, then picked them up. There were many of them, all carefully sliced open but still in their envelopes. There were many stamps from many countries. All addressed to his uncle, mostly to various London addresses. He looked at the envelopes before opening them, and he felt he was stealing into someone's private corner. His back began to itch where he could not reach it, and then he remembered that the parcel had been left to him. They were his. He was entitled to read them. Had been told to. Urged to.

The first letter he picked up was dated November 1930 and addressed to his uncle in Berlin.

I often wish you had never left. Every day I wish that. I miss the support your being here offered, and above all, a bit of intellectual stimulus. I am not sure you did right to follow your Hungarian student to Berlin, but then I may be prejudiced. I hope he finds time for his studies while you two roam the night-spots. Berlin must be so exciting now. The music, the new painters and writers must make you feel lucky you are there. Why can't they keep that turmoil out of their politics?

Mother is well, I suppose, but then I get my information second hand. She flatly refuses to have anything to do with me until I break up with HIM. I wish you all understood there is very little I can do about it. Less than very little.

Intellectually I know this love of mine may be doomed, but my emotions are all over the place, mostly up in the air. I am locked in a constant state of sexual heat. When we are in bed together and so close, the world evaporates into steam. I want to cry and laugh and scream and bite. Forgive the bluntness but you know what I am saying. He elevates me to heights I could never imagine really existed. None of the old 'Is that what all the fuss is about' virgins utter after that first time. Even when I come down with a bang whenever I see his inability to fulfil my soul, I can't resist loving him. His warmth, his pulsating energy, his irresponsible sense of fun and his childish enjoyment of the now. Surveying the devastation of my body every time he devours me makes him feel so proud. He wants us to get married, and I long to be his forever (I can hear your cynical laughter) and yet I hesitate. Self-defence, you will say, but I cannot do without him. I don't believe another man can do that to me, smell and taste like he does, give me the peace he gives me. Light the fire and put it out the way he does.

You'll say you never expected your bookworm of a sister to talk that way outside the library.

I agree.

There is this archaic bridge of religion I have to cross for him. You know I don't think much of religion. It's no more than an up-market club people join in order to belong somewhere. A temporary cure for fear. A safety valve in case there is a God after all. It's nothing, I think. Religion is a promise given by priests and rabbis. They promise you a better next world because they failed to give it to you in this one.

You say it is the tradition that counts and the obligation to one's heritage and family. How do we know who Grandma slept with while Grandpa was fighting in the Balkans? They misbehaved then too, darling brother, or else why were there so many laws and punishments for adultery? What if we are descendants of some Carpathian farm hand?

He used to come into town only once every month. Go out with his cronies and drink and dance in every joint, but these days he spends much time here, while I sit for the exams. He says I am wasting my time with history and he may be right. He has meals ready for me at the flat and won't let me lift a finger at weekends. The greatest delicacies appear, on silver plates from every famous restaurant in town. It's all done by his magic manservant Mihai who is his friend and a confidant and must have been a philosopher in some former life. Sometimes I go along with him to the Casino and watch him increase his debts, but he shrugs bad luck away with a quick little tilting of his beautiful head and says there's always tomorrow. He doesn't care. He must be the man Rudyard Kipling wrote about in If.

He introduced me to his parents, but you know all about that. By the way, he sends his regards to you. He well remembers your year at the University here and still says you have the brains of a professor. You never told me what happened during that weekend you spent alone with him up at his estate. Be a devil and tell all. He won't divulge a word, and I am beginning to think you two have something to hide.

Must dash now. I'm handing the French Revolution paper in tomorrow. I've got the political parties all muddled up. Wish you were here. Of course the people had nothing to do with it. It was the middle class, right?

He passed up a few letters and opened another. The date was 1933.

I hope this reaches you before you leave Berlin. Your last letter was riveting. Sorry to read your impressions of the decline in that city. Every now and then the sky seems to open over Germany and they produce a Beethoven or a Goethe or someone and then, alas, it closes. The country forgets its beautiful, pastoral soul and concentrates on making cars and cameras and scientific instruments. In the last few years they had that miracle again with the Expressionists and Brecht and now it's gone again. You used to love the decadence so. But since they won't let any of the Brucke artists exhibit any more and you say some are emigrating, I am pleased you have received your visa to England. I don't quite go along with your thoughts on the coming war. Of course the Iron Guard are bullies but no one takes them seriously. They are only imitating the SS or SA or whatever those brutes over there call themselves. It's like a new fashion but in bad taste. There is a fair proportion of Latin blood in us Rumanians and the regimented way of Nazi life won't wash here.

You said Jews are not too popular these days. You make this tragic statement sound funny, bless you. You asked me a direct question and here is the answer: Yes, darling brother, I have completed my crossing of that famous bridge and have been accepted by the Church. You know it means very little to me and that I have done it for love. We are getting married next month.

It is, I suppose, too much to hope you will be here. There will be no one from our so-called side, barring a girl who went to school with me and that cousin of ours the banker who has been a Christian for years. He has taken up shooting but looks more Jewish than ever.

It will be a huge affair and will take place in the country. All the big old names will be there. He says the honeymoon has been booked but won't say where. I have a sneaking suspicion it's Paris for a bit and then the South of France where the casinos are. He won't go to Baden Baden on account of the weather. Thank God for that. I will surely gain tons of weight with all that delicious French bread and cheese and wine, but who cares? I am no longer looking for a husband. They want to get the marriage over with as quickly as possible because his father is very ill. He is funny, though. Privately he calls me his intellectual ex-Jewish future baroness daughter-in-law. A title longer than his own. I have been taking riding lessons on the quiet to surprise him. I can't say I am enjoying that too much, but it might be different riding in the country. I know how you feel about blood sport and I promise you I shall never go hunting with him. He knows I hate getting up in the morning. I suppose I ought to be thrilled by the thought of becoming a bride but my heart feels heavy. One bit of news came from the University. It seems I have passed my exams, French Revolution and all. They thought my essay was a little radical.

Well, it will be goodbye to the world of academe and books and seminars.

He says my next job will be to concentrate on producing the heir. I wonder what sort of children we two will have. He wants them to have his looks and your brains. Take no offence. In a mousy way you have always been rather dishy. What a loss you are to all those nice girls in the old neighbourhood. Forgive the sisterly jab. I suppose I am a little nervous.

Write and tell me all about England. Since you love Dickens and Keats you are bound to enjoy living there. Do you still think there will be a war? Why can't people learn to enjoy themselves? If the world had been run by women there would have been no armies. Men love playing games and they are all cinema stars in uniform. Women could never like uniforms because they want to look different. Didn't you once say the stripes take one's individuality away? He looks very dashing in his, though. Yes, all right, like out of some schmaltzy operetta. I miss you a lot.
Your adoring sister

Next there was a lot of stuff from the South of France. Art Deco post-cards of trains and ships and long-bonnetted cars and couples on moon-lit terraces. Picture cards of palm trees and seascapes and sailing boats and one of the Hotel Negresco. She didn't say much. A few lines of re-gards and crosses and kisses and it was so good to see you again. Then there was a cable saying that the Baron's father was very ill, that they were going home on the Orient Express that night.

He put the thick envelope to one side and opened another with the estate crest at the top.

The date was December 1934.

The big news is I am going to have a baby. If it's a boy they want me to call him Peter, after my father-in-law. We are busy decorating the nursery and writ-ing off to schools all over the place. Thank you so much for Gone with the Wind. I could not put it down and I wept a lot. It left me breathless. What strength women possess when put in a corner. This must be a true tale. They say they are working on a film of the book. Apparently they still need someone for the part of Scarlett. Whoever it is, and whenever, I shan't miss it for the world. I can see so much of myself in her. Spoilt, wilful and without the slightest fear of God ... But I have never suffered.

You say very little about yourself. I am sorry about your Hungarian. Per-haps he has chosen America because of that weather you keep talking about. If he is as fickle as I think he is, he won't stay with his new lover for long. I know you are going through hell. I know you have tried to make him finish his studies, but then maybe he'd make a bad doctor. They can kill, unlike lawyers or poets.

There you are, far away and alone and dejected and hurting. What was it you said when I told you there was only one man for me? You said there are plenty of fish in the sea. Practise your sermons, darling twin brother. He isn't worth a tear. You will love again soon ... I only wish I could be there to talk some sense into you.

Starting your own company is a good idea. I am sure you will be a great success, and maybe one day you will come back a rich tourist, stay in the Athene Palace Hotel, and take us all to tea. I am not a business person, but do write and tell me all about it.

As you know, I have no news of Mother at all. Can you tell me how she is? People are emigrating left, right and centre. What sort of world am I bringing this baby into?

I wish you'd stop calling me Baroness or Your Excellency. I know you are joking but you never joke unless you feel depressed. It must be your Hungarian. You will have to grow out of it. I'm afraid there's no telling how long it takes one to recover from an amputation. Even if the severed limb was going to kill you it's still an amputation.

He is sweet and considerate and goes off only once a month on his Bucharest sorties. I expect he wouldn't be what he is without that ... but when he comes back it's a honeymoon.

Life is so good I feel guilty.

Another, dated 1935.

It's a boy it's a boy it's a boy. I am sorry my last letter was so muddled, but I had the blues. The doctor said it was normal. The name is Peter. You guessed it. You are now an uncle. Peter is a strong, masculine name, and his father is making plans for him already.

We have not taken any pictures of the baby yet but I'll send you one as soon as we do. He is, to date, the only blood relative you have in the next generation. I sent someone to Mother's apartment last week. It was empty and it seems she has left. Do you know where she might be? The neighbours said she had left the country and are trying to find out more. Dare I guess she has come to you? If she has, I know you will look after her. Perhaps you might talk to her of me sometimes. If you need any money or anything please cable. Or have you made your brilliant success yet? I do so hope you have.

From the sound of your last letter you are in love again. You are not making your usual foul, sarcastic jokes. The spineless, bitchy humour you ooze when you are lonely is missing. Tell me all about him. Is he divinely handsome and intelligent? Try not to get too obsessed with him this time, but you will anyway, won't you. You can't help yourself.

I have made practically no friends here. We have nice neighbours who live miles away but you know how I loathe shooting and camping. You and I are city animals.

No one reads out here and the state of music is grim. He bought me a new gramophone. It can play five records one after the other and you can listen to a whole concerto without having to get up. Well, I say get up, because I am in bed at the moment and the doctor wants me to stay there for a little while longer. It's nothing serious. Perhaps it's my body trying to help me to avoid these boring country parties we are always invited to.

Once a month, as is his habit, my husband goes down to Bucharest for the weekend. I suppose he needs to see his friends and visit his watering-holes, and he always come back happy. People come and go all the time. At the moment we are entertaining a cousin of his from Constanza. He is a jolly young man but his wife is a crashing bore who can talk of nothing but shopping and the latest issue of Vogue. She wears all her diamonds for dinner. In the country. She is a very beautiful girl and until she opens her mouth to speak her looks transport you to ancient Greece or Egypt. Long neck, long legs, aquiline nose and unbelievable eyes. Her croaking voice puts one off because she sounds like a little gosling who's caught a hoarse cold. In French, of course. I am being catty. Miao.

Has Margaret Mitchell written anything else? I hope she has. I would love to read something else by her. Like everybody else, I am dying to know what finally happened between Scarlett and Rhett Butler.

I read The Good Earth by Pearl Buck the other week. I am sure you have too. Her parents were missionaries. She lived in China for many years and seems to have managed to crawl right under their skin. Life in the Chinese countryside must have been horrendous. Up here they only play at farming.

I can hear they have finished their dinner down there. Any minute now they will all descend on me. The peace will be gone because they will feel obliged to humour me. They will tell me jokes and gossip and smoke and offer endless advice.

Write, write, write, darling brother. Tell me about Mother if she is with you. You have always been so close to her. Mention the baby to her if you think it will make her happy. I love and miss you.
Your sister

He folded the paper and took his glasses off and looked up above the fireplace where he thought he had seen the stained-glass window and the cross. There was nothing there now except the red-brick wall and someone's framed family crest. A feather and a crown and a fish and some tartan. He had read the name underneath once but had not retained it.

He liked his mother's turn of phrase. She could write but she was a chatterbox. She must have liked the sound of her own voice. She was a happy soul. There was nothing tragic about her. Nothing to cry about. She certainly had a high opinion of her twin brother, his uncle. No wonder he backed her to the hilt. Whatever his uncle had told him was a lie. Had to be. His father would never have told him she had left if she hadn't. Mihai, even Mihai, said he should have listened to the Baron. Hold it. He had not exactly said that. He said if your father talked to you about your mother you know what happened. Or something. It didn't matter now anyway. He was reading her letters for himself. He was taking an excursion into her life and character and he'd know all about her. Not second hand, from what others had said, but on his own.

So far she seemed to have been very happy with his father, but could have become bored. That was it. She must have tired of life in the country. It was plainly evident she considered herself above everybody. She was too clever and educated for them. She must have lost patience. Maybe she hadn't bothered to make friends, got bored and left them all, including the baby. She had said so little about the baby so far. Had she tired of him that early?

He picked up her photograph and looked at it for a long time, as if waiting for her to speak to him. Now that he knew something of her early life he felt sure he'd understand. Her own words were going to talk to him. Justify what she had done. Explain. Tell him what had made her disappear the way she had, without leaving a trace.

There were a lot of letters there and he did not want to read them all. The last batch had the white-on-red cross of Switzerland. He lifted one at random. The date was 1939.

Dark, menacing clouds are rushing in. They descend on this confused, unsuspecting planet and there's no sign of light anywhere. How quickly people forget the horror of war. Poor Remarque will be disappointed. I read somewhere he's moved to America. I can't blame him for leaving this bickering continent. Like an old horse it won't learn a thing. The Western Front won't stay quiet for long, will it? Soon my neighbours and yours will be fighting each other on some deserted plain. Each side killing the other for king and country.

From the sound of things you did not get the letters I sent via Turkey. I gave them to a diplomat stationed there. A Bulgarian. I suppose he forgot about them, or lost them. Maybe you'll get them later. Your letters are a source of life for me, darling brother. Who is going to look after Mother once you get drafted into the British Army?

I know you have been very successful and you always said you would make it but are you sure your people will look after her? On second thoughts Mother is a strong woman and will, of course, manage well on her own. She has always loved you more than life. Hopefully they won't send you too far away. Like Hong Kong or Singapore or India. Or any of the other faraway British colonies the Germans are so jealous of. People are saying the guarantees we have from Britain will not hold. They say England is finished. So far no one knows on whose side Rumania will fight, if she fights at all, but Germany's star is rising. In the meantime they are demanding more and more shipments of crops and oil from us. Everyone says this is going to be a long war. If the Americans come in on your side it might not be. Your side, I have written. Can you conceive it, you and me on opposite sides of anything? But that is what will happen because people say we will have to be on the German side. I am still not sure what this war is all about. I am writing this from Bucharest, and will send it via Zurich. I have found a safe way to do that.

My husband is in the mountains this week. As a matter of fact he has asked me not to write to you any more. He says to make sure you know it's nothing personal. Just security, I suppose. He has been in Germany on some mission. Didn't tell me what it was all about but he has, I think, changed since he's been back. He is more serious. He gets involved in discussions around the table these days. He talks politics and yet, without wishing to be condescending, I think his words are not his own. You hear it all, word for word, in every political speech Antonescu blasts his followers with. This man could well end up running this country. Imagine. He and those Iron Guard thugs. On the whole, they have, along with every other group, been in and out of favour so often you get confused. Officially we are still on Britain's side, but there are fears of invasions from Russia, from Germany, and the government might fall and then the fascists will get in. My husband believes in Germany. He says they are strong and efficient and organized. His attitude to me is strange too. Maybe it is all in my selfish imagination, but I feel almost totally ignored. I have moved into the Bucharest flat and have been here for weeks. He says the country is not safe enough. I suppose he thinks it won't be until his Iron Guard friends get to run things.

He has made friends with some German Luftwaffe officer from the embassy. A real New Order Nazi. Blond and erect and dashing and ready to preach that new German gospel to the world. Radiating blue, righteous eyes that have seen the light. Sentimental when off duty, though. They both love gambling and drinking and shooting and fast cars. They go out racing together. Maybe he has another woman.

Peter is going to a kindergarten close by and keeps asking for his father and his pony. Life in the country was much healthier for him, but for the moment the family insist on keeping him here in town with me. He is a bright little boy and helpful and loves a good story at night. I have never been much of a storyteller and right now my concentration wanders. Mihai our manservant is good at it and whenever he is here he obliges me.

My husband comes down once a month for his weekend but these days it really is his. I don't go out a lot and still live for the little time he finds for me. I try to let him have his space and say not a word about the gambling. I cannot agree with his opinions. Hitler's ideas will take Europe back at least a hundred years. He drinks a little too much and sometimes his temper is bad but I love him so much I forget it all when he takes me in his arms. Things cannot be too easy on him. They won't let him have an active command in the army and he thinks of himself as a chocolate soldier. My Jewish origins can't be very helpful to him either. He says the Reds in Moscow will target him and the aristocracy first and must be stopped. He says the Russians are sure to attack us and he won't be caught in an office when that happens. I wish I could do something for him. He is frustrated with his lack of activity here in town. He must be confused by all the alliances. Maybe this is why he drinks.

Still, on the bright side, my cooking has improved. I read a lot and I keep going through your letters. You are such an amusing writer. I have my music for company and, of course, there is Peter and sometimes, on sweet, rare occasions, I have my husband.

The city looks like a garrison with all the uniforms about. There are so many rumours around you wouldn't believe it. There are demonstrations for and against everybody. The government says there are no more Iron Guards in the town but no one is fooled by that. There is no shortage of anything. This is still a rich country and the shops are full. Seeing as we ship so much of our produce to Germany this must be a miracle.

I am friendly with the wife of the commercial attaché at the Swiss embassy. She is a Rumanian who was at university at the same time as me and recognised me in the street on my way to pick Peter up. She comes in to see me from time to time and it is through her and her husband's diplomatic bag that I can get these letters to you. There are many refugees from Poland here but people are disappearing daily, especially the Jews. The maid, who comes from the suburbs, is afraid to come in more than once a week because her husband is a known communist and they are, as you know, very unpopular here now.

For me it's almost a relief not to have her because it keeps me busy. My husband says it is spoiling my hands but then he is away so much he does not notice how we all age. I blame it all on this ugly, ugly world of politics and on the fear of war. The dictators want to replace God and with His demise hope is replaced by fear with no one to pray to for help. Fear brings out the worst in people once there is no religion. I shudder to think where all this will lead to, but then maybe it's just a bad day. Madness will come to an end soon. Do you notice how God and prayers are back in my vocabulary? Maybe I am lonely, and isn't He supposed to be up there always and for everybody?

I can hear you say I told you so and maybe you were right but I could only follow my heart and that was the way God had it mapped out for me. We have little choice, darling brother. Pray for me and for us all, that this madness will come to an end soon.

When my husband is here we have no arguments at all. I cannot bring myself to fight with him in front of the boy, and he is hardly ever alone with me any more. They have insisted on sending a girl from the village to play nanny and she lives just above me and is always here, although Peter still goes to kindergarten. She will soon be frightened by the rumours and go. I hope and pray you are well and wish he would come back to earth and be himself again. Life could then continue as it was before.

I suppose I am blowing things up a bit, but I am a woman and a mother. Write to me care of the Swiss embassy. Address it to Mrs Maria Bruckner. That is my friend. You can hand the letter to their people in London. It will reach me because the Swiss take these things very seriously. Pray, dearest brother. I do hope you were wrong. Forgive the down. It is one of those days. You know them well.

He was going to get up and curse. Curse his mother out loud for her fabrications. And then he felt a presence.

Something or someone was looking down at him from above the fireplace. Someone was watching. From where the stained glass had been.

Or maybe she was not lying. Maybe it was his uncle's work. Maybe the letters were a fake.

The old fox wanted him to hate his father.

Even now, from his faraway grave, he wanted him to hate his father. Him, or whoever had sent the parcel.

Annie? No. Annie had liked his uncle and she was dead.

Sunshine.

Sunshine was going to be punished for impersonating God's messenger. He was pretending, lying, cheating, and all the while he had been his uncle's disciple.

He felt tired. He could afford to have a rest because he had been doing God's work all these years. Despatching the sinners, the murderers, the liars and the thieves. Yes, that was why.

He had not been bad at all.

But now he was tired. Too tired to chase any more. He would leave Sunshine to the wrath of God himself.

He was going to take a long break as soon as he got out of here.

He looked out towards the garden and watched the scorching afternoon sun begin to devour the green. Flowers and leaves folded then burned while smiling at the sky, and the tops of the palms turned to yellow then split. There was not a cloud to be seen nor a hint of the trade winds. It had been a long day and it was far from over.

He felt drained but happy. The truth came to him at long last. The reason for the chase. The reason for the running. He was God's soldier. He had successfully eliminated some of God's enemies. Like the corporal and that woman in Venice and his uncle. But he had been wrong about Annie. He understood it all now, and he was going to help her. Really help her, because she was a victim too. There was still time because she was alive. Yes, he had tried. He had made her his wife and his friend but she had been too weak to understand what he was about and why. She had not known he was working for God even then. He did not hold that against her. How could he? He had not known it himself at the time. He had only found out why he did what he did a few minutes ago, when God revealed himself to him.

He would ring and ask for coffee and then read some more.

CHAPTER FOURTEEN

———■———

That's better, he said to himself when they had gone. The coffee was on the table in the library where he had asked them to leave it.

This time he sensed respect in the way they tip-toed in and out. They did not say a word, as usual, and for the first time in weeks he did not care. On the contrary. He couldn't wait for them to leave. He was no longer lonely because he had heard many voices that day. Sunshine and his uncle and a cheap imitation of his mother's voice from years back.

It was a lie, but it was her voice all the same.

He was certainly no longer alone. Or scared. And he felt he was coming to the end of his ordeal. Maybe it was not an ordeal at all but a pause in the running. Maybe it was God who had made someone hold him there. Granting him a break. Allowing him a look at himself and those who had run with him and from him and after him. He could watch them all through the distance of time.

Another from Switzerland, dated 1941.

Darling sweet brother
I have at last been allowed back into my apartment after three days of questioning. At least they did not send me to one of those transit places they keep undesirables in. Like Jews or gypsies or Communists. The Swiss lady Mrs Bruckner helped take care of Peter. The country girl from the village has now left me and gone back. The family are no longer interested. Under the circumstances of his current behaviour I shall not let his father near him. Not unless he is totally sober and even-tempered. I wrote to you about that in the last letter. About how he beat me in front of the little boy. You did not react to that and I thank you. Then again, with the war going the way it is, you might not have received it. How can the whole of Europe fold so quickly? The Germans seem invincible and I shudder to think what will happen to the world if they win. They are showing films about the bombing of civilians. It is all too reminiscent of Spain, but on such a large scale. You may not even be in London and I pray you are well. Suffice to say that my husband, having beaten me to pulp, does not communicate with me any longer. I have a sneaking suspicion he is ashamed of himself. Underneath all that bravado he is a kind man. I get messages from lawyers and henchmen and other followers. Mihai has been drafted into the army.

I have sold most of my jewellery and furniture and pictures to make ends meet. Now I shall sell the books and the records. There is a market for those and I don't really need them because I know them well. So well that I can go back and read or listen at any time, without the books or the records being here at all.

I could describe my situation as being under a loose sort of house arrest. But I am still a lot better off than many others. I have not been sent to any of those concentration camps people whisper about. I can still go out and about but there is no one I can visit and with little money the shops are no good. I have read all they have to offer at the public library.

There are no new books other than translations of guess who, and old classics you and I read many moons ago. Anything that might smell of opposition to fascism is out. But I spent a few dear hours with Hesse and Tolstoy and George Elliot. They have kept the French translation of Lorca. I suppose they forgot which side he was on now that all of Spain is with 'us'.

I read Don Quixote again and laughed and laughed. Someone may write a female version one day. A story of a woman dreamer who chased knights. Just as I did ha ha ha.

Another. No date.

People talk about the next world. Hell or the Garden of Eden, whichever it is you have earned. I am losing any faith I might have had in all that. Hell is not in the next world. It is here. So is Paradise. So is magic. You don't have to die to be in either. You wake up in the morning and if the head on the pillow next to yours belongs to someone you love you are in heaven.

I have never felt so alone in my life. Not lonely, just alone. You of all people know and understand what I mean. There are people, but I do not connect. Perhaps it has been like that since I changed my skin to be with him, and lost my family and friends. But at that time I was too consumed by the fever of love to notice.

Silly woman, you might say, but I would not have had it any other way. I often think of the happy days, short as they were, and they give me strength to go on. The memory of them tells me I am capable of being happy. You remember the bit from Maupassant's Une Vie? The bit where she says five minutes of happiness are worth years of suffering, or something. You know what I mean. We read that at the same time, remember? That summer at the seaside in Constanza? I should not beef. I have had more than a few minutes of happiness in my life. When we were children and I became your mother confessor I was happy. Yes, even when you discovered the way you were about women and men ... When you were shocked at the deep love you felt for the Turkish cook ... I was happy for you because the discovery put an end to your hesitation ... and then you went away and like the sparkle of a second childhood my husband came into my life. It is useless to think of him the way he is now. He is not himself and somewhere I know he will revert to what he was and I hope I shall be there to see it. Not to partake because I could not ever be a part of him again. There has been too much pain and he is not good for Peter.

Even if he gets his way and keeps him Peter will leave him one day when he finds out that his father is a dependent man. I should not hate him for being so weak. He cannot help that.

Mother must be an old lady now but I always see her in my mind the way she was when we were children. You remember how beautiful she was, how fussy about her clothes and her hats and her shoes? I think of Father the way he was when we went skiing. You I need not think about because you are a part of me.

I think of my husband when he was the spring.

He wants a divorce. He wants total submission with regard to Peter. I am to give up all my rights to my child.

Well, dear brother mine, my husband is in the depths of winter now. It would be easy to blame this horrendous war. It seems to change everything and everybody. And yet I feel he behaves the way he does because he is so feeble and easily led. I am convinced he still loves me, though. Why else would he want a child contaminated by Jewish blood for his heir?

He is putting me under real pressure and if things go much worse I shall have to capitulate. I am not weak but I am tired and those constant assaults hack at my soul. I must remain a human being. This sounds hysterical but you used to tell me I was all drama. You may have been right.

Do not send any records, darling brother. I have no record player any more. Send books if you can and make sure you come out of this war alive. And if, at the end of this nightmare, I am still with him, do understand. Love makes us fickle, my dear. If he ever needs me again I'll be there. Of course, he may not love me any more and no one can be blamed for falling out of love, can they?

The letter ended there, unsigned. He looked at the envelope and he saw that it had been addressed by someone else. His heart began to palpitate.

Another. His uncle's name and address were typewritten. Switzerland, the same year, 1942. He could not make out what the month was because the stamp was missing.

Dearest brother

I may not be able to write again for some time. I did not expect you to send me money and I hope you won't again. I did receive it and it did come in handy. I am lucky to have Maria Bruckner, otherwise I would have been in trouble for possessing enemy currency. I know you mean well but the people who play postmen for me are taking great risks. The last batch produced a fortune. I do not need any more.

This city has changed, and the friendly atmosphere there once was has disappeared. There is little laughter or chatter out in the streets and no one greets anyone. None of the people in the shops or the hotels, the musicians or the doctors we used to know, are left. Even that cousin of ours, the banker who converted, was arrested. Rumours are he was sent to a camp. Maybe out of the country. No one will help him because they all owe him money.

The gypsy bands and the country markets and all the charming light-hearted dust have gone. Uniforms and leather boots rule supreme and the so-called corruption squads are more corruptible than ever. If you appear to have money to spend on favours they won't believe you when you run out. As far as little Peter is concerned, our heads are above water and I am making great efforts to conceal the changes from him. He is a sensitive little boy and sometimes in the morning he cuddles up to me and asks whether I am warm enough. I am not writing much about him although he is at the top of my thoughts. When I think of him I want to cry. What sort of world will he grow into?

I have been taken away a few more times and yesterday my husband sent what must amount to an ultimatum. The child and a divorce for my freedom, or else. He can divorce me at any time. The judges will award the boy to him anyway.

The very fact he hides behind the law makes me think he might still have something of his old kind self buried inside him. They have started to come to my door every night so we have moved out of the apartment and are living with friends. I cannot tell you where in case this letter is seen by the wrong eyes. There are some kind people around still. I cannot stay too long because they are taking incredible risks. Also, I feel that these constant changes are very bad for Peter. A child must have some secure base somewhere. My husband and I communicate through the porter at the Athene Palace. He still comes to Bucharest one weekend a month to gamble. I am being followed but so far they have not discovered where we live.

They have learned a lot from the Germans here. About law and order and above all about papers and forms. They want me to sign some legal document which they will only show me after I sign. I may, I am told, look at it once my name is above the dotted line, in front of witnesses. I wonder why they go through this charade and for whom. In a country where you can have all you want for money. It can only be because my husband has insisted, and that means he still cares for me, right?

I saw him the other day in the street. He was with that German Luftwaffe officer of his and they were drunk. They beat up a taxi driver and in the commotion my husband fell to the ground. He looked so shocked and pitiful. Your stupid sister nearly rushed to give him a helping hand. I wonder whether he would have recognised me. I was wearing rugs. My clothes are far too big for me now. Well, I always talked about losing weight, didn't I?

Don't worry yourself about all that. I have plenty of clothes. I wear rugs only at night. That way I don't stand out in the crowd. If you're too elegant they stop you and ask for tips. There are more beggars in the streets than ever.

I read no books and I do not believe what the papers say.

I can no longer meet the Swiss lady Mrs Maria Bruckner in the open so we leave each other messages all over town and in the park. This hide and seek is fun. The woman is an angel, and if there is a God in heaven He will know. Remember, she was born a Rumanian and could easily get into serious trouble. I am afraid her husband has asked for another posting. They may be going to South America, far, far from all this madness. I think he has asked for Uruguay and although I shall miss them I hope they get out. That is why I may not be able to send you any more letters.

I shall continue to write to you, though. Writing seems to be a therapy for me. It takes one's mind away. I find that whenever I put something down on paper, bad as it might be, it cleanses my brain and makes me feel better.

Little Peter is definitely noticing things. I take him to play in the park and I cover his face, and mine. We walk at night to the ice-cream parlour but we never eat inside. He waits and I go in and get it and then we walk in the streets and lick.

I am trying to turn it all into a game and at first it was a big adventure for him. Sometimes we play at being poor and sometimes we play spot the uniform and take cover. Sometimes I have the feeling he knows it all. God help me, he might think I am keeping his father away from him even though he has not been asking for him lately. Not since the night I was beaten. He is a kind boy and I hope you will have the privilege of knowing your only nephew some day. He is clever and sensitive and good at languages. I am teaching him French.

He is big for his age and strong of bone and muscle, like his father. If you can do something for us you will have to hurry. I don't know how long I shall be free.

Sometimes I feel they know all about me and where I am and who I speak to. Like they are mocking me while they wait to trap me at will.

Otherwise we are healthy and with God's help we will survive this. Did I mention God again? I must be a fickle woman after all.

Is there any way you can get us out? This request, I know, is late and will be putting a heavy burden on you, but I have no one else. I have not been much fun lately and my letters are probably depressing. You will admit, though,

that I used to be amusing. Please tell me it's true. You said that often, remember? I wasn't always down like this, was I? There may be a way to get us out. The Red Cross or something. Think about it. After all, weren't you the one with the brains of a professor? Send no more money. Thank you.
Love

Lies. All lies.

He was breathing hard. The back of his neck was throbbing and from his stomach a bulge of pain came towards his chest. Could all this have been true? How come he didn't remember any of it? Had someone sent this stuff to torture him, body and soul? To destroy what little was left after being locked up like a dog in a kennel, far from the world? No. The parcel had been on his desk long before all this and Sunshine had no idea where he was.

Why had he not looked at these letters sooner? A premonition? Self-defence? Self-preservation? Annie had tried to make him. That showed she did not know what was in them. She would never have let him look had she known. She was always so protective towards him.

His skin was on fire and oceans of sweat ran down his cheeks and neck and back. He was overdressed. He must have a shower. There were only a few letters left. Six or seven envelopes. This wouldn't take but a moment. Suffering cleanses the soul. That was something the priest in the village had said. Not now. Not now. Later.

But from somewhere he heard a command: Read on.

What more could happen now?

He picked up another.

It was written in pencil. The handwriting was scruffy, as was the paper. Long, muddled letters that ached into misspelt words. There were very few full stops and no commas. He could feel someone's breath down his neck but was too scared to look ... Read on.

They have abused me and have dragged me down If I stop writing now I shall faint Yesterday I signed Peter away He will be taken from me any minute now and will see the sun and the fresh air and smell the flowers I did not do that because of the humiliations only for him I should have done it long long ago This is no place for a child They are killing us here brother including the little ones I am becoming a thief and a harlot and have submitted my body many times to many people for oh so little There have been many men in me and I will sell my soul too for a bite for the child but there are many who offer and no takers This morning a delegation of diplomats came to the compound and with them a Swiss priest who singled me out He said he knew my friend Maria Bruckner and would take a message out tonight We were arrested at the park I cannot say how long ago I do not remember Little Peter was sick but his temperature is down now How selfish of me to have kept him only you know I never meant him any harm I no longer believe in being right Just in doing the right thing and getting him out is right He is young still and will I hope forget he was ever in this hell.

There is talk of sending us out of the country to someplace Some say Turkey and others say Poland or Germany and death Anything is better than this I have lost my faith in the human race Grown men with families and a past drag fellow human beings into the gutter.

It is so easy to destroy a human being You shave a man's head and give him a number and keep him locked up and hungry and dirty and soon he will lose his dignity and become a nothing and then an animal while trying to save himself The struggle to stay alive makes you selfish In this condition you stop thinking and then you stop feeling and if this is survival I would rather be gone There is rape and people willingly have their gold teeth hammered out of their mouths and suffer incredible pain for simple favours like a suck at a wet piece of cloth or a rotten potato.

We are filthy and starved and cold and I thank the Lord for getting Peter out of here How wrong I was to delay signing the papers How selfish He hasn't spent too much time with me here and it will not affect him because children forget I hope I am sure his father has no idea what is happening here Have I told you I have finally signed that piece of paper? It was very official and had many stamps on it I was too tired to read it all but said that I did and that I understood before I signed and after He is no longer my husband and I am a divorced woman Good thing mother and father are not here to witness the shame of the first divorce in the family I have gone further down and am a fallen woman now The only ray of light in the past few weeks came from you and the letters you have written Until this morning I have kept them all They gave me strength and courage and something to remember the past and how I too was a person once Forgive me but I have now burnt them all It was so cold here last night and they lasted a few minutes No disrespect I remember each and every word and tonight I shall read them again from memory all to myself.

No word has come from you but I am sure you have moved heaven and earth to try and get us out At least be happy to know Peter is going back into the good world again and one day you will surely meet him and know him and explain Please be gentle when you do and maybe he should not know at all because I want him to forget I am so confused I shall leave the decision to you I think now I know I have managed to write something on the back of the document they made me sign I wrote don't tell the child or something to that effect If his father sees it he will respect my wishes when he is a gentleman again I hope no one will ever find out what happened to us and how low human beings can sink and how easy it is I wouldn't wish this on anyone's memory because the shame of it will drive those who know to seek refuge in madness No one would believe this anyway It is best dead like an ancient secret or curse.

Thank you so much for being there and holding my hand I have no more paper and the Swiss priest is coming back soon to collect the boy who is leaving with him I want to spend these few hours listening to my child I won't hug him too much lest he feels we are to part He is playing again in the corridor now and I shall listen to his charming laughter I make sure he is far from here when I sell myself and I do that for less than money Soon one of the soldiers will come to collect for the paper and pencil he gave me to write this and also for allowing me to give it to the priest My body is a cheap price to pay for this letter and even through the pain of a stranger's flesh entering mine I will know Peter is free He will grow into a happy intelligent man and I know in my bones you will know him Do not forget me brother and since I now do firmly and finally believe in God again remember me until we meet again wherever it is.

He threw the paper down on the carpet and opened the last envelope. He read it quickly. It was an official letter of sorts and came from the Swiss legation in Montevideo. It was addressed to his uncle and dated 1946 and enquired about the current address of Baroness Gordonitzu. The undersigned, a Mrs Maria Bruckner, said she used to know her in Bucharest during the war and was hoping dear sir could put her in touch without delay since Her Excellency Baroness Gordonitzu would surely be pleased to renew an old acquaintance.

He got up and went to the bathroom. He bent over the toilet and he retched. No one must see this or know of his reaction and he cleaned up and got himself under the shower before he realised he was still fully dressed, pin-stripes and all. Who was he hiding from? How could he hide when the room was full of people? Bodies and arms and feet and faceless voices in a million tongues who all spoke at the same time.

Shsha, he whispered. Shshsha. Shsha. Hush, Central European-style. No one must hear them or see or know what was happening. Your crappy lives and suffering and your lonely, painful death must be kept from the world. Mostly from me.

Mama does not want to hear of it. She doesn't want you to know about it and she wants me out of it forever. She said so. I saw. I almost heard her say it.

I shall go to the Chinese cupboard above the television where the booze it.

Grab the Scotch and get myself painlessly drunk.

A drunken beggar goes to jail but a drunken baron makes the gossip columns.

Annie's sort of talk, not his. Never his. Never once did he tell anyone else about his title. Who was he anyway? A has-been holder of a title from a red forest of petty thieves. A half-caste part-time criminal who made good at someone else's expense.

That was who he was. It was good to know. A relief to admit it.

After all the hopes his mother had pinned on him. He was worthless. A failure. He deserved to be where he was.

He could drink and drink himself to oblivion then sleep it all off as if nothing had happened. The way he drank when boarding a plane.

It was all a nightmare. Part of a conspiracy. He had had no messages from anyone. He had forgotten how to talk to people. If the doorbell rang now he wouldn't know what to say. He'd have to sit and think. After he had rested and made sure what stage of his life he was at. Was he a child, a soldier, a refugee or a businessman? Was he all four, one and the same?

He was here now in this house. He knew. But where did fact part from fiction, past from present?

Which were future events and which were memory?

He was asking too much of himself. No one could tell the difference. Only the Almighty and he wasn't always looking.

Peter Gordon does not live here any more.

Not in this house. Not in this body. This is not me.

Yes. This is not me. That was where it came from. What came from? This is not me. Someone had said that, but who?

It was his own voice he was listening to.

God, he must stop talking to himself.

He looked at his watch and saw the hands moving forward. They moved so fast he could follow them with his eyes. Couldn't someone make the day last a little longer just this once? He was not bored or alone or scared of the dark.

Outside, golden streaks began to cover the sea. They had mauve edges and were changing shape as they grew. He saw the Rottweilers run about in circles and they barked. They were only fed once a day to keep them on the alert. His meal was about to be served, too. He'd throw it to the others. It wouldn't be enough but he would show them how kind he really was inside.

Not yet. He had at least another hour.

He went into the bedroom and put his kimono nightgown on. Annie had given it to him after she read *Shogun*.

The voices were becoming whispers and he moved towards the window to watch the sun as it sank behind the burning end of the sea. Any minute now it would touch the water with an emerald flash and be drowned without leaving a ripple. The Caribbean would then be calm, then serene, then dark.

Like the surface of the Mediterranean. Not always but, yes, that time, just outside Menton.

It had been quiet there too, when they fished his uncle out of the water the morning he died.

CHAPTER FIFTEEN

He had expected to hear something, but not as soon as he did. He had not been back at his desk for an hour when the British consul from Monte Carlo called about the accident. He was an old Côte d'Azur hand who knew his uncle from way back. The company was looking after his investments. He had become rich and grateful. He said he was sorry to be the bearer of bad news. He'd only just heard.

The E-type Jaguar had British number plates and the local police had contacted him as soon as his office had opened.

'We were going to play a gentle game of tennis this afternoon,' the consul said. 'What on earth was he doing, driving up there late at night by himself? And why Menton? Don't you have a chauffeur down here full time?'

'We do, but yesterday was his day off. My uncle loves driving the Jaguar. I only got back from Nice yesterday and took a taxi to the airport because I didn't want my uncle to drive that far. He was very tired, I don't know why. I asked him to go and have a check-up but you know what he's like ... was like ...'

'Yes ... I am truly sorry, Mr Gordon ...'

'I'm coming out on the first available plane.'

'This is unbelievable.'

'Yes.'

'I'll meet you at the airport,' the consul said, not expecting to be turned down. 'Just let me know which flight you are on. Did you know there were witnesses?'

'Witnesses?'

'Yes. Someone saw it happen. A man and his wife.'

'What?'

'I shouldn't be talking about this now. I am sorry.'

'Did anyone talk to them? ... Did they say something? ...'

'That is the strangest thing of all. The police told me some of what they saw. The man said ... well, I'll wait until you come. I didn't understand any of it ... It's eerie ... You'll hear it all for yourself when you come. Maybe you can make something of it.'

'See you later.'

'Please accept my sincerest condolences. Your uncle was quite a man. I shall miss him.'

'Thank you.'

The office was stunned by the news and disbelieving calls came in from all over. Sunshine was safely away watching some tournament in Florida and his uncle's secretary called him there with the news. He was flying back but Peter wanted to get there first. Perhaps there was a note somewhere.

His uncle was an old fox. You never knew what he had up his sleeve. He'd sometimes lose his temper without warning, but he knew what he was doing. He always used his anger to manipulate others ... The old bastard.

They had had words on the last day.

'You're an opportunist,' his uncle had said. 'You don't care for anyone. How different you are from your mother. She had great courage. I am glad she never lived to see what became of you. I should never have made you change your name. You are a true Gordonitzu. Greedy, shifty, selfish and cold-blooded. Your father murdered her, you know. As good as ... He, like you, wanted his own pleasures above all else.'

He did not comment. He knew what was coming next. The old man had his own way of getting at him. Sharp, witty and offensive.

'As soon as I get back I shall change my will. Don't look so smug, Gordonitzu. You think the shares have already been transferred, right? You think you own the lot, right? Don't underestimate me ... never ... Do you hear?'

I am going to give you a surprise of my own, he had thought. Then his uncle's face fell.

'I did not mean any of it, Peter.'

He did not react.

'I am a little depressed. I am a very sick man. There are no surprises in my life any more. I even know when I'm going to die. And how. Death watches me and holds back and it's just a question of waiting for it. I have become used to it, but sometimes it hits me and then I lose my temper. I am sorry.'

Perhaps it was Sunshine's absence that made him miserable, but even that did not matter any more. He put his arm on the old man's shoulder.

'Don't worry about a thing, Uncle. You're going to be around for a long while yet.'

'The pressure is getting me down. Do pour me some whisky, Peter. I wish you didn't have to go back. I can't blame you, though. I have become a bore, an irritating old man ... Hard for you, I know.'

He was trying to apologise but it was all too late.

He was going back to London in the morning. It had to be done that night.

Any steep hill near the villa or further up around the Camargue would have been suitable. Narrow steep roads and high stone walls and a precipice on many corners. His uncle, when he drove, drove too fast. He had expected the car to last a few days longer. Give him a chance to get back to London and settle down in his office to wait for it to happen.

He had bored a hole in the brake-fluid tank. When he came out of the garage with the tools in his hand he thought he saw his uncle looking down at him from the terrace. He feared the old man was going to question him and he panicked and in his mind he struggled to find some excuse for being there at that hour. But his uncle just looked down at him and smiled and waved and said a loving goodnight.

The next morning they kissed goodbye and his uncle apologised for his last outburst. There was, he thought, a strangely relieved expression on the old man's face when they parted. He felt light and free back at his desk. He knew he would have to go back to France very soon and he did not unpack.

Everybody admired his behaviour when the news came. How brave he'd been, poor boy. How calm. How he'd made arrangements to go back to Nice on the next plane without betraying any of the pain he must have suffered.

The location of the accident, and the time, had plagued him all through the flight. That and the trouble he had, forcing Annie to stay behind.

She and his uncle had been firm friends for years. They met often and he allowed her to cook for him. Together with Sunshine they went out on the town whenever Peter was away. She was seized with hysteria when he phoned her with the news. She was sobbing over his desk within minutes.

'You killed him, you bastard ... you ... He knew you were going to kill him. He saved you from murder by killing himself ...'

'You don't know what you are saying.'

'There is retribution. Something terrible will happen to you.'

'I wasn't there, Annie,' he said, and he looked sheepishly at his secretary who nodded in sympathy. Annie noticed.

'You all think I am mad ... I'll show you who is mad.'

She pulled papers off the table and threw them on the ground. She smashed the telephone and tore the canvas of one of the paintings.

They called the doctor who gave her a sedative, but it took forever to enter her system.

'You don't give a shit,' Annie screamed. 'They ought to lock you up.'

'She is in a state of shock,' the doctor said. 'I wouldn't advise you to take her on the trip. Can you find someone to stay with her while you're gone? She shouldn't be left alone.'

The secretary volunteered.

When they put Annie to bed she was calling for Sunshine and showering abuse on him. 'Don't take it to heart, Mr Gordon,' his secretary whispered, 'she'll be all right tomorrow.'

'You stupid arse-licking bitch,' Annie snarled.

Outside, he cornered his secretary and asked:

'Should I postpone my trip?'

'Of course not. You must go to Nice as soon as you can. I am sorry it had to happen at a time like this.'

She was not fond of Annie. They had joined the firm on the same day.

He had his usual stiff drink before they took off.

'Haven't you been on this flight very recently?' the stewardess asked.

'Yes, I have.'

'I thought I'd seen you on board ...'

'Possibly. I was here the day before yesterday.'

'Can't blame you for coming back to the sun.'

'I don't get there as often as you girls do.'

'It's no more than a bus service for us, sir. In and out. Haven't been outside the terminal for over six months. We get to see the water and the palm trees but not to touch. Would you like some wine with your lunch?'

'No, thank you. Just top up the Scotch for me, will you, please? It's gone pale.'

'Never mix the grape with the grain.'

'That's right.'

What if his uncle had seen what he had done to the car? Or spoken to someone? Or, worse, written to someone before he took his plunge? You never knew with his moods.

Maybe he hadn't. After all, they were at peace when they parted.

He might have forgotten all about his last blowout. His memory was not what it used to be these days. Especially when he was depressed. He had nothing to worry about, he thought as the whisky sank into his system.

The consul from Monaco was waiting for him. They went straight to the police station. The witnesses, a French grocer from Villefranche and his wife, were puzzled by what they had seen. They were very talkative and eager to help.

'We were driving back from a family wedding,' the man said, as if in apology.

'We were driving very slowly,' his wife added. 'You had had a few drinks.'

'Well, yes. We were driving slowly and then we saw the Jaguar parked there, in the centre of the road ... In the middle of nowhere.'

'Let me tell them,' the wife said.

'Sure. Go ahead.'

'The moon was bright. It's full at the moment. When we saw the Jaguar there it was like daylight. The road was deserted. It usually is at that time of night. You could see the road and the trees and all the rocks below very clearly. You could even see the sea. You needed no lights at all, but of course we had them on ... My husband wanted to stop and see what was wrong with the Jaguar but I said don't bother, didn't I?'

'You did,' the grocer said. 'But I wasn't sure so I overtook the Jaguar very slowly and stopped a few paces ahead. I got out to see what had happened. Maybe he had broken down and was waiting for someone to come. As I approached I heard music blaring out of the windows. You know, serious music. The kind they play for important people. He sat there, his arms resting on the wheel, his head leaning back. "Are you all right?" I asked, and at first he didn't hear me. I repeated the question and then he turned and looked at me. He was a very elegant man and had this full head of white hair. He looked like someone who had just come to, or had just woken up. He seemed particularly happy about something. You know, his face had that last bit of a laugh or a smile you see on someone after they've heard a good joke, but I thought he looked pale. It could have been the moonlight that made him appear so. "Oh yes," he said. "I'm quite all right, and who are you?" He could have been drunk or something, and I must admit I was a little put out by his curt reply. Since I could see there was nothing wrong with him I did not answer him and walked away.'

'He is always helping people,' the grocer's wife said proudly. 'He's that sort of fellow.'

'Before I started my engine again,' her husband continued, 'his lights came on full and the Jaguar took off along the asphalt and overtook us like a rocket. I tried to follow but couldn't keep up. We only have a small Citroën, a Deux Chevaux. It is a very useful little car. Easy to maintain and drinks little, even if it is a bit on the slow side until you get going. Anyway, we followed and we could see his rear lights as he raced round all those sharp corners up there. I kept on going as best I could and I don't mind telling you, we were building up quite a speed, and suddenly there he was. His car was crawling as if he had no power. I got so close I nearly hit his rear end, but I slammed the brakes on and stopped.'

'I got a shock,' his wife said.

'Yes. You did. He drove in the middle of the road and whenever there was a straight run he accelerated as if to annoy us or stop us overtaking. I had no intention of overtaking him at all. Then, as we got to the sheer drop up there, you know, where the stone barrier was washed away last month, you know the place there, he slowed down again, stopped and then crawled on and swerved off the road. He did not forget to indicate. He drove onto the side of the road. Very slowly, as if he had meant to park on the thin air that bordered the kerb. Unhurriedly he went, and I sounded my horn in horror. Maybe he didn't know how narrow the road was. And then something strange happened. I will never forget it as long as I live. In the glare of my lights he looked back at us and I swear he smiled. It was all so very slow, you know. I saw his hand wave at me. His brake lights came on but the car did not stop. Slowly, like a slow-motion film-show, his front wheels came off the road and then, slower still, the rest of the car followed. The lights were on and I saw him waving his hand still. I jumped out and ran to the edge and saw him hit the first terrace there and then roll and roll past all the terraces all the way down. The moon was bright, his lights were still on and I watched him go further down and roll and go down until he hit the water and sank below the surface. Soon the sea was as calm as a swimming-pool. The car disappeared as if it never existed. There was nothing I could do. I just stood there in disbelief, sick to my stomach, mesmerised by the spectacle of death. Maybe he had had a heart attack.'

'Nothing of the sort,' his wife said. 'He just drove too fast where he shouldn't have and tried to park on air, but he waved, didn't he? He smiled, too, didn't he? Maybe he was high on something or maybe he imagined he could fly.'

'I am sorry,' the grocer said, 'so sorry . . .'

'I think he wanted to die,' the grocer's wife said. 'Maybe he committed suicide.'

'Thank you for your help,' the policeman said.

'Yes,' Peter said. 'Thank you very much.'

'Yes,' the consul said sadly.

He was taken to the morgue and identified the body. There was a peaceful, almost happy expression of relief on his uncle's waxen face.

'They often look like that,' the policeman said. 'Makes you think it's a better world out there. One last private joke at the expense of the living.'

They all thought the nephew was holding up very well.

After that they brought Sunshine in for questioning.

In his own mind there was no doubt. The old man deserved all he got.

He was defending society's moral code, not just the family honour.

This is for you, Father, he had thought as they pushed the metal drawer back in.

No doubt at all.

Annie changed a lot after that. She had never been stable in his eyes but after his uncle's death, for a long while, her ways became more erratic than ever. Her moods and expressions swung constantly. There were weekly changes, then daily. She was nine women in the body of one. Her conversations with him at home dealt with no more than bare necessities. Hardly anything at all. She went up to Scotland to stay with her father and then she came back for a week.

She went off again without saying where she was going, and stayed away for two months, but came back with a defeated expression in her vacant eyes. After that things became normal again. She kept house and talked and shared his bed, but he had began to tire of it all. She started a course in photography and another in drawing. She took up Chinese cooking. She was talking about studying archaeology.

He was, he reasoned, not made to have a part-time wife. He wanted to live.

These were the years of sailing holidays and expensive resorts and elegant, long-legged, bejewelled society women. At home he played along and she stayed in unless she was going to her classes or seeing Sunshine or going into the clinic to overcome one thing or the other. She was in a tearing hurry to educate herself. Everything became an obsession. She did not often mention his uncle again.

But whenever she did there was an undertone of hate or a vengeful look while her words remained slow and collected. If she still harboured any suspicions about him she did not say so. Perhaps her eyes spoke to him, but he did not hear.

Things were profoundly different now. He was alone in this house on the cliff and had read his mother's letters and had all the time in the world. He could wait for her words to sink in. Decide what the truth was. Who was right. Maybe read the letters again or watch Sunshine's cassette once more. Watch it carefully. He might have missed an important clue somewhere. The whole thing could have been staged. Like his kidnapping. A trick.

Another lie.

If Sunshine and Annie had known the truth why did they try to humour him? There was no hate in his uncle's lover's voice as he spoke to him on the video cassette.

He could have taken his revenge long before this. He could have trailed him to Jamaica if he really wanted to. Could have found him through the travel agent or the airline or his Diners Club card.

Or even through his secretary.

Everyone has his price.

Someone must have seen him before he was lured into the house. At the airport, in the plane coming over. In the hotel. Somewhere.

Sunshine did not really know the truth. Otherwise he would have made the effort to be there in person. He had always hated him and would have gone through hell to catch up with him. Would not have missed a chance to get at him.

He would have found him right here.

Strange, Peter Gordon thought to himself. He almost wished he had.

Or maybe not. God knew well what he needed now and maybe God had made sure he was going to have it.

He needed time on his own now. He chuckled. Alone.

Yes. Alone to think things out.

CHAPTER SIXTEEN

———■———

Dark rain clouds devoured the sun. It tried to shoot a few golden rays of light through the grey but failed. What was left of the great orange face up in the sky was now gone. The dogs rolled on the grass and barked at each other like two toddlers playing on some beach.

The rains came just as the garden sprinklers opened up. Someone must have goofed somewhere, he thought. What a waste this was, but why should he care? There was, the *Gleaner* had said, a drought on the island, but he wasn't paying the water bill.

Who was?

Funny, he thought. He wasn't that interested in finding an answer.

The identity of those behind his predicament was not top of his list any more.

Water fell on the roof and the void returned to the room. He had, while reading the letters, forgotten how still the place could be. Now the voices and the apparitions and the faces were all gone. He was alone with the rain, but somehow he did not feel as lost as he had done before. Maybe he was asleep. Maybe the old dream, the old nightmare, was about to descend on him. He listened in anticipation for those telling echoes, but none came. He was at peace.

Sunshine had said that Annie was alive. Well, if she was, she had no business being anywhere but here, by his side. In his arms. Where she said she had wanted to be for the rest of her life.

Long, long, long ago.

She had no real reason to be unhappy. Hadn't he tried to give her all she wanted? Hadn't he worked his backside off making a success of his life? What more could she want of him?

You don't understand, she used to say.

She had a problem. Something to do with her childhood. Nothing to do with him.

Something she must have inherited from someone.

Insecurity. Lack of self-esteem. Buried anger towards her mother which never erupted. Whatever. But why did she blame him?

He used to blow up at her and at the beginning she'd just curl up and look at him sadly and then he'd stop shouting and feel guilty and hug her and apologise.

Later on she started to voice her opposition and she'd get angry and raise her voice and finally her anger would come at him in a flood of yells.

At such times she was so livid he would just sit there and stare at her and listen.

'Why don't you answer me, Peter?'

'I can't talk to you. It makes no sense. You don't listen. You don't hear me. Not when you are like this.'

'Like what?'

'Like this.'

'You think it's me, all me . . . Only me all the way. I have a problem. You think I am ill. I am koo-koo in the head, you tell yourself . . .'

'Please don't scream, Annie.'

'Don't tell me what to do . . . I'll scream if I want to. You think you own me, you bastard, don't you? You think you own everybody . . .'

'How do you know what I think?'

'I know.'

'You are a genius.'

'Don't put me down.'

'You abuse me and yet you say I am putting *you* down?'

'Yes. You think you are so high and mighty . . . To you, I am a nothing . . . no more than a business transaction . . . Not a simple one, oh no. I am a transaction with a problem. So you sit up there and you wait for the crisis to blow over. Well, maybe I do have a problem, and maybe it makes me anxious and depressed and easy to manipulate, but at least I am doing something about it. I am seeing someone and getting help. I am getting better . . .'

'You call this better?'

'Yes. Better. Because I am getting help. You should do the same.'

'Stop trying to sell that analyst to me. Who do you think he is? God? He isn't God. He's just a man . . . An unhappy someone who sits there and listens to you and takes you back to that famous unhappy childhood of yours . . . Listening to you must make him feel better about his unhappy childhood . . . You keep talking about the same things over and over again . . . suffering the same shit again . . . talking and talking . . . as if talking about it will change the past . . . Talking about it will not make your childhood any better than it was . . . It's dead and gone now . . .'

'At least he listens to me . . .'

'Of course he listens to you . . . He can afford to listen to you because he gets paid for it . . . The longer it takes to fix you up the better.'

'Fix me up? You fucking bastard . . . fix me up? You do know how to make someone feel like dirt . . . Fix me up? What about fixing you up?'

'I do all right, thank you.'

'It's useless talking to you.'

'Then why do you bother?'

'Because I believe you can be helped. Because I believe there is some good behind all this mess of yours . . . You . . . you have problems too, much worse than you think. Maybe worse than mine. What do you do about your problems? Nothing.'

'Nothing? I do nothing? I work . . . I . . . I can handle things. I don't have to listen to some complicated jerk taking me to pieces to look for problems that are not there ...'

'Not there? You are mad ... You would go but you don't because analysis takes constant facing of the truth and learning all about yourself.'

'I know about myself ...'

'No you don't. You don't even want to know ... you are afraid to find out because you are a coward.'

'You think I am a coward?'

'Yes.'

'Thank you.'

'You smug son of a bitch ... I know what you are thinking ... you sit there and say to yourself it's all my fault and you ignore your own troubles. Pretend they are not there. Get rid of them by hitting out at others. Mostly at me. But not for long, Peter, because I will get better and when I do ...'

Usually she'd stop short of a direct threat.

Too weak. Could not face the thought of being on her own.

Or simply because underneath it all she knew she was wrong.

They were all wrong. Especially his uncle. He was firmly on her side.

The old man thought she was a rock. He had often told her how much his nephew would need her once he was gone.

Of course she started to believe it all. All the junk the analyst must have put in her head. On top of that she bought books. All those books about how to get on and how to talk and how to communicate and how to recognise your own worth and be happy.

She used to tell him she wanted to save him from himself. Make a real caring man of him. When he laughed it off she went berserk. She became, for a time, rude and outspoken and cocksure and tried to prove she could do without him. Said he knew nothing at all.

That was why she had left him in the first place. To prove she could do without him. To assert herself.

He used to talk about it with his women friends and they all said the same thing.

She has nothing to do, they said.

You give in to her every whim. She is bored and unfulfilled and unsatisfied with herself and she'll always end up blaming you for it, they said.

Or maybe she was always like that and you didn't notice, they said.

She has no friends. Can't make any. No one wants to listen to troubles all day. Not unless they're an analyst. An analyst gets paid for it, they said.

Tell me about it, he thought, and he laughed.

They said:

She's a lucky woman.

My husband would never stand for that. He'd have kicked me out for less.

You must love her to death.

You spoil her too much.

You live in a boat without a tiller.

With all your power and your money you really have nothing. You live like a dog.

She's too selfish, too busy with herself to have any friends.

They said all that.

And they said:

You make it worse by playing into her hands. You are too safe. Are you scared of her? Do you think she will ever leave you?

God, he hoped she wouldn't, but he never, never admitted it.

He thought she was friendly with Sunshine because he was a weakling himself and needed to lean on her. Or maybe because she needed to play mother to someone. Whenever Sunshine was around she acted the tough guy.

Get out if you want to, she'd say.

Drop dead, she'd say. Go find someone else to take your moods.

Sometimes she fancied herself as a psychologist. Talked big words, quoted books and cases and analysed him for hours on end. Telling him how much help he needed. How sick he really was.

That was the time she began to talk a lot.

She was going on a crusade for him. Something like that. But before she could save him he'd have to hear all about himself. She did not spare any punches. Day and night she talked to him about himself and who and what he really was and how she was going to save him from himself.

'You are cold, you don't feel things like other people. And that is because you are afraid to touch on something inside you. You go through the act of emotion to please someone or to get somewhere or make a woman open her legs for you, but you have no love in you. I used to think everybody had love in them, but I was wrong. I thought you were afraid to show love because you were scared of rejection. But I know now there is nothing under your skin but flesh. You cannot give and you cannot receive closeness. If only you knew the joy in being able to ... You should get help. You can, you know. You have no idea how great analysis is. Sure, it's difficult at the beginning, but little by little you feel more comfortable with it and with yourself. You open up and look at yourself without pain. You miss out, Peter.

'Remember the time I thought I was going to have a baby? Moments that should have been the happiest in my life were shattered. You didn't say you were happy. You didn't say how marvellous for us. All you said was I suppose I'll have to marry you now. How I cried after that, but I cried alone. You said you were joking but you were serious. You couldn't stand another child in the house because you are a child yourself. You were born without shoulders. Today I am happy our child was never born. What a prospect to have a weakling like you for a father.

* * *

'Your passion is carnal. It knows no feelings. Like a robot. You don't make love, you fuck. You have this thing about orgasm because you want to prove what a man you are, not because you care. You give me a roof and food and clothes and money and a bed. You take me whenever you think it's pay-day ... Value for your investment. Rent. You keep asking if I've enjoyed it ... You never wait for me to answer. You don't treat me as an equal. I'm just an employee. A paid person who has moved from the typing-pool into your flat. And I am guilty because I reached the pinnacle of joy when you put that ring on my finger. I thought, he'll show his real self now. He'll give me love. But it never came and now I know you don't have any love to give. Not to me. Not to yourself. Not to anyone. Anyone who can talk about his mother and his uncle the way you do knows no love.

'I stayed with you all these years because I did not believe it. Because I waited for something to erupt in you. Feelings. Something. Any emotion, even hate. Anything. I thought you were going through periods of adjustment. To England, to having a family, to your work. To having money and then to me, and I waited.

'But you needed no adjustment to anything. Adjustment means acceptance. Compromise. Giving a little. Things that leave you cold. Nothing moves you. Perhaps you should live on your own. With robots you can manipulate at the push of a button. And still I waited because I felt there was something in there. There had to be. How I long to be there when the door finally does open on your insides. I keep threatening to leave because I want you to stop me. Tell me you can't do without me. Tell me you need me.

'But then you think you need no one. Perhaps you really don't.

'How would it be if you were ever to be on your own? Really on your own?

'Other people's emotions embarrass you. I've seen you read books. You home in on the action. On the plot. On how the characters cheat or kill or fuck or make money. You skip the dialogue, the thoughts, the expressions. What the characters feel is of no interest to you. But life is not a balance sheet, Peter. You will one day learn that for yourself. As long as there are people around who need you, and use you in return for being used, you will continue to be bored by what lives in our innermost selves. Detachment, that is what you thrive on. You have never ever been alone. It will be good for you, Peter.

'If they had caught you dabbling in foreign currency all those years ago, if they had thrown you in jail, perhaps you would have been different. As long as you trade with people instead of communicating with them, you will not see them for what they are.

'You will never know what it means to miss people.

'And more than anything, you will never look and examine and see yourself.

'You are a poor, lonely, miserable, misguided thing in the shape of a man.

'Any suffering you might have undergone you've pushed out of your mind because you are afraid of mental anguish. You cannot deal with it. It is this sort of pain, the one that comes from thoughts and feelings and, yes, the brain, that makes us different from animals. But I shall be there when you change. I may, if God gives me resolution and strength and time, be the cause of your change.

'You like beautiful things. Paintings and carpets and boats and beautiful women. Maybe you even like flowers and trees, but for you there is a price-tag on everything. You acquire beautiful things. You never think of what has gone into creating beauty. The tears and the sweat and the doubt. And yet you come from a family that appreciated art for the right reasons. On your mother's side. The woman you said lied and deserted you. Your uncle, the man who gave you everything . . . You said he was a fox and a cheat.

'Who would you believe, Peter? Yourself? That twisted carcass that is you, the thing that mistreated you all these years? Or maybe you've found something else now. Something new. A conscience. These voices you hear in the night. Your other self trying to get out of that stubborn prison you locked yourself up in. You are a sick man. A very sick man. You can get help. You have time, Peter – not much, but you have some. Use it and think. Perhaps there, somewhere inside the labyrinth of sighs that troubles you so, lies what will tell you who you really are.

'You did not kill him, you know. He did it for you. Not really for you, but for himself. And not because he had cancer . . . no. He could not live with the legacy your mother had left him. He could no longer fight the guilt of the survivor. The guilt he had felt, the helplessness, the use-lessness that had plagued him ever since her last letter. That dirty last note she scribbled, the note you wouldn't ever wish to read or keep be-cause it is unclean and wouldn't fit into your scheme of things. Soon, if you get help, you will be a free man again. Show me what you can do with your freedom. Show me you have learned humility. If you get treatment I'll be waiting for you. A little older and harder perhaps, but waiting, like most of us women have been taught to do.

'I shall not try to replace your mother for you. I will no longer spoil you or protect you from aches and pains the way I did when we were young, because you will have to learn to do without my protection.'

She had talked and talked and talked. Yes, she talked incessantly then, but not today. This wasn't her. How did she know he was going to be a free man again? And the things she said could not have come from her. Well, some of them, maybe most of them, but many of her words were someone else's. Maybe his own. He remembered most things she had said and when she had said them, but this last bit was not her . . .

How did she know about his mother's last note and what was in it?

He must be dreaming again. Dreaming as usual.

And all the other things she had said. Yes, she had often tried to hurt him, but she had never said all that.

She had reduced him to nothing, but out here she wouldn't have dared. Not face to face, she wouldn't.

She'd only say these things in silence. Have her words come out of his own mind.

Outside, the rain stopped falling as darkness swept from the sea into the garden. The moon hid behind a thick layer of grey clouds. It's the rainy season, he thought.

They were coming in with his dinner now.

Peace reigned. He did not hear them come or go. Maybe he had dozed off. He went into the dining-room and found his cold cuts and the salad where they usually were. By the tray lay another parcel. He felt it. Hard plastic. Must be another video cassette.

Could only be from Sunshine. That was his style. But he couldn't work up any curiosity about it. It had been a long day and he yawned as he got up to go to his bed. He left most of the food on his plate. If there was someone else in the house they could have it.

He put the parcel by his bedside. He'd watch it in the morning when he was alert. See what else the tennis coach had to say. Or leave it under his pillow and let the words flow into his head during the night. The way good children can learn their Bible, without the effort of reading. Mihai had told him about that when he was small.

It was going to be a peaceful night. He felt it in his bones.

No one would stop him having a rest. There was much to think about, but he would do it in the morning.

Later, he lay on his side and looked out of the window. The sprinklers came on with the darkening evening sky, and he deliberated on how soggy the lawns would become in the night. Then, as if commanded by his thought, the sprinklers stopped. He had powers. He did not even care who it was who had locked him up. Too much had happened in the last twenty-four hours. Something was afoot. They must have realised he was too important and too well known to be kept there forever. Otherwise they wouldn't have allowed Sunshine's parcel to get to him. Maybe they were going to release him soon. They would apologise and say it was all a mistake. He would not need to use his powers to get himself out.

The moonlight shone above the calm water that spanned endlessly beyond the fence. He watched the Rottweilers by the tall palm. They stood dead still, like a pair of statuettes frozen by time. For the first time in years he felt no fear. Maybe he was just tired. They too were waiting for the night to end. Perhaps they were afraid of the dark, he thought, before his eyelids became heavy. He smiled as his head hit the pillow.

He slept.

CHAPTER SEVENTEEN

■

The bright morning sun splashed through their window and expanded the sitting-room. The man wore a white cricket jumper that was a size too small and a pair of white cotton slacks. He was tanned the way ski instructors are tanned, and had an arresting toothy smile. His arms were wiry and strong and, in contrast to the rest of him, a budding bulge of stomach hung over his belt. He sat, his handsome face focused on a little gadget on the table. It resembled a microphone of sorts, and emitted a whining crackle like a short-wave radio.

'Move away from that thing,' the woman said. 'You're hogging it. I can't hear a thing.' She had pale alabaster skin and wild, thick pepper-and-salt hair. Her large olive-green eyes were intense. She had the short, nervy movements of one who has recently given up smoking or drinking. Her voice was husky.

'Nothing's going on.'

'What sort of night did he have?'

'Very quiet. Slept like a baby. Nothing. Didn't dream, didn't scream.'

'Are you sure?'

'Of course I'm sure. I've been up most of the night. He slept well and late.'

'Thank God for that. Oh, thank God.'

'Don't go religious on me now, Annie. He is getting close, but he isn't there yet.'

'Six weeks is long enough. He's had time to digest the letters now.'

'Digest? How? He only saw them yesterday afternoon. He must accept them. Believe them. This will take time . . . He is in a state of shock. That is why he had no nightmares.'

'Those letters will be nightmare enough.'

'When he takes them all in they will. Not before. There may be an explosion next. Up or down. Only then will we know. He needs more time.'

'Good God, what have we done?'

'It's a little late in the day to be thinking of that . . .'

She shot out of her chair and looked at him, then she sat down again. Her face was pale and she looked shaken. She put her hand on his shoulder.

'What was that you said, Sunshine?'

'Nothing.'

'Yes you did. You said it was late in the day to be thinking of what we have done . . .'

'Not we, Annie. You.'

'But you went along with it . . . All the way, you went along . . . You never said . . . I thought you agreed . . . I thought . . .'

'You thought . . . Did you ever ask me what I thought?'

'I am asking you now.'

'It's late in the day . . .'

'You said that before . . .'

'It was always going to be a risk, Annie, but you knew that well. You said so yourself. Dammit, Annie, you were going to save him . . . Make a man of him . . . This was your idea.'

'You never talked like this before.'

'Maybe I'm too tired.'

'Too tired for what?'

'To agree with everything you say . . . like I always do.'

'Sunshine . . . What's come over you? You never said anything to me . . .'

'I had no opportunity. You did all the talking. You used all those complicated psychological words and theories . . . half the time I did not know what you were talking about . . . but you were so sure, so convinced you were going to save him from himself . . . You were besotted with your idea, your plan.'

'Not really mine, his uncle's.'

'You never said.'

'That's right. I didn't.'

'Why not?'

'I don't really know. No special reason. I suppose I didn't want to pass the ... I don't know ... It's my responsibility anyway, whoever thought of it ... You see, his uncle thought his system needed a shock. Underneath, he said, Peter is good.'

'He was no psychologist ... of course he thought Peter was good. He had to think that. He never saw him for what he is ... He saw him as a reincarnation of his sister ...'

'Oh, he knew about him ... Believe me, he did ... Especially towards the end. I'm so scared, Sunshine, what if ...'

'It's too late for regrets.'

'You're so cold, Sunshine, so businesslike ... What have I done?'

'Maybe you should have asked that question before ... Before you convinced yourself you were embarking on some crusade to save Peter ... A mission he was going to thank you for one day ...'

'Well, will he or won't he?'

'I don't know.'

'Oh God, I hope he will ... I hope so much he will ... It was torture, you know ... All this ... It wasn't simple ...'

'You've always been a great organiser, Annie. Want to come and run my business?'

'Don't poke fun now, Sunshine.'

'You used to like my jokes.'

'Not now, Sunshine ... Not just now. I must know about you first ...'

'What is it you want to know about me?'

'Are you with me?'

'Hold it. I think there is movement up at the house.'

Peter Gordon stretched until his shoulder-blades creaked, and opened his eyes. Out in the garden, scores of colours swarmed into view. They began to merge with the green – red and blue and yellow and pink and mauve and more and more. Shapes. Happy, gossamer-thin shapes danced in, and he thought he saw a rainbow sneak out of the spray of water and blend with the flowers. It was late morning. The sky was clear and the sun was on the quarter mark. The sea was a smooth sheet of pure emerald. He looked at his watch. It was eleven o'clock. He dropped the bedside clock onto the floor and lay down again. He thought he saw himself walk in the direction of the bathroom, but he hadn't moved.

From somewhere in his body he felt the surge of an oncoming bout of energy. He felt rested and strong, and he expected to see them soon and hear that 'Good morning, Mr Gordon, sir', but there was nothing, and then he remembered it was too late for that. They must have come and gone while he slept. He wasn't sure whether he'd had his nightmare or not. He sat up again. No. He had not dreamt at all. He had not gone to the window nor had he screamed at the view. He smiled to himself. His head felt clear and he lay back and whistled 'As Time Goes By'.

'He's happy,' Annie said. 'That's what he whistles when he's happy. Thank God there's no damage. We've passed the first test, haven't we, Sunshine?'

'Early days yet.'

'What do you mean?'

'We'll have to wait and see where it ends.'

'I hope it ends right now. I wish we'd never started this.'

'Do you want a husband or don't you?'

'Are you with me again, Sunshine? What do you mean?'

'Nothing ... I was simply quoting you ... isn't that what you said when you came up with this plan, how you would force him to change ... get your husband back again?'

'You're being a bitch, Sunshine ...'

'Stop it, will you.'

'We should have asked for advice from a professional ...'

'Yes. Why didn't you?'

'I should have talked to my analyst about it. He would never have agreed. And my father didn't like it at all. When I told him we'd have to fake my death he was livid. He said I was playing with fire ... He only agreed because I said it was the one way to get Peter back.'

'You can be very convincing ...'

'God, what have I done?'

'Don't start all this again now, Annie. It will soon be over.'

'Over? Over? What do you mean, over? What is going to happen?'

'We don't know yet, do we? Let's put it another way. You said it couldn't have been any worse for you before, didn't you?'

She nodded.

'Well, then, let's see this one to the end, shall we? You have no other choice. My guess is he'll go to pieces when everything really sinks in.'

'You're a sadist.'

'I am not.'

'Yes you are. You hate him. I can feel your hate every time you talk about him. You hated him all along. You are jealous of him . . . You are looking for ways to avenge his uncle . . . Beating him up was your idea . . . You suggested it.'

'Come on, Annie . . . You said we had to keep surprising him before we made him read . . . I don't know any more. I'm tired. Maybe I did suggest beating him up for the wrong reasons. It was as good a way to surprise and shock him as any . . . I don't know . . .'

'You just said he'll go to pieces.'

'What do you expect a man to do when you shove all that in his face, huh? Sing a song? Of course he'll be hurt, but then you may achieve what you set out to achieve, no? Didn't you say you were going to rebuild him the way you wanted him to be, like educating and moulding a child, but that first you must bring him down . . . down to earth . . . It's this coming down with a bang that should be shattering him, in case you've forgotten. It will break him into pieces and then you can pick them up again . . . Assemble him from scratch . . . Make him whole the way you want him to be. That's what you said.'

'I did?'

'Yes. You did. This was your scenario, remember? Save him . . . Keep him in that house . . . Isolate him . . . Find ways to stun him . . . Find ways to hurt him. Leave him no option but to look into himself . . . Then, when he's been on his own long enough, startle him some more and then make him read the letters that will hopefully shock him and bring him down . . . The letters will hurt him much more than the beatings did . . . Yes. I remember now. I suggested it because I thought his pain would make you stop while you still could . . .'

'What? What are you saying to me, Sunshine?'

'You heard what I said . . . I tried to stop you but you carried on . . . You insisted on going on with it . . . on giving him the letters . . . forcing him to . . .'

'I thought you were with me on everything.'

'I couldn't stop you. Nobody could . . . Nothing. Not even his pain after they were through with him . . .'

'I don't know what has got into me. I'm scared. We've got to stop this . . . while the going is good. Let him go now . . .'

'Too late, girl . . . You can't do that now . . . it's dangerous. You don't stop in mid air. Things crash when you do . . . What do you think happens to a plane if all its engines are turned off at forty thousand feet? It will glide for a bit and then drop out of the sky.'

'You're a prophet of doom ...'

'No I'm not, but we must not pounce on him now. Whatever we do we must let things take their course.'

'Go on ... let's try.'

'Try how, Annie?'

'Call him.'

'Call him?'

'Yes. Call him on the telephone. Say something. Anything that comes into your head. Tell him ... I don't know ... Tell him he can leave.'

'That's not a good idea. Not halfway through this thing.'

'It is. We can ... We'll know more ... We can gauge his mood better that way. Call him, Sunshine.'

'You are manipulating me again, Annie ...'

'Do it for me, Sunshine. Please ... Please do it for me.'

A strange sound came from the library. At first it was like electronic music, then it turned into an urgent shriek propelled by panic.

It was the telephone.

God, he had forgotten what the thing sounded like. No one ever called him there.

It rang again and again and he jumped out of bed, ran to the library and picked it up and barked, 'Gordon here.' He barked it with authority and confidence. Just like he used to.

'Get yourself ready, Mr Gordon,' a voice said. 'You are leaving.'

'Would you repeat that?'

'You can go. Get yourself ready. We're making all the necessary arrangements for you. It will take about an hour. Is that enough time for you?'

'Where am I going?'

'Where? What do you mean, Mr Gordon? ... I was hoping you'd tell me that. You can go anywhere you like, Mr Gordon.'

'Wait a minute. You can't just come at me like that. What's the catch here?'

'No catch. You're free. Let us know where you wish to go. We'll do the booking for you. We'll arrange the tickets.'

'I want to think about this. I want some answers. I'll call you back.'

'What is there to think about?'

'I'll call you.'

He slammed the receiver down. The voice had definitely been Jamaican to begin with, but there was a strange discipline in it, a firmness that was too English. The islanders' softness was missing. He must have imagined it. Oh, no. He wasn't going to dance for them every time they felt like playing their flute. He could play games too. He wasn't leaving here. He had things to do. To finish off. Now that he'd had a good night's sleep he'd be able to do them. He had powers. He'd show them who they were tampering with.

But first he must work out if it was true. He'd call them and see if they'd talk again.

He picked the receiver up and growled a firm 'hello'.

'Yes, Mr Gordon, sir, anything we can do for you?'

'I am staying right here for now,' he said. The other voice had calmed down. It was local all right.

'But why?'

'As I said, I need some answers. I will be asking the questions. I'll call you when I'm ready to talk to you. Now leave me alone. I am staying here for now, understand?'

He slammed the receiver down, then picked it up and slammed it down again. He repeated the action many times because it made him master again. Marvellous, he thought. He'd keep them guessing. That would show them, whoever they were. The shoe was firmly on the other foot.

'That doesn't seem right at all. On the one hand he sounds aggressive, but on the other he stays put like a lamb. He does not act. My husband would have grabbed his chance and come bursting out of there. Wouldn't you?'

'He is in the process of changing. Of becoming another man, Annie. Teething troubles, that sort of thing.'

'You are making fun of me again.'

'No I'm not. It's his self-defence mechanism working. Or trying to, if you'd only give it a chance. His old personality is trying to resurface, fight the change ... You bring him face to face with the most painful memories of his life ... You confront him with that past you wanted him to know and accept, but you don't give him the tools to deal with it, do you? He can't face the world half naked. Calling him was not a good idea. It could brake the process you have so carefully thought out ... We should have waited.'

'Another man ... You said he was becoming another man?'

'Isn't that what you wanted?'

'Yes, but I didn't mean another ... you know, a different man ... I wanted the same man but changed ... Not changed ... the same man as he really is, inside ...'

'Make up your mind, for God's sake. I hear a different story each time you ...'

'Let's not argue, Sunshine, please let's not argue. Not now. Not ever. Not us two ... We've been through far too much together. I must think. I am scared.'

'The die is cast, as the prophet said. It's up to Peter and the gods now. You've put all the ingredients in there. All we can do now is wait for the cake to bake. Wait and watch. You must not prod or interfere or egg him on. Strictly observers, that's what we are now.'

'He sounded so sure of himself. Too sure ... As if he had not been in any trouble at all ... As if he was in total control, and yet we know he isn't ... Something is about to happen.'

'Probably.'

'But what?'

'But nothing. Can't say, girl. Can't say. He's just been through one hell of an experience. It's going to take its toll on him. He'll go up and down. He'll go through many stages. We'll have to wait and see.'

'His breakfast is cold by now. He hates cold eggs.'

'If he doesn't like it he'll call.'

'Do you think he'll read the letters again?'

'Maybe. I can't say. Maybe not. He took his time reading them when he did. You said he was no reader ... You said he always skipped pages to get to ... you know ... the saucy bits ... But not this time. Of course he took them in ... He understood them well enough. Don't you remember how he reacted?'

'I wish I could forget.'

'Therapy is often hard to take ... Painful. Ugly, even ...'

'What do you know about therapy, Sunshine?'

'Oh, I know ... I was there too.'

'You had therapy?'

'Yes. Me.'

'You never told me that.'

'I don't want to talk about it right now.'

'I didn't know you had problems.'

'I didn't have problems. My parents did. They could not accept my being a homosexual . . . Long after I accepted it. So they sent me for therapy. Thought it would put me on the straight and narrow . . . Make me normal . . . Find a girl and fall in love and get married and have children. Isn't that a scream? They thought . . .'

'Did you have a rough time of it? Did you suffer, too?'

'At first I did. The man I went to see was no good. You'd be surprised how many analysts are no good. Don't make a face, Annie, he meant well, but he had more problems than I did. Came up with all sorts of theories. Brought out every bit of misery . . . his misery . . . and tried to make out it was mine. Tried to put words in my mouth, thoughts in my head that weren't there at all . . . That was torture . . .'

'You poor man . . .'

'I was not poor and I was not a man yet, not then. I was a boy of fifteen who didn't get turned on by girls, that's all.'

'And then?'

'Then they found me another therapist. He was a doctor too . . .'

'A psychiatrist?'

'Yes. A psychiatrist. But he didn't give me any pills . . . He was good. He helped me. In fact, I had a ball. But you wouldn't agree . . . You figure one must suffer first. Go through all the whys and this and that just to find out you have a problem that can never change . . . But I don't want to talk about it now. This exercise is all yours, so let's concentrate on your husband, shall we? Just be patient. You may win.'

'May win? May win? What does may mean? Be definite, for Christ's sake.'

'I am definite. I said I don't know.'

'Don't joke . . . Is anything going on in there?'

'He's having a shower. Relax, girl, please. Your therapy has confused him . . . It's a contest, you know. A competition between two or three different Peter Gordons. Keep cool. In the end, like a tournament, it's the nerves that win, not skill.'

'You've been away from tennis for years. Stop talking like a coach. We are playing with a human being, Sunshine.'

'You are playing.'

'I won't listen to you any more.'

'Sure you won't. You never do. You don't need to because you know it all . . .'

'Is anything going on up there?'

'Not that I know of. He must still be in the bathroom. All I can hear is water.'

The glass compartment filled with steam as he showered. The hot water streamed down his body and he shampooed his hair and tried to sing, but his mouth filled with the bitter taste of the lather. He did not feel too hungry yet, but then he had never had more than coffee for breakfast before he arrived in this house. Maybe he was assuming his old habits again. Maybe he was already free. He turned the water off, as his other hand pushed the door open and found the towel.

He shaved slowly and then he went back into the bedroom and dressed. His label-studded suitcase gazed at him from the top of the cupboard as if it were hinting at him. PARIS. BANGKOK. HONG KONG. NEW YORK. MADRID.

He winked at the names and repeated them to himself and hummed some tune. He wasn't sure which.

On the bed lay the video cassette he had slept with and, as he put his jacket on, he took it in his hand, walked into the library and threw it hard at the screen. The glass broke with a grey puff of smoke. He thought of calling them to tell them to replace the set, but there was no need. He had learned that they always knew what was going on in the house. Maybe they had a way of watching him. Let them come and fix it if they wanted. This was not his house.

He went into the kitchen and poured himself a cup of coffee. He sipped the bitter black liquid and then walked into the library. He picked the photographs up and looked at the one on top. He thought he saw a hint of a smile on his mother's lips. You're proud of me, huh? he whispered.

There was a picture of his uncle as a young man, and he remembered him and thought how little he had changed. The bastard ate like a pig but never put on any weight. These people never change, he thought, and he was jealous and remembered his uncle's transparent smile in death. That time in France, in the morgue. What morgue? Someone was putting ideas into his head again.

He was no killer. They were maligning him. His thoughts were maligning him. He was going to tell someone all about them. Maybe Father. That was it. He'd tell his father and his father would punish his thoughts for putting bad ideas into his head. But the Baron was in Bucharest. It was one of those weekends. He'd have to tell Mihai the manservant. He was so easy to talk to and he always knew how to listen and his answers always made sense.

'Mihai,' he called out loud. 'Someone put coffee in the cup. Where is the hot chocolate?'

Behind the photographs there was a wad of letters and he looked at them for a while, and then he realised they were written in a foreign language.

Maybe French.

'You can read French and tell me what they say, can't you, Mihai?' he shouted. 'Come in here at once and tell me what they say. They are telling lies about me again.'

'He is speaking Rumanian,' Annie said. 'We'd better get in there quickly.'

'Hold it, please hold it.'

'Last time he spoke Rumanian he was on fire, remember? If we hadn't gone in there to make him take those pills he would have died ... His fever was so high he didn't even know we were there. Something is wrong.'

'It's happening.'

'What is happening?'

'The process you were hoping for. The change.'

'Why is he speaking Rumanian?'

'Because he is going through his life. He is in his Rumanian stage now.'

'He's gone quiet again. Tell me, Sunshine, what happened when you went to therapy that second time?'

'Now? You want me to tell you now?'

'Yes. You said you had a ball ... I want to know how come it was such fun.'

'You really want to know?'

'Yes. What did the second therapist do?'

'He made love to me.'

'No!'

'Yes. He did.'

'What a cruel son of a bitch ...'

'He wasn't that at all. I was lucky.'

'Lucky? You're crazy ... What an irresponsible bastard. He ought to be exposed. Sued and struck off the ...'

'Not at all. In fact he did me a favour.'

'A favour? Are you out of your mind? There he was, in a position of responsibility ... of authority ... taking advantage of a young, innocent boy ...'

'Oh, you're wrong. That second time was a few years later ... I was not that young any more, and I was far from innocent ... and quite willing. More than willing ... I may have initiated it, you know ... I gave him the come-on ... I am not sure who seduced whom ...'

'Still, he ought to be shot.'

'Not at all. He did me a favour, I tell you ... He realised nothing could change the way I was ... what he did helped me accept it ... helped me understand I would always be like that ... He knew that the best way to save me from pain was to show me there was nothing wrong with being homosexual ... You see, he could have kept me there for years and years in an attempt to make me look for reasons and causes and at the end of it I would have remained what I am ... Oh no, Annie. He was good for me ... He helped me ... If I had any doubts about myself before then ... if I suffered because I was different ... he put an end to it because he slept with me and that made me see there were others, even people like him, in high places if you like, who are that way and that made it acceptable. Not to my parents, who knew nothing of it, but to me, Annie. I needed to accept the way I was and learn to live with it, and being with him did just that. I went to see him for a few months and then we parted company. I had no qualms about myself after that. I knew who and what I was ...'

'Jesus Christ.'

'Don't Jesus Christ me, Annie. I wish some of these other so-called analysts would do the same ... tell their patients to forget about the causes and accept that their problems are there to stay ... Maybe teach them how to live with them ... Don't you think people know what they are like and why? Don't you think they *know* they have a problem? What they don't know is how to live with it ... When people get used to living with a problem it often grows smaller and smaller and sometimes it can shrivel and disappear ... Above all it makes people take responsibility for themselves ... not run for opium every time they feel bad ...'

'Opium?'

'Well, yes. Food, drink, drugs, depression ... anything people run to when they can't face a problem.'

'You don't know what you are talking about ...'

'Maybe I don't, but I believe what I'm saying ...'

'I had no idea ...'

'That was what I was trying to tell you before, Annie ... If only you could have helped Peter live with his past without going into it so deeply, he would perhaps have learned to have accepted that it was as much a part of him as his legs or his hands ... and then he might have become what you wanted him to become, whatever that is.'

'He must know about his past before he can learn to live with it.'

'Don't you think he knows? Don't you think that somewhere inside himself he knows? Didn't you say he has nightmares?'

'Yes, he does, but he never remembers what they are.'

'I am not surprised. No one wants to remember misery.'

'He was not himself. Underneath he was never himself ...'

'So what if he was not himself ... how many people are? Does that give you the right to write a programme for him ... the right to play God?'

'What do you mean?'

'Don't you know how much he needed you? He needed you like ... I don't know ... like a mentor, a mother, a ... and you used your hold over him to get him to dance ... You are worse than my psychiatrist was ... He did not use his authority at all ... He did not have any authority over me. Anyway, he made me happy. What you are trying to do will not make Peter happy, if that is what you want ...'

'Of course it's what I want ... What do you mean?'

'Do you want him to suffer again?'

'Suffer again?'

'Yes. By forcing him to remember that horror you make him suffer.'

'You poor, misguided man ...'

'Yes ... that's precisely the trouble. Many analysts really believe they can help people and want to help them, but instead they make them dependent ... they give them aspirin ... For years and years they talk about the causes that created the problem ... The bit the patient knows about best ... the painful bit that troubles him most ... is the cause ... His tough childhood, his uncaring mother ... His parents fighting ... His bullying older brother or whatever it was that started it. Don't you think the patient knows all that anyway? Why don't they deal with the problem itself? After all, the causes died years before but the problem will always be there. Why don't they teach the patient to accept it and live with it.'

'Some people need to go into the causes and understand them before the problem can be dealt with. That is why they go to therapy.'

'Yes, but not forever ...'

'You poor boy ... You talk like Peter. He doesn't believe in therapy either.'

'Good man.'

'Good man? I thought you hated him.'

'I never took to the gentleman but I am beginning to admire him ... I suppose his crime was that he decided to have nightmares instead ... The nightmares are his way of dealing with what happened to him ... his self-defence ... That way he tried to take responsibility for himself ... the sort of thing some analysts object to because it makes the patient too independent ... No more opium ...'

'You are beyond hope, Sunshine.'

'You haven't listened to a word I've said, have you ... but I know you mean well. Still, I wouldn't worry your pretty head about me ... Hold it. Hold it ... I think I can hear your husband talking again, Annie ...'

'Let's go and see him now.'

'I don't think that's a good idea.'

'Shut up, Sunshine ... Get off your backside and come with me now.'

The letters were talking to him. Words and lines ran in front of his eyes and effortlessly they formed sentences, but they ceased to be visible. They were written words that converted into sound.

'Mama,' he said, 'you promised we could go to the park today. We can spend my money on ice-cream if you don't have enough. I am rich now, Mama. I am so rich you wouldn't believe it. Richer than your cousin the banker. I can buy all the ice-cream in the park. Every pony in Rumania ... Come on, let's go.'

'I am busy now, Peter. I am writing a letter to your uncle in England. He will come soon and take us away. You can stay and listen to my letter if you promise to be still. Very still. We will go to the park later.'

Her voice was faint and soft but it was sweet and it talked of what they had eaten for dinner last night. A blow-by-blow account of every course and how it was cooked and how it tasted. Then she talked about politics. About the king and the government and the Russians. Why would his uncle want to know about that? Then she told his uncle about a book she was reading. A fat, heavy book she had got in the public library. A book without pictures. He sat on the floor and looked up at her as she wrote and the words she was writing hovered all over the room and he could hear them as soon as they formed on the page. She was so pretty, he thought. He was a lucky boy. He did miss the pony and Mihai and the gate and the country but the thought of the ice-cream after the walk in the park pushed the country out of his mind and he listened. He listened so intently he did not hear the door.

All of a sudden the television turned itself on and Annie appeared on the broken screen. She was so large he thought she would walk out of the set towards him. He acknowledged her with a smile and a slight movement of his arm, and he saw her nod in recognition. This must be the cassette they had sent him last night, but how could it work with that great big hole in the middle of the grey glass?

Never mind. Accept. Fool them into thinking he was playing along. Ask questions later. In any case, he was God's servant and anything was possible. She was talking but she was not looking at him. She must have had this recorded before she went to the clinic. The time he went off sailing with that woman. In Palma. The one he had thought of settling down with. The one who got cold feet when he told her Annie was dead.

Annie was never a coward. It was strange to look at her knowing she was dead, but then he had seen dead people on television before. Humphrey Bogart was dead, yet his voice was as good as new. He had watched *Casablanca* not a week before.

Who was she talking to? Was she really alive like Sunshine said? Dead or alive, he must tell her to hush. Mother must not be disturbed. He had promised to keep still. Who was Annie talking to? Why was she not looking at him?

'What is happening here, Sunshine?' she was saying. 'Something strange is going on.'

You bet something strange is going on, he thought to himself. Amusing. Let her see how he had fared these past six weeks: never knowing who was talking or why, to whom and when. How he had suffered. Was she talking to Sunshine? What was Sunshine doing there?

Of course he was there. He had to be. Sunshine was filming it. Making the recording. That was why she was talking to Sunshine. Sunshine was the cameraman.

'Get on with it, Annie,' he said. 'Listen to Sunshine. Get it over with and do it quietly. Mama is writing to my uncle in England. Shsha.'

'I am here, Peter. Here with you. What is he saying, Sunshine?'

Sunshine did not answer. Peter said:

'Of course you are here. You are angry again. You are angry because I did not come back in time for your funeral. I am always late for funerals. For my mother's funeral, for your mother's, for uncle's and for yours. I was at sea, you know, and they buried you too quickly. The sea-to-shore radio was out ... no one told me what had happened until I called from Palma. Sunshine came to meet me at the airport after they cremated you.'

'I am not dead,' she said from the broken screen, just above the buttons. Her image grew and grew and she came away from the matt glass and approached him, to make sure he was listening.

'Don't shout, Annie,' he said. 'I can hear you.'

'I am not dead,' she repeated.

'Of course you are not dead, Annie.' He must humour her. Agree with everything she said. Coax her. Make her feel at ease. All this was upsetting. Guilt and regret were welling up in him and he knew he must try to make her disappear. He touched the buttons in panic and frantically pressed playback. But she refused to go away and was still there bigger than ever and close and talking out loud. She was angry, but she was not looking at him. Maybe she was angry with someone else. He was now the servant of God and he was good and quiet. She was nervous, that was all. Nervous and frightened. Of course she was. She always raised her voice when she was nervous. She looked over his shoulder and talked to Sunshine. She was calling Sunshine by name. He'd best sit there and let them fight it out. She was angry because of the letter, or because he was late for the funeral or something. Or just angry with herself. But it was Sunshine who was getting it now. He could ignore them and wait for the cassette to finish. With her fury aimed at someone else his vision became clear and his worries evaporated and he remembered that time, when he had not gone to her funeral.

They had docked in Palma where he had chartered the boat. The hazy mid-morning sun hit the cathedral beside the palm-lined road. Large brown ancient stones, arched Arab windows and gargoyles looked down on him. Closer, the smell of fish emanated from the nets that lay on the quayside to dry. The man at the yacht club had messages for him and he telephoned his office.

'I am sorry about Annie,' his secretary had said.

'What do you mean?'

'Didn't you get my cable? She is dead, Mr Gordon. Three weeks to the day.'

The time it had taken him to circle Minorca and double back.
'You're crazy.'

'We couldn't reach you. I sent someone to the islands to look for you when your radio went off the air. We even chartered a helicopter.'

'Annie dead? Are you ... What happened?'

'She left the clinic and went up to Scotland. She shot herself in her father's house. Apparently there was a loaded hunting gun there ...'

'Where is she now? I want ...'

'She was cremated last week, Mr Gordon. That was what she wanted. She left instructions with Sunshine and her father. The whole thing was done very quickly.'

He ran back to his boat. On deck he saw the other woman applying a layer of make-up to her tanned face. 'I am going back to London this afternoon,' he said, and he told her.

'How awful ...' she said.

'Yes.'

'We'd better not be seen together after this.'

'What do you mean?'

'There will be a scandal.'

'I don't understand ...'

'I mustn't be involved. You must think of my husband's position.'

He could not think of anything. She was gone from the boat within the hour. He did not try to make her stay. She was a coward, but he didn't care. He was in a state of shock. How he packed his things and how he booked his flight and got to the airport he could not remember.

On the flight back he drank an entire bottle of Scotch. How had she managed it? Weren't they supposed to be watching her twenty-four hours a day at the clinic?

'You need a million eyes to watch them,' the doctor had told him once. 'Accidents happen all the time. They can be very cunning. They can talk people into anything. Even discharge themselves ...'

They, he thought. Annie is they. She discharged herself and went to Scotland and killed herself the same way her mother had. Got her father to leave the house. Used the same gun. And yet her analyst had said something else.

The bastard had said she was getting better. Her condition was curable, he had said.

She fooled them all in the end.

He remembered his trip back to London. At the airport, he saw Sunshine waiting for him in the arrivals hall. He sobered up as soon as he saw him.

'You look like you've been on holiday,' Sunshine said.

'I have been on holiday.'

'While your poor wife was crying out for help.'

'Who the hell do you think you are?'

'I am her friend. And I am angry and frustrated and sad. I should have been there with her. I feel guilty. I feel the way you should be feeling.'

'How do you know what I feel?'

'You can flaunt your whores out in the open now.'

'If you came all the way here just to fight with me I'll take a taxi.'

'Did you know she left me a note? She asked me to look after you. I saw her the day you wrote that horrible letter. You told her to look for a place. You said you were finished with her. She was a discarded, broken wreck . . .'

'Do you know how often she wanted me to go? How often she screamed at me in public . . . Humiliated me . . . How often she told me to drop dead . . .?'

'That's hardly relevant. She was not well.'

'Oh, grow up, Sunshine. The marriage was over. Had been for years. I'd finally met someone I could . . .'

'How can you talk like that now?'

'How else do I . . . I didn't know. I wasn't there. She was all right when I saw her last. Well enough to send me to hell.'

'Why couldn't you come back and talk to her? Be a decent human being?'

'It's none of your business.'

'The note she left me makes it my business.'

'I can't turn the clock back.'

'I want to believe you feel something behind that arrogant exterior of yours. Annie believed it. You think you are so clever. Success has gone to your head. If she could have seen you now she'd have lived. She would have known you're not worth dying for.'

He didn't want to listen to any more of this. It was a good thing Annie's father was in the flat. He must have been devastated, but he did not show it, and not once did he accuse his son-in-law of causing her death. If anything, he showed compassion. He was there for him and stayed with him for weeks. Cooked and cleaned and talked to him as though nothing had happened. Almost apologised for being there. Eerie. He must not think of that now. Forget. Forget.

He looked at Annie's face in amazement. The camera loved her. It caressed and recorded every lovely bit of her haunting face. She loomed so large she looked virtually alive. He could feel her anger, hear her nervous excitement, smell her almost. She did not look unhappy. She looked strong. They must have recorded this before she received his letter. She was not depressed or even sad. She seemed frustrated, but she didn't look like someone intent on taking her own life. If anything, she seemed encouraged by something. She stood there firmly, her legs apart, a carefree yet accusing hand pointing at Sunshine who was right there with them in the room. Somewhere behind him. He did not dare look.

But Sunshine had said she was alive. How could that be?

It was all far too confusing for him. He busied himself avoiding her in case she was displeased.

'Let's go to the park, Mama,' he whispered.

'I am writing a letter now.'

'What shall I do in the meantime, Mama?'

'Look at the pictures and be still.'

He looked at more pictures and listened to his mother writing.

There was his father and his Bugatti and there he was himself. In his school uniform. He remembered the day that picture was taken.

Mihai had taken it up on the estate, in the country.

The weekend the Alsatian had bitten him. Right after they took the picture.

A shudder coursed through his body. The sharp pain of that bite came back to him. He looked at another picture. It was himself riding his pony. He could almost smell the grass on which the impatient little hoofs stood, anxious to go. Had Mama taken that one? Could be. That was before. Before what? He strained to remember. It was before something unpleasant. Better not think about it today. His face would give him away and that would upset Mama.

He looked up and he saw Annie. Having stepped firmly out of the screen she now walked around the room, then stood there right above him. He saw her lips moving. On her face was a look of compassion, of pity, as if she was commiserating with someone. Her eyes were sad and encouraging. It will be all right, her eyes said. Let me help you, her eyes said. Let me rub your neck better. He wasn't feeling bad. She must be feeling sorry for Sunshine. She had told him he was lonely these days. She said he had put on a lot of weight and was no longer as handsome and lithe as he used to be. Sunshine missed his uncle. Love of his life.

How come she never felt sorry for me? he asked himself. Because I am big and strong and fearless and impregnable and nothing can touch me. Because I am her torturer and her king and her prison guard and because you don't feel sorry for people who live on a pedestal. You worship them or you hate them.

He had not invented any of it. She told him all that herself whenever they had a fight.

And now she stood there, close to tears. A new kind of sadness. It wasn't self-pity; it wasn't the hard-done-by look. He could not make out what it was. He couldn't talk because Mama had told him to be quiet while she wrote her letter. And Annie wasn't going to talk either. What was he so concerned about? It was all on television. He could play it again later, when he had more time. Who was the recording made for anyway? He looked up again and saw she was talking quietly but he couldn't hear a word. Maybe the sound had gone after he smashed the screen. It would soon come back now that there was such magic in the room. In the meantime he could pretend to look at his mother's photographs or read the letters. Annie wouldn't mind that. That was what she had wanted him to do.

'What is happening to him? Now and again he looks like he knows me, like he knows what is being said, and then there's this blankness in his eyes. I am scared, Sunshine.'

'You never listen, Annie. I told you it wasn't a good idea to come in here just yet. He is moonstruck ... We have walked in on his dream ... Look, he is studying the pictures. He is in some other world. We should go before he wakes up.'

'He's awake. He's not dreaming. I know the man well ... God, how pitiful, how lost and sad he seems. He's afraid of something ... What have I done?'

'We should not be here, I tell you. We must break it all to him slowly. Perhaps he did see you for a moment. He knows you are alive. He watched that video I sent him. He reacted to it, remember? He said thank God she's alive. Yes ... He would have known you were here, but not today. Right now he is so far away you couldn't reach him if you tried. Right now he is on another planet ... in another dimension. He knows nothing of you or me ... nothing of the present ...'

'Of course he does. He spoke to me. Didn't you hear? He mentioned my name.'

'Maybe he did. Why shouldn't he? You are a part of his past ... Maybe he was going through his life with you when he mentioned your name. I didn't hear ... I was in the kitchen. I told them to come up and get rid of the dogs. You said he has a thing about dogs.'

'Did he eat his breakfast?'

'I didn't look.'

'Why is he so quiet? Why isn't he saying something? Anything. This isn't like him at all. I wish he'd get mad or shout or knock his fist on the wall ... He isn't himself ...'

'Of course he is not himself right now, Annie. His emotions are locked up inside him, but they are slowly coming out. Soon they will burst out.'

'Oh, yes ... Please God, yes ...'

'We should not be here when it happens, Annie. I am warning you.'

'Do you think he can hear us?'

'Not a word. I told you. He is in another dimension.'

Not a word. Another dimension. Ha. Who did they think they were kidding? Of course he could hear them. Not every word, but he could hear. The soundtrack was bad on this cassette. They should have placed the mike closer. Anyway, that rubbish they were whispering to each other had nothing to do with him. He was snugly immersed in his childhood, and he could be with people who loved him and soon the video would be over and it would be quiet. He would be alone with his mother, in the flat in Bucharest, waiting to go to the park. He had not seen all her letters yet. Some were still unread. Soon he would be a witness to her conversations with her brother. Brains of a professor, he thought, and he chuckled.

'Did you see that? He smiled.'

'He must be having some happy thoughts.'

'You have a cruel streak in you, Sunshine.'

'I am here because of you ... For you. I am even doing this for you. He is the cruel one, not me. He would not hesitate to kill me if he knew

I was here, and I would deserve it ... He isn't aware, you understand?
Not of me, not of you, not of anything around him. How many times
do I have to tell you he is somewhere else, in another time? His expressions are no more than spasms that travel through his mind. Short,
momentary spasms. That smile was probably a short happy thought.
Like a baby in its sleep. Maybe he remembered something good. He
might burst into tears next.'

    'Let's get out of here.'

    'Yes, let's. He is reading the letters again.'

    'Hold it, Sunshine. Wait.'

The handwriting was clear on this one. His mother had used a pen.

Dear brother

*He is such a good little boy and I live in daily fear for him. He knows things
aren't right at the moment. His father does not come in to kiss him goodnight.
He does not take him out, but Peter roams through the house and he hears
things. Something must be troubling my husband. He is in a permanent state
of drunken stupor and everyone save Mihai is scared to approach him. I must
not let little Peter see his father like this or he'll lose respect. I do not agree
with King Solomon about not saving the whip. A frightened child cannot love
and a battered son will become a battering father. I want him to love his father.
I pray to God he won't hit me again in front of the child. It is all my fault,
I suppose. I am not the wife he needs. I have tried but I am no hunter or hiker
or racing enthusiast and my so-called parties must be a bore to him. If only we
could talk sensibly and find a compromise. But how do you talk to a bottle?
What do you say to a man who bursts into your dinner party and curses your
friends? Bookworms, he calls them. Intellectual communists.*

    *The politics in this country seem as confused as ever. One day we are to
be guaranteed by the British. The next thing you hear is an ultimatum from
Russia. The Iron Guard who were supposed to disappear are back in strength.
Some of the ministers back them. In the end they will have to go with the Germans. In the towns there are so many refugees and beggars and food prices are
soaring. There's no peace for the wicked.*

    *I have to take Peter away. I am going to take him to the flat in Bucharest
for a while. I am going to suggest that soon. Maybe I am over-reacting. I'll
let you know. Wait before you write again as I don't know where I'll be. You
are in my thoughts always, but my place is with my son now. I'll write happy
things again soon. It will all clear up again, you'll see.*

Your adoring sister

That was all before. Before she went to that frightening place she wrote about. She was not writing her letters in sequence. Or maybe he had made a mistake.

The pain had eased and he looked up. On the cracked screen he saw Annie again. The screen kept growing and so did her shape. She looked almost real, and this time he looked straight into his eyes.

'Get on with your stupid recording,' he shouted. 'Finish it and get out. Can't you see I am busy?'

She did not move. Just stood there and looked. She must be in one of those black moods of hers. But he'd need to sit this one through.

He bent forward to switch the set off. Again he touched all the buttons and twiddled all the knobs, but he could not make her go. Where was that remote control?

If he couldn't get rid of the vision he could ignore it.

She had often accused him of ignoring her when it wasn't the case at all. He would listen to his mother instead.

He picked up another letter and held it close to his ear, but Annie refused to go away. She stood still, her face suffused with pale horror. How long could a video cassette last?

She was wasting it, standing there saying nothing, doing nothing. He heard Sunshine's voice. He took a deep breath and he listened.

'Let's get out of here,' the man whispered. 'Now!'

He must have run out of video tape.

'That's right, Sunshine,' he thought to himself. 'You shut your camera and get her out. You and she belong somewhere else. It's not your turn yet. You haven't happened yet. If I can help it you'll never happen. Get her out.'

He thought all that but did not say it. And yet things were happening.

He heard the shuffle of feet and then the door slammed shut. Annie was gone. The screen was empty at last.

He must have passed God's test. He had more power than he knew. It had nothing to do with money or position or success. He had made them disappear. It was magic. Gypsy blood in his father's family?

He laughed. He could turn machines on and off by sheer power of thought.

He could get rid of dogs and open locks just by wishing. He knew that he had the love of his mother and with that he would make things happen.

Other things. Other people and places.

If he played his cards right he could design a different future for himself. Leave all the bad things out of his life. Get rid of the nightly horror of his dreams.

No corporal. No Venice. No escape to England.

No Mr Gordon or Annie. No Sunshine. No one at all.

He could stay right in this house forever. It was familiar and safe. He must rest and digest it all. He got up and went back to his bed. He lay down in his clothes and covered himself and closed his eyes.

CHAPTER EIGHTEEN

'We shouldn't have gone in. You never listen.'

'I couldn't help it. My heart went out to him ... Is anything happening?'

'He's gone all quiet. He must be reading again.'

'Listen, Sunshine, I am worried about him. I am worried about the whole thing. You can't spring a man's past on him without warning. Not this sort of past.'

'Isn't that what I said to you before?'

'It's horrible. We're making a lion find out he is a dog.'

'But that is what you planned, isn't it? It will bring him down to earth, you said. Teach him humility. Make him human. Isn't that what you wanted? Isn't that what you always beefed about?'

'Not if it's going to destroy him.'

'Destroy him? That's a little far-fetched.'

'You are trying to be nice to me, aren't you?'

'What is done is done ... This was a risk we were going to have to take.'

'We? Not we ... We risked nothing ... Only he did, Sunshine. He cannot be blamed for his mother's suffering, nor should he be punished for it. He's going to hate himself for something other people did.'

'He's hated the wrong man before, and a little punishment is good for the soul. He thought his uncle had invented horror stories about his mother to discredit the Baron. He killed him for it.'

'There was no proof, Sunshine.'

'I don't need any proof.'

'You are turning against him again. You keep changing sides, Sunshine.'

'Not when it comes to facts. He did kill his uncle ...'

'It was an accident ... He killed himself.'

'Even then it was Peter's fault. His uncle had to live all those years with his sister's fate on his conscience. Yes, maybe he was relieved to die that way rather than be eaten by cancer, but the guilt of having survived was too much for him. Peter could have helped him by sharing it. By being a real nephew ... Maybe the guilt of surviving gave him cancer ...'

'Why doesn't he say something? Do you think he could do himself an injury? It's so quiet in there.'

'Maybe he needs another shock. Shall we send the woman in again? That will ...'

'Don't you dare ... don't even think it, you cynical bastard.'

'I am only trying to help, Annie ... believe me. Sending her in might shake him in a positive way. It would be something good for a change. Don't you see? He thinks she's dead. Seeing her again would soften the blow ... he'll understand what really happened. It wouldn't kill him, though. Finding out you were alive excited him no end, but it did not harm him. He'll catch on ...'

'Catch on to what, Sunshine?'

'Catch on that it was all make-believe. A game ... Pretend, you understand?'

'I can do without your help. You are no help at all. You are as confused as hell. Everything is maybe this and maybe that. Anyway, you're not sending the woman in there. It was bad enough the first time.'

'I do believe you are jealous.'

'I am not jealous.'

'Possessive, then. You have to let go, Annie.'

'The woman is not going back in there and that's final.'

'Have it your way. You always do. Anyway, it's your show.'

'I am beginning to see why he hated you, Sunshine.'

'He hated everybody.'

She threw some more accusations at him and he answered but he did not try to contradict her or defend himself. Later they sat where they were, staring into space like a spent old couple. They sat and said nothing and they listened for a hint of life from the microphone. She thought Sunshine looked pleased with himself, almost fulfilled. Could she have been wrong about Sunshine? Peter hated everybody, he had said. And then she remembered the time, years before, when Peter's uncle suggested what he thought could save her marriage.

'More than your marriage, my dear,' the old man had said. 'It will save him. He is consumed by hate. By a desire for revenge against an enemy he cannot identify. This frustrates him and leads him to hit out at any-one or anything he thinks is in his way. You see, he has been forced to bury his own feelings for so long he has forgotten he has any. He has created his own world, his own set of rules, in which good and evil are opportunities for him to indulge himself. Moral codes and religion and decency have nothing to do with it. What's good for him is good, and what is bad must be eradicated. That is how he has managed to destroy the memory of what actually happened to him. In his mind there is room only for safe memories. He can survive only with the past he has created for himself. The truth could save him, but it could be a disaster for him, too.

'That is why you think he is insensitive. He cannot afford to care. If he did he would know how soft and compassionate he really is. You see, he was good and considerate and sympathetic as a child, and once the dam he has built to hide all that from himself bursts open, it might destroy him.'

'What about taking him to an analyst?' she had asked.

His uncle said:

'It will take fifty years to unlock Peter's mind, by which time, if it works, it will serve no purpose. No. If he ever got stuck on some desert island all by himself with all the letters his mother wrote to me it might work. He might be forced to dig into himself, in his own time and on his own terms. Do it slowly. That unlikely situation might be his salvation, and yours, if you cannot accept him the way he is. Accepting yourself, my dear Annie, is to mature at last. To accept your husband the way he is, is happiness.'

She had not accepted Peter the way he was. Now she was destroying him. She had put him on a desert island, but she could not blame his uncle for it. He had only been talking. This house of cards could fall anywhere and at any time and it was her responsibility. She had built it on an idea she may not have fully understood.

'His uncle understood him better than you know.'

'Maybe.'

'I wish his uncle was alive.'

'So do I. Christ, so do I.'

'I have been playing God,' she said quietly. 'In the old days they burned women at the stake for less. Much, much less.'

'Come on, Annie.'

'Will this ever end?'

'Yes. It will.'

'Go on, say it.'

'Say what?'

'Be your usual helpful self. Say it.'

'Say what, Annie?'

'Say it will end one way or another.'

'I am your friend and I care for you ... Whatever happens, darling, this will take time. We won't go in before tomorrow. He needs another night on his own.'

'I won't allow that.'

'Quiet,' Sunshine said. 'Something is happening over there.'

A stubborn sun stuck to the middle of the sky and refused to budge. All the shadows had gone. The light and the heat had turned the earth into a steaming, flat surface that spanned all the way to the sea. Inside the house it was unbearably hot and he shot out of the sweat-drenched sheets. His skin itched and he walked around the room throwing things about and shouting abuse. He went into the library and threw books about and kicked the broken television screen. He went to the bathroom and sprayed his face with cold water. He began smashing glasses on the tiled floor.

Beyond the barbed-wire fence, he saw his mother being driven towards the lawn in the big family car. She must have been in Bucharest for her Easter shopping, and he ran towards the big picture window to greet her. On the way he hit objects of furniture and flower vases and he fell on the big bed and started to tell her about the pony and the bicycle and his excursion into the village with Mihai.

Ridiculous, he thought. She wasn't there at all. Couldn't be. How could he be talking to his mother while he lay on his bed face down, in a house miles and years away from the estate?

What estate? There was no estate. There was only Community Farm 603. No. All that was in the future still, and he had control of his future. How many people could learn from their mistakes and never have to make them because they had the power to change the way things were going to be? He was a blessed boy. Community Farm 603? Never.

That was one bit of future he would change. That and the bit about his father losing the estate to Mihai the manservant.

And a few other best-forgotten items.

He lay on his back and looked up and saw his mother more clearly than ever. Out of the corner of his eye he saw how the rest of the world had become a blur. He wasn't certain what part of the estate they were on, but all that mattered was her face and voice and what she had to say. So far he had only heard her speak to her brother. The one who had gone to England before he was born and was always writing to her. He'd have to be patient and good and wait until she could talk to him alone and be all his. His alone.

Maybe if I ask her a direct question, he thought. Yes.

'Why are we going to live in Bucharest, Mother?'

'We are not going to stay there for the rest of our lives, darling Peter. Just for a little time while the war is on. There are many important people who come to see your father up there on the estate and he needs to see them in secret. Would you like to see a film-show this afternoon? Yes? That funny man with the moustache and the walking-stick and the big shoes, remember? We can see him again, if you like, and then we'll have a chocolate ice-cream. Your father asked me to take you out every afternoon until we find a school for you. You'd like to go to school here in Bucharest and play with other children, wouldn't you? I went to school here, Peter; so did your father for a time. Mihai? No. Mihai went to school in his village. Only lucky people go to school in Bucharest. Maybe he had to help his parents on their little farm. Of course I need you to help me too, darling. That is why we are here together. Your father will come and be with us as often as he can until we go back to the country.'

He got up and paced the bedroom. He listened to her and sometimes he thought he was dreaming, and then he gathered more things from the floor and out of the drawers and threw them away from himself because they had nothing to do with him. The passport and the lighter and

the wallet and the books all belonged to a future he would change anyway. They made him angry. He took the papers and the documents and
he threw them into the fireplace. He would set them alight later. The
present, such as it was, belonged exclusively to the times he spoke to his
mother. For a few minutes he was incensed. He kept throwing things
on the floor and kicking them and then he lay down again and curled
up and listened to his mother. He had to be quiet because her voice was
so faint. He had to concentrate very hard to catch each and every word.

He didn't think she wanted to talk about the other place. That bad, ugly
place where they had slept with all those people. Where they pretended
to be poor because she said they were playing a game and being poor
was part of the game. It was fun there most of the time. He did not need
to wash up or say his prayers and no one told him off for being filthy.
There were lots of people there and they all played the same game of
being poor and pretending they were hungry. But despite all the fun,
he knew his mother did not want to talk about the place. She used to
make him hide under the bed or behind the door and he stayed there
for a very long time until she told him he could come out. It was their
special hide-and-seek game and sometimes it lasted so long he would fall
asleep where he hid. A lot of people slept in the bed and he was never
cold or lonely. It might have been a game but his mother didn't like it.

It wasn't half as much fun at his boarding-school, where there were
many beds parked in a row along cold, stony walls, one bed for each boy.
This was the same school his father had attended and had hated. They
got up in the dark and went to bed while the sun was still out. His uniform had to be kept clean and mud removed from his shoes. They said
prayers together and were caned a lot and often he wondered why she
sent him to that school, especially after what she had written to her
brother in England about schools. He knew she had. The letter was right
there with him. Magic. He might still be a little boy, talking to his
mother, but he could read the letter she had written to her brother in
England.

He raced into the living-room and picked the letters up. He selected
one. He knew he had not seen it because it was still in the envelope.
He opened it. He'd read and he'd listen.

There.

Darling brother
He came to stay with us here in town yesterday. It was almost like in the old days, because he was laughing a lot and he played with Peter and took us for tea at the Athene Palace. There are no shortages of any kind here. The Germans are paying us well for the oil we are sending them from Ploesti. We are getting a lot of Italian films these days and the other day we saw the Marx Brothers. Someone must have slipped somewhere. The public laughed like mad, including the Germans.

This morning my paradise began to crack. He started saying he would like Peter to be sent away to boarding-school. I think he is far too young for that yet. Besides, I do not agree with boarding-schools. Do you think I am being selfish? He says it will make Peter independent and tough and self-reliant and all that, but he went to that school himself and none of that happened to him. He used to tell me amusing stories about smoking and drinking and midnight feasts.
    I suppose he's forgotten all that now.
    Maybe he is right. I am so happy to have him here I forget everything the minute he smiles and takes me in his arms. I cannot see straight.
    Still, I am afraid we had a filthy argument abut it today. Luckily Peter was out with Mihai touring the back streets in search of pre-war champagne. They have ran out of it up in the country.
    He says he has little time to come here and be with his son. The school can and will provide Peter with the discipline he needs. What about love? A child needs love and cuddles to give him strength and confidence. He needs to know someone cares for him. He needs to be shown. And as for discipline, I can do that too.
    He called me a spoilt bitch and stormed out of the house. I refused to let this get me down and I concentrate hard on remembering the good times we had before the subject of the school came up. I know I shall hear more about that but I shall fight it tooth and nail. You can write to me here at the flat. I don't think I shall be going up to the country before Christmas.
Love

Forgot to tell you something. We are having a tremendous season of ballet and music and opera in town. The Italians were here last week and next week the Bulgarians are coming. Did you know they have a great opera house in Sofia?
    You would have loved La Bohème, being so fond of Puccini. I did not miss one performance. The Germans sent some incredible orchestras. You would never believe such people could perform such music.
Love again

Sorry. Do you remember Alfredo saying he felt as if a thousand serpents were torturing him? Or was it Violetta? I do not remember because they have not performed Traviata at all, but this is how I feel when he is being mean to me.

I shouldn't really say that. He must be having his own problems, but he is too much of a gentleman to tell. If people in high office are confused, what must he be thinking?

If only he could share his life with me. My fault my fault my fault. Music and books hardly go with gambling and the hunt.

I promise this is definitely the end of this letter. Love yet again from your twin sister. I do go on a bit, don't I? But I am so happy to know you do love me.

Love again

There were no more letters. He must have read them all because now he was leafing through postcards again, and then he saw the cable from the Red Cross.

It was addressed to his uncle and dated 1947 and said simply:

'According to the records it was Auschwitz. Regret.'

It was signed by some name he had never heard of.

On the envelope there was scribble in his uncle's handwriting.

'*Ordenung muss sein*', his uncle had written.

Order must be kept.

Rubbish. It could not be notification of his mother's death. She was here with him. Sitting there. She was writing letters and speaking to him.

Besides, Sunshine had said in his video that she was definitely alive.

He had said someone was alive. Must have been her.

And above all, he could hear her quite distinctly. Right then he could hear her speaking.

'You are not going to any boarding-school,' she said.

So there.

Then how come he was sent there after all?

Had some of his future sneaked out of control? Had some of it happened anyway?

Something was wrong. The world had conspired to confuse him. Given that he was a messenger of God they were going to set a lot of traps along his way, but he must never succumb. They were testing him. Like in the Book of Job.

They would try to turn him into a frog. Or a chicken.

Bewitch him off his guard and make him forget his mother and his mission.

Test him. Investigate his soul. Make sure he deserved to have his mother.

Make him believe he did not need a mother by making him think he was a grown man.

He took his shoes off, went back to bed and covered himself and curled up.

He must sleep now. He had the power to make himself drop off this very second. Like a child. Sleep the future away.

CHAPTER NINETEEN

First there was a scream that started somewhere behind the cast-iron horizon that surrounded him. He knew he was not alone because he could make out the faces of the others. He heard them groan and some-one said something that sounded like water. Then someone fell down and he heard a throaty gurgle and a gush of foul-smelling air came up at him from someone's lips and then there was silence. The cast iron came closer as the whole world contracted with a metallic squeak. People moved closer and backwards and uttered hisses of fear until they saw it was a mesh of barbed wire, not a steel wall. There was another scream, longer than the first but closer to him and not as loud. He looked about him and saw naked knees, mostly covered with tatty woollen stockings eaten with holes. He saw bare feet below him on the cemented floor. Feet larger than his own. Some had old shoes which opened at the front to reveal pale toes and dirty, long nails. There was an unbearable stench about, a mixture of urine and bad breath and old sweat. Someone bent over him and his hands touched the soft tepid flesh of a cheek. A forced smile bore down on him, revealing yellow teeth, and then the mouth narrowed as another scream invaded the crowded space, level with his eyes and all those knees. His hands, he thought, looked small, and his arms were covered with a torn blue sweater far too large for him. He was not cold but he was hungry and he said so again and again and hands came down and covered his mouth and stopped the air and he thought he was suffocating. He wriggled his head and the hands gave way and he looked up. There, way above the heads, there were more moans of helplessness and many, many tired eyes that sometimes looked down at him with painful silence. He heard the sound of feet tapping on the cold floor. Soft, tired tapping which grew louder and louder, and then he heard nothing and his vision went blank. He heard the barking of dogs somewhere near and he was seized by a paralysing panic. He grabbed at the legs closest to him and felt for a familiar shape, but the legs moved away and when he tried to hold on they kicked at him. On the floor, a few paces away from where he stood, there was a little doll. He had seen that doll before but now its head and one of its arms were missing, and it lay trodden on the dirty floor. Someone close by, a foot above his head, started wailing. A long, monotonous whine that made him shiver. It was cold.

There were no doors in the room he was in. Only blankets that did not stop the draught that came blowing in from the long canvas corridors. There were many corridors, he thought, and people walked along them, slowly dragging their feet.

His dream moved him away and left him sitting on the floor of some other place. There were two iron beds in the room and he was made to crawl under one of them. A pair of long, polished leather boots pushed him there and a man's voice said keep the boy there or he'll die. He knew he couldn't die on the floor because someone had told him when you die you fly. You grow wings and fly through a blue warm sky into the clouds. And then the bed started to creak and he heard someone groan in pain. The bed moved violently for a while and then it stopped and the boots came down and kicked him and marched out. He heard some-one laugh as the rug door was lifted and another pair of boots came in and climbed onto the bed.

Fire. There was fire somewhere nearby, but it did not smell of dry grass or slow-roasting meat as it did up-country. There were sobs from above him and he stayed under the bed, pulling his knees up to his chest, and waited. He was scared. He always curled up when he was scared. He saw many boots marching in and out and the bedsprings croaked in between. There were curse-words and heavy breathing and a cough and then an-other. Someone slapped someone else's flesh and he heard sobs. He thought of that other place where he would stand with all those knees, a woman's body dangling from the top of some mast somewhere on the perimeter. He had not seen it himself but people were talking about it.

They said she had climbed up there and hanged herself before anyone could get to her. They said her hands were limp and her head lay on her chest and her eyes were open. She is dead, someone said, and he did not believe it because he could not see. He had strained to see but he was too small. And now he was under the bed and he tried to imagine the woman. He knew that if she was really dead she would grow wings and fly and none of the people said anything about wings and he concluded they were all lying.

But that was earlier and now he was lying under the creaking bed, waiting for the last pair of boots to leave. He rubbed his chest and his legs and did not feel the cold and then came another scream. Right above his head. He heard a slap and then the last pair of boots emerged and walked out.

Arms scooped him up from under the bed and all of a sudden the room was filled with faces he did not know. Amidst the fear and the sobs that emanated from the people he felt softness and gentle hands that stroked his head. Somehow they all knew his name. Someone gave him a lump of hard candy sugar to suck and the sweet saliva lingered and cleared his head and soon he was up on his feet and running along the corridors, towards a strong pair of arms that slapped his face, then pushed him back where he had come from. There was someone there to whom he used to go. To whom he brought his complaints and his fears. He felt the mark of the hand that had slapped him and saw stars. A strange whistle implanted itself inside his head and he forgot where he was going and who it was he belonged to. He walked, his body swaying, and he fell into someone's arms and the whistle ended. The confusion had gone without a trace, as if he were sitting in front of a blank wall without a yesterday to remember.

Later there were many naked, emaciated bodies around him and from the ceiling came gushes of cold water. The assembly was sprayed with a white liquid which had a strong smell. Someone rubbed his body with a hard, chunky bit of soap which formed bubbles all over his skin. There were holes in the ceiling through which he saw the water dripping down, and he stood under one and saw the foam roll off his shoulders, down his tummy and legs to the shining, slippery concrete floor. Everywhere there was the close feeling of other bodies who lingered under the water as if they were in Paradise. As if they were making themselves ready to grow wings and fly up to God. There was subdued laughter, and he was sure death was coming soon. He felt his back and his shoulders for a sign of the feathers and the wings that were coming to him any minute now.

There was a mirror on the wall and he squeezed past the bodies and stood in front of it. He looked at himself. He was very small indeed. He had forgotten how small. Someone must have punished him for something and reduced him to the size of a dwarf. He strained his eyes to look at his face. But through the steam a blank oval shape looked back at him. There were no eyes, no nose and no mouth. The head was clean-shaven and there were no ears. If there were no eyes, how could he see anything? he asked himself, but then maybe he was dead already.

The face gave a shriek and his hands grabbed its sides and the shriek continued and he thought it must have come from inside his own head. He hit at the skin that covered the face and came upon a nose right in the middle. A little higher than where it should have been.

He turned round and ran back to where the bodies were and looked up, and there too there were no faces and no hair and he did not know which of the bodies he had come with. He was alone and he wanted to cry but he couldn't. Maybe, he thought, he could not cry because there was no mouth for his cries to come out of and no eyes for the tears.

How was he going to be able to eat without a mouth? Hunger came gushing into his throat and he held his breath.

Without a face no one would know who he was and no one would recognise him or want him.

Then the fear went away. I am a man now, he thought. I need nobody.

But why was he so small?

Maybe it was all an illusion, a dream. Or maybe all the others were giants.

Someone tucked him into a cot. He stretched his arms to touch his face and see if it was there. There were other people in the cot with him, and then he realised it was not a cot at all. It was a big bed and a spear-like mattress-spring stuck into his back and he moved and kept moving away from the pain. Everybody moved.

Let me sleep, someone shouted, and he moved his hand about his face and it felt a pair of eyebrows and the two hills of his cheeks and a mouth. The nose had been there all the time. He found a pair of ears just where they were supposed to be and he sat up in excitement. I found my face, he shouted, but someone pulled him back again and said sleep now. Every time you move you shake us all. The springs are shot, you understand? At least he was no stranger here. Someone knew him well enough to order him about. Or else he was still a child. Children were ordered about by everyone. Children saw the world from the level of an adult knee. Yes. A child, he thought, but then again how could it be?

Again the bed-spring tried to dig into his back but he was a big man who could take pain and he did not move.

He was warm and wet. He imagined a river of blood streaming out of his back. It spread under his body and it was comforting. He was just about to drop off when someone fished him out of the river and an angry voice said if you have to go out just get up and go. Don't piss on me. If it's urgent use the floor like everybody else.

This is blood, he said, but the words came out in someone else's voice. He had to repeat himself because his own sound would not come, and it appeared no one heard him. The blood kept coming out of his back. He felt no pain.

He was swimming in a lake of red matter. Blood, he thought, and he shuddered. The liquid was cold now and did not stick to him. Maybe he was being punished for wetting his bed. Maybe they had made him smaller still. Small enough to sink in a bowl of soup. If that was so he would soon hit upon a piece of meat or pasta or a segment of bean. Soon he was swimming in soup and he thought maybe he was a magician. He was very hungry and swimming there he could gobble something before anyone noticed. But then if he was that small maybe he could swim in the soup forever and eat everything in it and no one would notice at all. He opened his mouth and something swam in and moved about on his tongue. It was cold and slippery and he spat it out and saw a tiny green frog splashing as it swam away at speed. It got to the rim of the plate in no time and jumped out. He felt a wave of nausea rising in his throat and he held his breath. Hands pushed him deep into the wet world, and further down it kept getting warmer and warmer. As he reached the bottom it was piping hot.

He must have been mistaken for a rabbit or a leg of a chicken. He must get out of there or at least make them see him. Make sure they knew he was a man. Otherwise they would surely cook him alive. Or drown him. It was dark all around him and wet and sticky and hot. His lungs were filling up with all that liquid and fear crawled into him. He wriggled and shook and kicked. Then all of a sudden his body was dry. He was swimming inside an enormous bubble of air. No. He was flying and he knew he must not stop moving his arms or else he would fall down.

His limbs were beginning to hurt with the effort and he stopped for a second and felt himself falling, gathering speed as he went down.

He looked and he saw sharp rocks pointing right at him like fingers, and carcasses of dead beings with arms and legs and open, worm-filled bellies. He must start moving again or soon he would crash into the rocks and no one would ever find him again. Ever. How could he have been flying without wings? He felt his shoulders. There was nothing there. He was not dead yet, but perhaps he was in the process of dying.

CHAPTER TWENTY

He jumped out of bed and went to the window and screamed.

'THAT WAS NOT ME. NOT ME NOT ME NOT ME!'

Why was he saying that? Sure it was him. What was wrong with being him?

His face felt flushed and fresh and his heart palpitated like it used to at the end of a birthday party, the moment the guests were out of the house and it was proper to open the presents. With the expectation of a new toy he had been dreaming about.

Or the moment he'd bite into a ball of ice-cream seconds after it was served.

Or at school when he was about to be told his team had won a game.

Things he could be proud of and brag about to his mother and Mihai.

His mother stood there before him in all her youthful splendour. Intense yet soft rays of love streaming out of her in his direction. Hugging, teasing, beautiful rays of affection.

He stretched his arms out to her.

She loved him today and always.

No one could separate them now.

He ran out of the bedroom and into the library and lay down on the carpet.

It was the middle of the afternoon. Time for his nap. There were people there. His mother, it must be his mother. She was talking in a tongue he did not understand to a man he did not know. But all that did not matter because she was looking at him and her warmth devoured him and her smile belonged to no one but him.

'Good thing we came in,' Annie said.

They saw him slumped on the floor, his head resting against the chesterfield. His eyes were peaceful and as he saw them and acknowledged them his face contorted into a faint smile. Not one piece of furniture was in place. Crushed plants lay in heaps of battered earth which mingled with smashed pottery. In the bathroom the water was running out of all the taps including the shower.

He looked at her and she glimpsed a flash of recognition spark in his eyes.

'If he moves about he'll hurt himself. There's broken glass all over the place. Poor soul.'

'It's over,' Sunshine said. 'We'll soon know.'

He had never met the man but he knew who he was. From somewhere far back through the corridors of his memory he recognised him. Yes. It could only be his uncle from England, his mother's brother. He was tall and tanned and his muscular legs bulged through his white cotton slacks.

My uncle is sizing me up, he thought. After everything Mama wrote to him about me he wants to see for himself. I'd better be on my best behaviour. Father did say he had the brains of a professor. A professor is much cleverer than a teacher.

He must have come for a visit. His mother often said he would. Maybe he had just arrived and now he was being shown off. She always said such beautiful things about him in her letters and he must never let her down.

Like he did the time he wet his sailor's suit at a children's party she had organised.

He did not need to look at her. For as long as he could remember he had not seen her standing as close and as still as she did now. Her face had changed a little and her hair had assumed a different shade. Something like dry straw. She must have come in straight from the hairdresser's. That was why he had not seen her all day. She didn't take him there any more. Not after the time he wandered all over the salon and nearly suffocated under one of the big dryers when the helmet-like contraption collapsed over his head with its hot air blowing.

She must not tell his uncle that. How she had lost her temper and slapped him across the face.

She wouldn't.

She hadn't even told his father.

'We are going home, Peter,' she said, and came closer. What could she mean? Was this not home? Where was home if not right here?

She was testing him. He'd best pretend he was asleep.

She often used to complain about his habits. How he had kept her up insisting on keeping the lights on. Insisting on just one more story. Just one more cup of chocolate. Just one last kiss.

Look how easy the boy is, she would whisper to his uncle. I have no trouble with him at all. Sleeps like an angel. Look. She bent over him and touched his forehead. Smooth, strong, gentle long fingers. She loved playing with his locks and tickling his scalp and making him laugh. That was how she used to wake him up in the morning, but morning was long past. Yes, it must be afternoon, time for his nap. The sleeping-time he hated most.

He could insist he wasn't tired at all. No, not today.

You will grow tall and strong like your father if you sleep in the afternoon, she used to say. Sometimes she'd bribe him with a promise of sorts. Sweets. A film. Ice-cream after dinner. A bedtime story with Mihai.

But not today. He would expect no rewards today. Today he would do as she wanted even before she asked.

He had slept well. He had had one of his bad dreams but had forgotten it. Maybe he had not dreamt. His dreams came only at night.

He gave her one of his deep, loving, sweet smiles which he knew would melt her insides, and she smiled back. There was, he thought, a tear in her eye. She was happy. She often cried when she was happy. Christ, he had had an accident while he slept. He had wet his pants, but he must pretend it hadn't happened. Stay right there until it dried. He must smile. Make every inch of his being smile. Smile harder and better and make it last.

'Have you seen his eyes, Sunshine? Have you seen the kindness, the affection, the love in his eyes? The contentment? It's working, Sunshine. We're winning. It's there. All of it is there. All that tender character you said he did not have. Under that brute force of his there is compassion. There is understanding and support and that great love I have been waiting for. Tenderness he has always had but was unable to show. Just look

at his eyes, Sunshine, please look at his eyes. Oh God, it is working
. . . It is happening . . . The months of deception that often made me
hate myself . . . Oh, it's all coming . . .'

'You may think you are whispering, Annie, but you are shouting.
He can hear you. Calm down.'

'He's asleep, poor darling, but he'll soon wake. And then I'll have
my man back. Pure and positive and strong. Just like his uncle said he'd
be. Look at his hands, his chin. Look at him. I've never seen him so
pale. He has been locked in here for ages. Far too long. He loves the
sun. He needs it.'

That language again. English. That was what it was. His uncle lived in
England and was an Englishman now.

'Have you packed your bag, Peter?'

What bag? He wasn't going to boarding-school yet. That was coming later. Much later. Anyway, he wasn't going to any boarding-school.
She had promised.

'Don't bother him with details, Annie,' the man who must have
been his uncle said. 'We'll have the stuff packed and collected later.'

Annie? Who was Annie? That was not his mother's name. But there was
an Annie. He'd heard the name before. A woman who died. No, she had
not died. It was in a dream maybe. Or a bedside story. He'd ask Mihai
about that. Mihai would know. Mihai knew everything.

'Where is your jacket?'

'Don't push him,' the man said. 'The plane doesn't leave until nine.'

They must be taking him somewhere. It was a foreign language they
were speaking, but somehow he knew what they were talking about.
Where were they going? School? Not in a plane, surely. Were they going
to England? Why couldn't they stay here on the estate. It was warm and
familiar and had been in the family for years. He knew every corner.

'Where are we going, Mama?'

'What is it he's saying?'

'You are supposed to understand Rumanian, Annie. The lessons
you took . . .'

'That was a long time ago. He can speak English.'

So that was how he was going to impress his uncle.

Of course he could speak English. Or could he? Where did he learn?
No matter. He could pretend he spoke it. Mimic. Drawl it like

Humphrey Bogart.

Make her proud and make her laugh. Lisp. Yes, she liked that.

'I speak English, Mama. Look. Hello. Goodbye. Nice to see you. English, see?'

'I've come to take you home, Peter,' she said, and she opened her arms to him and he looked at her and stretched his arms and yawned. Make out he just woke.

'There are two big dogs out there, Mama.'

Why did he have to say that? Now his uncle would think he was a coward.

Maybe she hadn't heard. Maybe she was so surprised he could speak English that she had not digested the bit about the dogs.

'They have gone, Peter.'

'I slept ... I slept for a long time, Mama ...'

'I am Annie,' she said softly.

Sure. She could be anyone she wanted to be. Pretend. Yes, she liked those games. Like they pretended to be poor in that place. He'd play along too.

'Give him time. He is confused,' the man said.

Confused? He knows exactly where he is. He knows who he is and at what stage of his life. There is no more confusion. He is at peace. He closes his eyes and relaxes his face muscles. Should he feign sleep again? Or suck his thumb and pull it out immediately? He does that often when he knows she is watching him. It shows her he is good now and will never be naughty again. He will make her so proud. There will be a toy or a chocolate by his pillow when he wakes and she will forgive him everything. He'll do anything. Even go to boarding-school. And once he is good everything else will be good.

He opens his eyes and looks some more. Not at her but in her direction, like he always does. He stretches with the sweet pleasure of what is to come, and he looks and waits for her to disappear under the weight of his eyes.

He knows what will happen next. It has happened many times before. She will look at him as he sleeps and she will smile. When he wakes again she will extend her arms to fish him out of bed and hug him. And then the warmth of her will form a glow of safety and envelop him and all else will vanish.